DARK PRINCESS

SHADOWS

THE CHILDREN OF THE GODS
BOOK EIGHTY-NINE

I. T. LUCAS

Dark Princess: Shadows **is a work of fiction**! Names, characters, places, and incidents are products of the author's imagination or are used fictitiously and are not to be construed as real. Any similarity to actual persons, organizations, and/or events is purely coincidental.

Published by Evening Star Press, LLC.

EveningStarPress.com

ISBN: 978-1-962067-58-4

MORELLE

"I have passed beyond the veil before my time," Morelle's mother said. "But time has no meaning here. It has meaning where you are, though, and it is time for you to wake up and experience the new world I sent you and your brother to. Ell-rom needs you."

Morelle was still reeling from the revelation that her mother was no longer among the living. Was she now telling her that Ell-rom was in danger?

"Who is threatening Ell-rom?" She felt anger electrifying her blood, readying her to wake up and fight to protect her brother.

"Nothing has changed over the thousands of years you were in stasis, my daughter. Your grandfather, the Eternal King, still wants you and Ell-rom dead."

That statement should have been the most jarring of everything her mother had told her, but it was not.

Since Morelle was old enough to understand her and Ell-rom's hybrid nature, she had known the Eternal King would kill them if he ever discovered that they were his grandchildren, born from a forbidden affair between the Kra-ell queen and his son.

What distressed her more was the revelation that her mother was gone and Ell-rom was in danger. Still, she shouldn't let this strange dream alarm her. It was probably not true, and her mother was, in truth, alive and well, ruling the Kra-ell with a strong and steady hand as she had done throughout Morelle's life.

What had prompted the dream, though?

Had she perceived some new danger threatening her mother?

Was that why she was dreaming that the queen had died and was speaking to her from beyond the veil? Or was the danger aimed at Ell-rom, and had she projected it onto their mother?

Her brother was too kind and pious for his own good, so his being threatened was not surprising.

No Kra-ell could afford to be so trusting. In their culture that was perceived as weakness, and for those in positions of power, it was like painting a target on their backs.

And what was that about thousands of years in stasis?

"You must have misspoken, Mother. This is just a dream. I could not have been asleep for so long."

The queen assumed her customary haughty expression, which terrified most of her subjects but not her daughter. "Walking the Fields of the Brave does not diminish my faculties, child of mine. If anything, it makes them sharper. You have just regained awareness but have been in stasis for a long time, much longer than you should have been. Your grandmother delayed and sabotaged the settler ship. She did it for her own reasons, but inadvertently, she saved your and Ell-rom's lives, so I am grateful to Ani, queen of the gods, even though what she did was not enough to save her son, your father."

The anger in her mother's voice sounded more familiar than anything she had said so far, but it was tinged with sadness, which, in life, the queen of the Kra-ell would never have allowed to infiltrate her tone.

"I am sorry for your loss, Mother. I did not know how deeply you cared for our father."

"I did, and I still do. We might not have been fated as he believed, but we produced two wonderful children who bound us in life and death. Bonds of love never die."

Perhaps her mother was dead after all because she would never have spoken of love when alive. The Kra-ell did not believe in such soft emotions, only loyalty and duty.

"I am surprised you still feel so strongly about those

bonds in the afterlife. I thought that we are unburdened at death."

It was one of the reasons Morelle hoped for death to claim her. To take one's life was a sin, and even though she was not a great believer in the Mother of All Life, she was not so rigid in her disbelief as to take the risk and be relegated to spending eternity in the Valley of the Shamed.

"In time, we forget the details of what caused our greatest joys and sorrows," her mother said. "But we carry their echoes through many rebirths." She smiled. "You are an old soul, Morelle, and your burden is heavy, but you should not allow it to rule you. Find a way to turn it into strength. You will need it."

"I am tired, Mother," Morelle admitted. "I feel like I have been struggling through endless epochs. I want to rest."

"This is not how this works, my child, and you do not get to choose when the cycles stop. Besides, Ellrom needs you, and this time around, you will not fight alone. Listen..." Her mother's voice began to fade.

"Listen to what?"

"Just listen." The dreamscape around her mother began to dissolve, colors bleeding away into nothingness.

And then Morelle heard it.

Someone was speaking next to her about strange things that she could not comprehend, even though she understood every word the male was saying.

"That's why I think artificial intelligence is the future," he said. "It is divorced from feelings and therefore should be able to always choose the truth. It will take time and effort to clean it of biases, and I'm not sure how we can make that part of its algorithm, but if we manage it, we will finally be free from the power grab of the illusions we create."

She had no idea what he was talking about, but it was nice to listen to something other than the thoughts swirling in her head.

"Who is he?" she asked, but her mother had already faded away, leaving her alone in the darkness.

The voice continued, weaving tales of a world similar to the one Morelle had left behind and yet so vastly different that most of what he was describing did not resonate with her. She lacked the context to connect his words with familiar images or processes.

Still, as she listened, she felt a pull toward wakefulness, curiosity warring with her reluctance to leave the comforting oblivion of the dreamscape.

As the darkness around her began to lighten, transforming into a soft, warm glow, Morelle became vaguely aware of other sensations, like the weight of the blanket covering her supine body, the gentle whisper of air that did not sound like wind but rather like something mechanical, and other noises that seemed artificial rather than natural.

It made sense, given that she was in a stasis chamber inside of a pod, surrounded by a variety of life-supporting equipment, but who was the male speaking to her?

Was it one of the gods back on Anumati? Broadcasting through the speakers in the stasis chamber? But then, why was he talking about strange and unfamiliar things?

Her mother had said that thousands of years had passed while Morelle had been asleep in stasis, so maybe things at home had changed beyond recognition, and that was why she could not understand most of the things the god was saying.

How was he speaking in Kra-ell, though?

Had the gods who had been exiled to Earth adopted Kra-ell as their official language?

That was not likely, even though their rebellion had been on behalf of the Kra-ell. It wasn't as if their Kra-ell collaborators had been sent into exile with them. The Eternal King had only punished his people who had risen against him. He made a peace treaty with the queen of the Kra-ell and even supplied her with the ship to take settlers to Earth.

She was dreaming.

That was the only explanation.

"...and that's why I think we need to focus on educating the younger generation," the voice was saying. "If we can teach them to think critically, to question and verify facts, we can combat the spread of untruths."

Part of it resonated with her, and part of it sounded like gibberish.

"What do you think, Princess? Ready to join the fight for truth when you wake up?"

Morelle had never thought of herself as a princess because no one had ever regarded her as such, and being of mixed blood, she would never have become her mother's successor, so perhaps this wasn't a dream after all.

But how did the god know that she was the queen's daughter?

Did he also know that she could never ascend to the throne?

If she were fully Kra-ell, she would have been the crown princess, her mother's successor, but as a hybrid abomination, all she could do was hide or run, and she had done both.

By sending her to Earth, her mother gave her a chance to change her destiny, but first, she needed to wake up.

2

BRANDON

The steady beep of the monitors provided a soothing backdrop to Brandon's mutterings. He'd been talking for what felt like hours, pouring out thoughts and feelings he had never shared with anyone.

After spending so many years in Hollywood and faking everything from who he was to what he believed in and what mattered to him, it was refreshing to just speak his mind, even if the person he was talking to couldn't hear a word he was saying.

Maybe that was why he felt free to do so.

If Morelle had been awake, he would have most likely assumed the persona everyone was familiar with and expected, and he would have charmed her with tales sure to fascinate her.

"You are a very good listener, Princess Morelle," he said, "I wonder if you can even hear me and, if so, if you can understand what I'm talking about. You come from a world that's so different from this one, and what you were told about Earth before embarking on this journey is no longer true."

He leaned back and sighed. "If you were awake, I would talk your ear off about all the wonders of our modern civilization and how bright humanity's future is thanks to all the marvelous innovations the clan has been slowly introducing to humans ever since we deciphered portions of Ekin's tablet. I would boast about the lofty ideas of democracy and equal rights that we have been propagating. But since you can't hear me, I can admit the truth, and it's not as pretty. Rot is festering everywhere nowadays, and so far, we have been able to bring light and prosperity to just a portion of this planet's inhabitants, but not enough. A large chunk of this planet's population is still living in poverty and misery. Barbarism and savagery are rampant and growing, and I don't know how we will ever be able to fulfill our mission of spreading the light to every corner on Earth. There just aren't enough of us, and humans are not picking up the slack. On the contrary. the children of those we have lifted up are letting themselves be seduced by the darkness."

He leaned closer to the hospital bed. "But that is not what you need to hear from me, right? I should be coaxing you to wake up, and instead, I'm giving you reasons to stay asleep."

He leaned back, studying Morelle's peaceful, unresponsive expression.

"I wonder what you're dreaming about. Are you reliving memories from thousands of years ago? Or are you somewhere else entirely, free from the weight of history?"

"Hold the door open!" someone yelled.

Alarmed, Brandon rose to his feet. "I should check what the commotion is about. I'll be right back."

Outside, he was met by a flurry of activity, with Ellrom bursting through the door that Julian was holding open, the unconscious Jasmine in his arms.

The prince's face was a mask of barely contained panic, but Kian and Brundar, who walked in right behind him, didn't seem as concerned.

"This way." Julian directed him to one of the other patient rooms.

Brandon pressed himself against the wall, giving them plenty of space to pass. As the door closed behind them, he turned to Kian. "What's going on?"

"Jasmine is most likely transitioning." Kian settled into one of the waiting-room chairs. "She fainted in the bathroom at my mother's house." He stretched his legs in front of him. "What are you doing in the clinic? Did you get hurt?"

"I'm fine." Brandon sat down next to him and gestured toward Morelle's room. "I came to visit our sleeping beauty. I thought it wasn't fair that her brother was getting all the attention while she was all alone in here."

Kian nodded. "It's nice of you to think of her. She has no one to be with her, and that's not good. Maybe that's why she's not waking up."

Brundar, who had remained standing next to the entry door to the clinic, shifted his weight to his other leg, which caught Kian's attention. "You can go, Brundar," Kian said. "Thank you for your help."

The Guardian dipped his head and left without a word.

"Strange fellow," Brandon murmured under his breath. "Sometimes I think that he's playing a role." He chuckled. "If Brundar didn't exist, someone ought to invent a character like him."

Kian smiled. "It seems to me that it's possible to take you out of Hollywood but not Hollywood out of you. You think about everything in terms of movies."

Brandon couldn't argue with that. "I do, but it will fade with time."

"I don't think it will." Kian glanced at the front door of the clinic. "Perhaps you would like to add to your script that there are Guardians outside."

Brandon tensed. "Are you expecting trouble?"

"Not really, but I'm being cautious. For the time being, I want to make sure that no one is harboring ill intentions toward the twins. At least now they are both in the same location, so I can dedicate fewer Guardians to them. It's not like we have any to spare."

Kian's answer didn't alleviate Brandon's concerns. "Do you think someone might try something even after the Clan Mother compelled everyone to keep the twins safe?"

"I've learned to always expect surprises." Kian sighed, rubbing a hand over his face. "Like Drova being behind the sabotage and thefts."

"You'd suspected her for a while," Brandon pointed out. "It shouldn't have been a surprise."

Kian let out a breath. "We believed she was involved, but we didn't think she was the mastermind behind it. The most troubling part was the way she managed to pull off so many incidents. I will schedule a council meeting soon and inform the council members of what we are dealing with."

Brandon didn't want to wait. "Don't keep me in suspense, Kian."

"It turns out that Drova has inherited her father's compulsion ability, and it only started manifesting recently. She used it to get Parker, Lisa, and Cheryl to do her bidding. The girl is incredibly dangerous, but at the moment she's just a misguided teenager, and I'm not sure what to do with her."

Brandon felt a chill run down his spine. "Her age shouldn't be a consideration. She needs to be approached with the same caution that was used when we approached her father."

Kian shook his head. "We put Igor in stasis because there was no way to redeem him. Drova is young, and she is Jade's daughter too. With the right influence and education, she could become a great asset to us. In a way, the same is true of the twins. We don't know yet what they are capable of, but given who their parents were, they should be formidable. In their case, though, I hope that being related to us will make them loyal to the clan."

"Has Ell-rom started showing any signs of compulsion ability?" Brandon asked.

He remembered their prior conversation about the twins when Kian mused about Morelle being the dangerous one and possibly having abilities they were not prepared for.

"Not yet, but it's too early to say that he doesn't." Kian sounded nonchalant, but Brandon sensed that he knew more about the prince's emerging abilities than he was willing to share.

That was fine. Eventually, he would inform the council.

"What about your plans for faking the twins' deaths? Is that still on the table?" Brandon asked.

"Aru has not reported finding the pod yet, and we want to keep it that way. Jasmine convinced him that it was better than trying to fake something and getting discovered. We concluded that it was better to wait until another pod was discovered with everyone inside dead and report that. If several pods are found in the same condition, the higher-ups might assume that all the remaining settlers are dead and decide that there is no need to search anymore. The problem with that is that they will recall our three new friends back home, which the gods don't want to happen since they are now all mated to immortals, who cannot be taken back with them."

Brandon nodded. "Would we need to fake their deaths as well?"

"Is there another option?" Kian asked.

"I guess not." Brandon glanced at the closed door to Jasmine's room. "I feel for Ell-rom. With both his mate and sister unconscious now, he must be going out of his mind with worry."

3

KIAN

Kian gave Brandon a curt nod, but his mind was on the experiment about to take place later that evening. The gods were impatient to test removing the tracker from one of them and transferring it to the captured trafficker, and the truth was that Kian was eager to get on with it as well. But for that to happen, Julian needed to get back to the keep along with Merlin, and Bridget needed to take over the village clinic to care for Morelle and Jasmine.

In fact, Kian decided that he needed to accompany the doctors to the keep and supervise the procedure, even though his presence was unnecessary, and he would rather spend the evening at home.

Then again, tomorrow was Saturday, so he could compensate by doing a little less work in his home office and spending more time with his family. After all, Sari and David were going back to Scotland on

Monday, and he didn't want to miss out on all the family lunches and dinners that his mother and Syssi had planned.

As if summoned by his thoughts, Bridget rushed in. "Hello, Kian. Brandon," she said in passing.

"Thanks for coming," Kian called after her.

She nodded as she opened the door to Jasmine's room, and a moment later, a dejected Ell-rom was ushered out.

He looked lost and stressed, and given what lived inside of the prince, it was important to keep him calm.

It wasn't that Kian was worried about Ell-rom lashing out with his death ray and killing random people, but until they could put the guy through thorough testing, it was better to play it safe.

He rose to his feet, walked over to Ell-rom, and put a hand on his arm. "Take a deep breath and relax. It's perfectly normal for transitioning Dormants to lose consciousness, and your mate is tougher than most. She'll make it through."

Ell-rom's shoulders felt like they were made from granite. "Why did they tell me to leave? What are they doing in there?"

Kian led the prince to a chair next to Brandon. "They are not hiding anything alarming from you. It's perfectly normal for Bridget to kick the worried mate out of the room while she is hooking the patient up to the monitoring equipment. She is quick, efficient, and she doesn't want anyone disturbing her workflow."

Letting out a long breath, Ell-rom sat down. "I understand all of that logically, but my heart can't stop racing. I feel lost without Jasmine."

"I get it." Kian sat down on Ell-rom's other side.

He still remembered how wrecked he'd been during Syssi's transition. It was much easier to give advice when it wasn't his own mate's life on the line.

"In a day or two, you will look back and realize that you were panicking for nothing." Kian imbued his tone with as much calm and confidence as he could, hoping it would ease Ell-rom's fear.

The truth was that he wasn't worried. If Jasmine encountered any difficulties, his mother would come and give her a 'blessing,' and she would be fine.

"We haven't lost a single transitioning Dormant yet," Brandon said. "And some of them were much older and in relatively poor health compared to Jasmine. You really have nothing to worry about."

Ell-rom cast Brandon a grateful smile. "Thank you. That puts things in perspective."

"Glad to help." Brandon clapped Ell-rom on his back.

"So, what now?" the prince asked.

"Now we wait." Kian crossed his arms over his chest.

The next few minutes passed in silence as they waited, and then Bridget and Julian emerged from the room.

"All done," Bridget said. "Jasmine is exhibiting the classic symptoms of transition, and her vitals are strong. I don't expect her to remain unconscious for long, but I've learned that every Dormant is different, so I can't make promises."

"Can I go to her?" Ell-rom asked.

"Of course," Julian said.

"I'm coming with you." Kian followed him inside. "Do you need anything?" he asked.

Ell-rom shook his head.

Kian chuckled. "You'll want to stay by Jasmine's side until she's out of the critical stage of transition, which means that you'll need a change of clothes and some toiletries. I'll pack a bag for you and bring it over."

"I couldn't ask—" Ell-rom began, embarrassment clear in his voice.

"Don't worry," Kian cut him off. "I'll have Okidu pack your bag, and I might send him to bring it over or I may come myself."

The tension in Ell-rom's jaw abated. "Thank you. I appreciate your thoughtfulness."

Smiling, Kian gave Ell-rom's tense shoulder a light squeeze. "Syssi's transition is still as fresh in my mind as it was when it happened, but I've also seen many others since. I know the protocol. Can I get you some coffee? Maybe a bottle of water?"

Ell-rom shook his head. "Thank you, but I don't need anything right now other than for Jasmine to open her eyes and look at me."

Kian's heart squeezed in sympathy. "I'll pray to the Fates for Jasmine's quick and successful transition."

"Thank you," Ell-rom whispered.

When Kian returned to the waiting room, Brandon rose to his feet. "How is he?"

"Distraught, as can be expected. It's never easy watching someone you love go through this."

Brandon nodded. "I bet, which makes me wonder how Jade is taking Drova's betrayal."

Kian chuckled. "You wouldn't know looking at her, but it's not easy. She pretends to be the tough Kra-ell, who is a leader first and a mother second, but she can't fool me. If I had suggested putting Drova in stasis, Jade would have risen against me despite the life vow she swore to me."

Brandon looked surprised. "Are you sure? Their whole existence is about honor and duty. They don't believe in love."

Kian wasn't sure that was the case. Certainly not with Jade, but she hadn't discovered it until after meeting Phinas and falling in love with him. She had also loved the sons who Igor had ordered slaughtered, and she'd acknowledged that a long time ago. Unlike most people who were followers and accepted dogmas without questioning them, Jade had a strong personality, she was a leader, and she made up her own mind about things.

"The Kra-ell might have beliefs and customs that are very different from ours," he said. "But they are more like us than they realize. They are not made from stone, and they love their children, or at least those who can think for themselves do. Jade loves her daughter, and she loved the sons she lost. She would give her life and her honor to protect Drova. Not that I have any clandestine intentions for the girl. For now, she's under house arrest, and we will figure out a more permanent solution later."

"Like what?"

Kian shrugged. "I don't know yet. I can only handle one crisis at a time."

4

BRANDON

After Kian left, Brandon returned to Morelle's room and settled into the chair by her bed. "Hi. I'm back," he said, "It's been quite a day. Your brother's mate is transitioning, we've got a rogue compeller on our hands, and here you are, still sleeping through it all." He chuckled. "I don't suppose you'd consider waking up and adding to the excitement?"

Morelle remained still, her chest rising and falling in a steady rhythm. Brandon sighed, leaning back in his chair. "No rush," he murmured. "But when you do wake up, I hope to be here. Someone needs to catch you up on seven thousand years of history, right? And let's face it, I tell a much better story than any of my brethren or a dusty old history book. I can turn it into a script and make it come alive in your imagination. Actually, that's not a bad idea. I should produce a series called *Seven Thousand Years*. Nah, that's a lame title. I need something catchier."

He settled in, preparing for a long night even though no one expected him to stay.

In fact, he probably shouldn't.

Morelle wasn't his mate, and it might be improper for him to stay with her as if he had a claim on her. On the other hand, Kian had Guardians posted outside the clinic because he suspected someone might harbor ill intentions toward her and her brother, so having an additional layer of security would probably be appreciated.

Not that he was much of a fighter. He had given the Guardian force a half-hearted try in his youth, but he had quickly realized that he enjoyed entertaining his fellow Guardians much more than sparring with them.

Still, he just wanted to stay.

There was no one waiting for him at home, and he could do his brainstorming for ideas right here next to Morelle's bed while telling her all about it and helping to stimulate her mind.

His gift was turning anything he talked about into a fascinating story, and he could talk for hours. That was one of the things that made him such a successful producer. The problem was that the public around him had changed in ways he hadn't foreseen, and the material they wanted to consume was getting dumber and dumber. The plots he had seen approved for production recently would have been thrown out only a couple of decades ago, but today's viewing public didn't want to watch anything that engaged their minds or challenged their beliefs. They wanted the same crap shoved down their throats and said, 'Thank you, we want more.'

It was disheartening.

His chances of producing a history series for any of the main networks were nil unless he used thralling, and that was against the rules. Besides, it would flop, and then he wouldn't be able to produce anything more anyway.

Even if he gave the series a satiric twist, it might still not get green-lighted because there was no audience for it.

Hell, who cared?

He had a captive audience of one.

Brandon wondered what Morelle would be like when she finally opened her eyes. Would she be anything like her twin brother?

Ell-rom seemed intelligent, regal, and kind—a good guy who no one felt threatened by. For some reason, Brandon had a feeling that Morelle would be much more commanding, and that was fine by him. He liked assertive females, as long as they weren't too stuck-up and full of themselves, and most importantly, they had to be not only smart but also open-minded.

Too many people were stuck in the little boxes they created for themselves or that others had created for them. Even the smartest of humans often felt more comfortable inside their little mind enclosures than risking independent and critical thinking that might alienate their friends.

There was comfort in conformity.

"*Millennia: The Story of Us*. Now, that's a catchy title. What do you think?"

There was no change in Morelle's expression. Perhaps he could pop into the next room over and ask Ell-rom what he thought of it?

"Nah, first I have to come up with a list."

Brandon pulled out his phone and opened it to his note application.

"*Eons Unfolded*." He wrote another title and then lifted his gaze to Morelle. "No, nothing? I thought this was a good one. How about *Chronicles of a Civilization*?"

There was no response. "Can't blame you, Princess. They all sound lame. I need a title that will tickle people's curiosity." He chuckled. "Unfortunately for me, *A Game of Thrones* is taken."

As he looked at Morelle's peaceful expression once more, he had the absurd urge to kiss her full lips, but even though it sounded great in a fairytale kind of way, doing so without her consent would be a violation. He wouldn't even dare to kiss her forehead.

The most he would allow himself was to hold her hand.

"You need to wake up, Morelle, and tell me that you want me to kiss you, or just take the initiative and kiss me. I'm easy. I know it's absurd, but since you probably can't hear me, I can allow myself flights of fancy."

Sighing, he looked down at his notes and added two more short titles. "*Epochs* and *Timeline*s. I like *Epochs*. I should test it on InstaTock. Imagine being able to step into key moments of the past, to see and feel what it was like. I wonder what Ell-rom would think of that idea."

He thought about the stories he would tell Morelle and the wonders of modern Earth he would describe. There was so much to share, so much that had changed since the settler ship had embarked on its journey through the galaxy. And yet, in many ways, the fundamental struggles of humanity remained the same, just on a much bigger scale.

In the grand scheme of things, there was nothing new under the sun, but on the personal level, the Fates sometimes delivered surprises, like a sleeping hybrid princess whose mystery and beauty captivated him.

It was like something out of a fantasy novel.

Hell, it would be a great script for a sci-fi movie.

5

MORELLE

The male's voice continued to wash over Morelle, a steady, soothing presence in her semi-conscious state. His words ebbed and flowed like gentle waves, carrying fragments of thoughts and ideas to the shores of her awareness.

"You need to wake up, Morelle, and tell me that you want me to kiss you, or just take the initiative and kiss me. I'm easy. I know it's absurd, but since you probably can't hear me, I can allow myself to fly."

What did kissing him have to do with flying?

But that was the less important question. Why did he want her to kiss him?

Did he find her appealing?

Her mother's words from before echoed in her head. "You are beautiful and perfect, half goddess and half Kra-ell, and there are joys in life that can only be experienced through the flesh."

Morelle had never kissed nor had she been kissed, and perhaps her mother was right, and she should try those joys that had been out of her reach before. She hadn't been allowed to show her face, let alone engage intimately with anyone.

"*Epochs* and *Timelines*," the male said. "I like *Epochs*. I should test it on InstaTock. Imagine being able to step into key moments of the past, to see and feel what it was like. I wonder what Ell-rom would think of that idea."

Ell-rom. The name sent a jolt through Morelle's hazy consciousness, triggering a cascade of memories. Suddenly, she was a child again, huddled with her brother in the dark corners of the temple, whispering secrets and planning mischief. They had been each other's whole world, bound by blood and shared isolation.

In the depths of her mind, Morelle saw flashes of their childhood games, elaborate fantasies woven from scraps of overheard conversations, and forbidden glimpses of the world beyond their sheltered existence. She remembered the warmth of Ell-rom's hand in hers, the silent understanding that passed between them with just a glance.

All they had was each other, Morelle realized with a pang of longing. And now, in this strange new world, Ell-rom was waiting for her.

The thought sent a ripple of anticipation through her.

As Morelle hovered in this liminal space between dreams and waking, she felt a subtle shift within herself. The fear and reluctance that had kept her submerged in the depths of unconsciousness began to recede, like mist dissipating in the morning sun.

In its place, a tentative curiosity began to bloom.

Who was this male who spoke so tirelessly? His voice had become a constant in her twilight world, a beacon drawing her closer to the surface of consciousness. How did he know her language? The question tugged at her mind again, demanding attention now that she was almost sure he wasn't a construct of her mind, a figment of her imagination.

Did the people of Earth speak Kra-ell now? The possibility sent her thoughts spinning. Could it be that the settlers had conquered the planet, imposing their language as the official tongue of the land? For a moment, Morelle entertained the notion that perhaps only her and Ell-rom's stasis chambers had remained sealed, suspending them for millennia while the world changed around them.

But no, that couldn't be right. The memory of her mother's words surfaced, clear and sharp amidst the fog of her thoughts. The entire ship had been delayed, a machination of Ani, queen of the gods, wife of the Eternal King, and mother of Ahn. The complexity of divine politics intruded on Morelle's contemplation, bringing with it a host of troubling memories.

The more her past resurfaced, the more agitated Morelle became. The tranquil void she had inhabited for so long was dissolving, replaced by a swirling eddy of emotions and half-formed thoughts. The calm she had clung to was slipping away, leaving her adrift in a sea of uncertainty.

If her dream world was to be as tumultuous as the waking one, what was the point of remaining asleep? The desire to see the face behind the voice grew stronger, pushing against the inertia that had held her for so long.

Morelle focused her will, struggling to open her eyes, to break through the barrier between sleep and wakefulness. But she discovered that awakening was not as simple as deciding to open one's eyes. Her efforts felt like pushing against an immovable weight, each attempt leaving her more drained than the last.

The strain of it pulled her back into the depths of sleep, the sensations of the waking world fading anew.

Yet something had changed. Instead of the peaceful oblivion she had known for so long, Morelle's dreams were now filled with vivid images. She saw Ell-rom smiling and reaching out to her. The sight filled her with a bittersweet longing, a mix of joy at seeing her brother and sadness at their separation.

How long had he been awake?

And then there was another face, one she didn't recognize but felt drawn to. It was a male who looked like a god, with warm brown hair and kind blue eyes that seemed to look right into her soul. Despite the fading edges of her self-awareness, Morelle knew this image wasn't real—it was a face her mind had conjured to match the voice that pulled her toward consciousness.

Still, these visions stirred something within her, something she hadn't felt in what seemed like an eternity—excitement. And beneath that, tentative and fragile, was a flicker of hope. Hope for a future she had long since abandoned, hope for a world that might hold more than the pain and isolation of her past.

As Morelle drifted in this space between worlds, caught between the pull of sleep and the growing urge to wake, a decision crystallized in her mind. The next time she heard that voice, she would answer. She would summon every ounce of strength she possessed, push through the fog of unconsciousness, and open her eyes and say something, anything, to bridge the gap between the world of dreams and the reality that awaited beyond.

But first, she needed to gather her strength.

Morelle let herself sink back into the comforting embrace of sleep, but this time, she held on to the images and emotions that had surfaced. She clung to the memory of Ell-rom's smile, to the warmth in the imagined god's eyes, and to the sound of the voice that had become her lifeline.

6

KIAN

"I'm excited," Anandur said as he parked the car in the keep's underground. "Utilizing a trafficker to benefit humanity in any shape or form is just such beautiful poetic justice."

Opening the passenger door, Julian chuckled. "In this case, the trafficker is going to benefit gods, not humanity, but I agree with the sentiment."

"I vote for testing new drugs on them," Merlin suggested as he waited for Kian to get out so he could follow. "There are so many scumbags out there who have done so much harm to people that using them to test potentially lifesaving drugs and treatments is the least society should take out of their hides." He got out of the car and closed the door behind him.

Kian agreed with every one of the proposals, but he didn't feel like joining in the idea fest. It was bad enough that he was forced to wade through the despicable sludge of humanity, and his Guardians were doing all they could to clean up as much as possible, given their small numbers. He didn't want to immerse himself in it any further.

Then again, that exact sentiment had allowed trafficking to flourish. No one wanted to touch the problem or even talk about it, while millions suffered.

When they reached the clinic, Aru, Negal, and Dagor were already waiting for them.

Aru's expression was pinched, and the frown lines on his forehead were so deep that they looked like a permanent feature, but naturally, they were not.

As soon as the god smiled, the creases smoothed out.

"Gentlemen," Kian greeted them with a nod. "Or should I say gentle-gods?"

That got a chuckle out of Aru. "Gabi uses gentle-male. She read it in one of her romance novels about vampires or shifters. I'm not sure which." He rubbed the back of his head. "What baffles me is why she still feels the need to read those books when she has the real thing right here." He pointed at himself.

Dagor grinned. "Face it, Aru. You just can't live up to the fantasy males in her stories."

Aru lifted a brow. "And you can?"

The god puffed out his chest. "Frankie says that she can't read any more romance novels because the heroes pale in comparison to me."

"Lucky dude," Julian murmured. "Now you've made me feel insecure because Ella still enjoys them."

So did Syssi, but it didn't make Kian insecure, and he even liked reading a few chapters here and there to get a good laugh. It had never occurred to him that he should feel offended by it. Maybe he was too obtuse to realize that he should.

Whatever.

Syssi said that reading relaxed her, and that was what mattered.

"So, did you decide who is going to do it?" Merlin asked.

"Dagor." Aru clapped the god's back. "He's the lowest ranking among us, and anomalies in his tracker's transmissions will be less suspicious."

Merlin turned to the god. "I've removed hundreds of trackers from the Kra-ell, and none of them suffered any negative side effects, but I've never removed one from a god, and you might be different. Has anyone told you that extracting a tracker carried risks?"

Dagor shook his head. "I don't think it does. The idea behind the trackers is for our people to be able to find us. No one expects us to get rid of them to run away on some primitive planet."

Kian wasn't so sure. Governments usually cloaked censorships and infringements on the privacy and personal liberty of their citizens in benevolent-sounding policies and arguments about ensuring safety. In the case of military personnel, they didn't even bother with lame excuses to hide their intentions.

He put his hand on Dagor's shoulder. "There might be risk involved, and Merlin wants to make sure that you consent while being aware of it."

The god nodded. "I'm willing to risk it so the three of us will be free to move into your village with our mates. I want Frankie to live among a community of people who know what and who she is. I don't want her to be a nomad."

"Same here," Negal said. "If you have second thoughts, I'll do it."

"I don't." Dagor walked up to Julian. "What do I need to do?"

"First, we need to put you through the scanner to find out where exactly the tracker is located. Since Merlin has done so many extractions, he is the one who will do that part. I'll perform the transfer. If all goes well, the tracker will transmit normally from its new host, and your commander will be none the wiser." He turned to the rest of the group. "Do you want to watch?"

Kian nodded and then turned to Anandur. "Call the dungeon to bring our guest up here."

"I will do better than that." Anandur headed in the opposite direction. "I'll escort the vermin myself."

As Kian followed Dagor and Merlin to the imaging room, he thought about the potential outcomes of this experiment. Success could mean freedom for the gods and a chance to integrate them fully into the clan's community. Failure, on the other hand, meant coming up with a new solution.

Faking their death was still an option, but it wasn't a good one.

In the imaging room, Merlin gave Dagor another thorough look. "Good, I see that you've followed instructions, and you're not wearing any metal on you." He scanned the rest of the group. "Everyone else, if you are wearing any belts with metal buckles or metal buttons, please stand at least ten feet away from the machine."

Kian had been through enough of those to know that, and he had come prepared.

Negal cursed under his breath and proceeded to remove his belt. "I forgot about that."

"That's okay," Merlin said. "No harm done." He turned to Dagor and pointed to the MRI machine. "Lie down and try to remain as still as possible during the scan."

As Dagor settled on the narrow platform, the machine hummed to life, its rhythmic thumping filling the room. Kian watched the monitors, but the images meant little to his untrained eye. Merlin, however, leaned in close and muttered something incoherent.

"There," the doctor murmured after several long minutes. "Left thigh, embedded in the vastus lateralis muscle. Quite an ingenious placement, really. Easy to implant, difficult to remove without significant muscle damage, but naturally, that wasn't the intention since gods heal so fast. They just wanted it well hidden."

Aru's eyes narrowed. "Will you need to put Dagor under to extract it?"

Merlin shook his head. "A local anesthetic will do."

As Aru released a relieved breath, Kian lifted a brow. "Why were you concerned with Dagor being anesthetized?"

"Because I wasn't sure that it would work on him. Our bodies repel foreign substances that are perceived to be harmful."

"Your body might react the same way to a local anesthetic," Kian said. "Maybe we should get him drunk? I know that you can consume alcohol and feel its effects."

"That might be an option," Aru agreed.

After Merlin completed another full MRI scan to confirm nothing was missed, and Dagor emerged from the machine looking unperturbed, Kian wondered whether the god had heard what was discussed. The gods' hearing was even better than immortals', but the machine had been loud, and it had probably drowned out their conversation.

"What now?" Dagor asked.

"Now, we put you in the operating room," Merlin said. "I thought we wouldn't need it, but because of the location of the tracker, I prefer to do this in a properly equipped OR."

7

ARU

"Can you wait a moment?" Aru asked Merlin when Dagor went to change into a hospital gown. "I want to run up to the penthouse and bring a few bottles of whiskey in case your anesthetic doesn't work on him."

Merlin gave him an incredulous look. "I will test it before I begin. I won't operate on Dagor before I'm sure the area is numb."

"Test it on me," Negal offered. "Inject it into my finger or something, and let's see how long it stays numb."

"Good idea." Merlin motioned for Negal to sit down. "I have a hunch that whatever works on immortals will work on you just as well, but testing is always preferable to assuming, right?"

Negal nodded.

Merlin gathered his tools, including a small syringe

that was filled with liquid. "The lidocaine will block the nerve signals in the area."

He cleaned Negal's hand with antiseptic and then pinched his finger. "The base where the nerves are located is the best location." He took the syringe and inserted the needle. "I'm injecting the anesthetic just beneath the skin."

Negal didn't even wince, and he didn't react when Merlin repeated the procedure on the other side of the same finger.

"How bad was it?" Aru asked.

"It was just a small pinch, and now it stings." The trooper chuckled. "Stop hovering over me like a mother hen. We are soldiers."

"Right." Aru crossed his arms over his chest.

For some reason, little hurts suffered in civilian circumstances seemed larger than major injuries suffered by a soldier in battle. That reminded him of what his commanding officer at the time had told his unit during training—it was all a mind game.

"Okay." Merlin brandished a wicked-looking tool. "Let's see if that worked." He prodded Negal's finger. "Did you feel it?"

"I felt no pain."

"Close your eyes." Merlin waited for Negal to comply before doing it again.

"Well?" Negal asked. "What are you waiting for?"

The doctor chuckled. "It works. The question is, for how long? I need two minutes to take the tracker out, and it will take a few minutes longer for Gertrude to staple the wound."

The door to the dressing room opened, and Dagor walked in wearing blue hospital booties and a hospital gown that he was clutching in the back. "This thing is so drafty." Noticing Negal sitting in a chair and holding his finger up, he frowned. "What are you doing?"

"Testing the anesthetic for you."

Dagor shifted his gaze to Aru. "What, no whiskey?"

"It seems that the anesthetic is working," Merlin answered for him. "No booze needed."

"Oh well." Dagor climbed onto the hospital bed, flashing everyone as his gown parted in the back. "I'm ready to be liberated from the tracker, Doc."

"One more moment." Merlin used his tool to prod Negal's finger again. "Still numb?"

Negal nodded.

"Excellent." Merlin put the tool aside. "Now, I want everyone except for Gertrude to get out." He shooed them away by waving both hands.

Reluctantly, Aru left together with Negal, who was

still holding his finger up. "You can put it down, you know," he told his friend.

Negal shook his head. "I will when the feeling returns." He opened his mouth, exposing his elongated fangs. "Who needs surgical tools when I have these, right?"

He nicked the finger on one of his fangs. "Damn, it is still numb. Why isn't my body rejecting whatever Merlin injected me with?"

It was indeed odd and a little ridiculous. Perhaps Negal was just clowning around to reduce the tension.

The procedure itself was nothing, but what followed would significantly impact their lives, and Aru had been a ball of stress lately.

"I don't know." He opened the door to the waiting room. "Maybe it doesn't recognize it as something that needs to be repelled."

Kian greeted them with a raised brow. "Why are you bleeding?"

Negal looked at his finger, licked the drop of blood that had welled over the wound he'd made, and then showed it to Kian. "It's not bleeding anymore. I just wanted to check if the numbing was still working. Surprisingly, it still is."

"Interesting," Kian murmured. "Evidently, your healing speed is not much faster than ours."

Aru knew that it was, but he was tired of discussing the subject. "Is the trafficker ready to receive the tracker?"

Kian nodded. "He's heavily sedated. We don't want him panicking, although given what he did, we should let him suffer both the fear and the pain. He doesn't deserve our mercy."

As the minutes crawled by, Aru started pacing the small waiting room while Negal and Kian passed the time scrolling on their phones.

When the door finally opened and Merlin emerged with a tray and a tiny object on top of it, Kian rose to his feet.

"How did it go?"

"It took some digging, but the anesthetic held on for most of it, and Dagor only had to suffer through the suturing. He's resting now." He headed toward the room where the trafficker was waiting. "Extraction was successful. Now, on to the implanting. Cross your fingers, gentlemen."

"That's odd," Negal said when Merlin closed the door behind him. "How come my finger is still numb?"

Kian shrugged. "Maybe he gave you a very strong dose. Bite it again."

"Nah." Negal finally put his hand down. "I'm glad that I'm so susceptible to the anesthetic. When Merlin removes my tracker, I won't feel a thing."

"I just hope this works," Aru said. "If not, our trackers are staying in our bodies, and we will be packing and getting ready to go."

"It will work." Negal leaned back in his chair. "We need to start looking for humans to carry our trackers and figure out how to compensate them for their efforts."

"That's the easy part," Kian said. "We will also need to implant them with an additional tracker that we can monitor so we can make sure they are doing what they are supposed to."

"Good thinking." Aru cast him an appreciative look. "Also, compulsion will have to be used to ensure that they don't try to remove the trackers and disappear."

Kian nodded. "Talk about a morally gray area. I would have suggested using captured traffickers for that, but I don't want to let those monsters loose."

When the door opened again, Julian emerged, pushing the gurney and motioning for the Guardian to take over. "You can put him back in his cell. When he wakes up, he won't know that anything was done to him."

The Guardian nodded and took over, pushing the gurney out of the clinic.

"Shouldn't Dagor be out of there by now?" Aru asked.

"He's probably waiting for one of us to tell him that

he can go." Merlin opened the door to the back of the clinic.

Negal lifted his hand. "Why is my finger still numb?"

Merlin frowned. "It shouldn't be. Let me take a look at it."

Aru left them in the waiting room and headed over to the surgery room to check on his friend.

8

ELL-ROM

As the minutes ticked by with agonizing slowness, Ell-rom became acutely aware of the silence pressing in around him. No one had come to check on him and Jasmine or to offer words of comfort and reassurance.

He understood why, of course.

Kian was at the keep, overseeing the tracker removal experiment. Annani was occupied with her daughters. But the knowledge did little to ease the ache of loneliness that settled in his chest.

He held on to Jasmine's hand as if, through sheer force of will, he could tether her to the world of the living. The steady beep of the heart monitor provided a rhythmic backdrop to his silent prayers, a desperate litany to the Mother of All Life to keep Jasmine in this world and not take her away from him.

"Great Mother, creator of life, please guide Jasmine safely through her transition. She is everything to me."

The words felt strange on his tongue, a mixture of a familiar ritual and raw emotion. Ell-rom loved Jasmine with every beat of his heart, but he hadn't realized the depth of his attachment to her.

He could barely breathe without her.

She looked so peaceful, as if she was only sleeping, but she was unresponsive, unconscious. He longed to see her eyes open, to hear her voice, to feel the warmth of her smile that somehow made everything seem brighter, more vibrant. Without her animated presence, the world around him felt dull, devoid of color, and unwelcoming.

"I miss you." Ell-rom gently squeezed Jasmine's hand. "I never realized how much I've come to rely on you. You are like a bright light in a dark room. You make my life worth living, my Jasmine."

The moment the words left his lips, Ell-rom felt a jolt of awareness.

This was a novel feeling, wasn't it? This sense of purpose and the joy in simply existing.

He frowned as he delved into the murky waters of his fragmented memories. Had life on Anumati truly been so bleak? So devoid of hope?

Images flashed through his mind: dark corridors, whispered conversations, the constant weight of secrecy and fear. The isolation had been all-encompassing, suffocating. He and Morelle had been two anomalies in a world that had no place for them.

Morelle. The thought of his twin sent another pang through Ell-rom's heart, and guilt gnawed at him.

Here he was, upset because no one was visiting him and Jasmine, while she had been all alone in her room for days on end.

"Jasmine, my love," he said softly, leaning in close, "I'm going to step out for a few minutes to check on Morelle. I'll be right back, I promise." He pressed a gentle kiss to her forehead, lingering for a moment before reluctantly releasing her hand.

As he stepped into the waiting area, he saw Bridget in her office, but she was turned around with her back to him, her swivel chair facing the cabinet behind her desk, and her phone clutched to her ear.

She laughed at something the person on the other side had said, which sounded oddly out of place in the somber atmosphere.

Not wanting to disturb the medic, Ell-rom quietly made his way toward Morelle's room.

He didn't hesitate before depressing the handle, but unlike almost every other time he had visited his sister, she wasn't alone, and seeing the back of a male who was leaning over her sent a bolt of adrenaline surging through his system.

In an instant, Ell-rom felt his protective instincts flare to life. The familiar burning sensation started building behind his eyes, and his fangs began to elongate.

The stranger turned around, his eyes widening as he took in Ell-rom's threatening posture. Recognition flickered across his features, and he quickly raised his hands in a placating gesture.

"It's me, Brandon," the male said, his voice steady and sure despite the tension in the air. "Calm down, Ell-rom."

He blinked, forcing himself to take a steadying breath. He'd met the guy during the welcoming party, and he was sitting with Kian at the clinic when Bridget told Ell-rom to leave Jasmine's room.

"What are you doing here?" Ell-rom asked, his voice low and tinged with a growl he couldn't quite suppress.

Brandon's posture remained open and non-threatening. "I'm keeping Morelle company." He smiled, but it looked a little forced. "It didn't seem fair that you were getting all the attention while she was all alone in here. Julian said that she needed someone to talk to her, and well, talking is my thing. I can talk for hours."

The explanation was reasonable but not logical.

Brandon had no reason to be in Morelle's room.

Nevertheless, Ell-rom forced his fangs to retract, consciously relaxing the tension in his shoulders. "Julian is correct," he conceded, "and I thank you for the effort. But it seems a little odd to me that you would dedicate your time to a stranger."

Brandon's smile widened, a hint of self-deprecation creeping into his expression. "Ah, well, I suppose it might seem that way. But I'm a storyteller at heart. It's what I do, what I've always done. And Morelle," he gestured toward the still form on the bed, "she's got seven thousand years of history to catch up on. Who better to bring her up to speed than someone who can spin a tale better than anyone else?"

It sounded great. His sister needed all the stimulation she could get, and if Brandon was telling her about Earth's history, maybe Ell-rom should join the lessons. He did not want this stranger with unknown motives alone with his sister.

He moved further into the room, his gaze shifting between Brandon and Morelle. "I would love to hear some of those tales you have been spinning for my sister."

If Brandon was offended by the implied accusation, he didn't show it. Instead, he sat down on the lone chair in the room and leaned back. "Oh, a bit of everything, really. The rise and fall of empires, great discoveries, the triumphs and follies of human progress. Did you know that humans have walked on the moon and that soon they will walk on Mars?"

Leaning against Morelle's bed, Ell-rom crossed his arms over his chest. "I did not know that. But since I come from space-faring people, and given the technological advancement of humans, I am not surprised." He turned to look at his sister's peaceful expression. "Has she responded to any of your tales?"

Brandon shook his head. "Regrettably, she has not. I thought that I saw a ghost of a smile. That was why you found me leaning over her when you came in. I wasn't doing anything I was not supposed to."

The fact that Brandon was apologizing for something that hadn't even occurred to Ell-rom aroused his suspicions again.

Ell-rom frowned. "Like what?"

Brandon chuckled. "I keep forgetting how new you are to our culture. There is a very popular fairy tale about a sleeping princess and a prince who wakes her up with a kiss. I admit to being tempted, but I would never do such a thing without a lady's consent, and since Morelle is unconscious, I can only dream of her waking up, taking one look at me, and deciding that she wants to kiss me."

That was such an honest admission that Ell-rom felt his suspicions fade. "Are you enchanted by my sister, Councilman Brandon?"

"What can I say?" The media specialist lifted his hands in defeat. "She is magnificent." His expression turned serious. "Don't worry, Prince Ell-rom. I swear on my honor that I will not do anything inappropriate. I'm here to help Morelle in any way I can, and Julian and Bridget approve." He lifted his finger and pointed at the camera mounted near the ceiling. "It's not like we are really alone in here. This room is constantly monitored, and so is Jasmine's, so don't do anything you don't want the esteemed medics to see."

The truth was that he had forgotten about the cameras, which he shouldn't have, given that he had spent a lot of time in a room just like this one.

"Thank you for reminding me."

He took Morelle's hand in his and was shocked when the contact sent a rush of memories flooding through him. Chasing each other through the empty corridors of the temple, getting scolded by the head priestess and sent to their room, spending countless nights huddled together in the dark, whispering stories to each other and finding solace in each other's presence when the world rejected them.

"I'm sorry I haven't spent more time with you," he murmured, his thumb tracing small circles on the back of her hand. "A lot has been happening."

Brandon watched the interaction with sympathy in his eyes. "You must have been very close."

Ell-rom nodded, not taking his eyes off his sister's face. "We are two halves of the same soul, or as the head priestess used to joke, the mirror image of one another. Morelle was my whole world for so long. We only had each other."

A comfortable silence fell between them, broken only by the soft beep of Morelle's heart monitor. After a few moments, Brandon shifted in his chair. "I've been thinking about your story—yours and Morelle's. It could make a great script for an epic fantasy. Two beings, born of two worlds, hidden away, lost in space for thousands of years, only to emerge into a completely different era. It's the kind of tale that could captivate millions."

Ell-rom looked up sharply, a flicker of alarm passing through him. "Our existence must remain a secret."

Brandon laughed. "It would be totally fictionalized, of course. Names changed, details altered. But people will connect with the struggle for identity, the search for belonging, and the power of siblings' bonds. It's universal."

Ell-rom was intrigued despite thinking that this story should never see the light of day. "Is this what you do? Create fictional stories?"

"Among other things, yes." A spark of enthusiasm lit Brandon's eyes. "I've been in the entertainment industry for longer than I care to admit. Producing films and television shows. I love providing windows into other worlds and other lives, shaping perceptions, challenging beliefs, and inspiring change."

The concept of sharing stories, of connecting with others through shared experiences—even fictionalized ones—was oddly appealing. It contrasted with the secrecy and isolation that had defined so much of Ell-rom and Morelle's existence.

"I wish you could create a story about us, but it is too dangerous. I don't know if Earth's broadcasting is monitored on Anumati, but if it is, we can't risk even a fictionalized and altered version."

9

BRANDON

Brandon was slowly starting to relax, though his heart was still racing from the initial shock of Ell-rom's entrance. The words that had popped into Brandon's overactive mind upon seeing the prince enter Morelle's room had been chilling—the Grim Reaper, the devil, a demon.

Ell-rom had looked truly terrifying when he'd thought his sister was in danger, and the sight of those fiery eyes would surely haunt Brandon in his nightmares for days to come.

Now, he had no doubt Kian was hiding Ell-rom's true abilities, and he was doing so because the mellow-looking, genteel prince was potentially far more dangerous than he seemed.

The transformation had been startling—one moment a creature of nightmares, the next a confused and concerned brother. It was a jarring juxtaposition that left Brandon feeling slightly off-kilter.

After Ell-rom had ascertained that Brandon posed no danger to Morelle, the prince had returned to looking like he had on the podium earlier that day— a nice guy who wasn't quite sure of his footing and was looking to Annani, Jasmine, and Kian for direction.

Talk about misleading appearances.

Brandon found himself wondering just how much of Ell-rom's gentle demeanor was genuine and how much was a carefully constructed façade.

The thought sent a chill down his spine.

Did Morelle know what her twin was capable of?

If she retained her memories, she had to know. The siblings had had only each other for company, and unless they had been kept apart for some reason, they must know everything about each other.

Whatever Ell-rom's talent was, Brandon was sure it was nothing good. He hadn't imagined the raw power he'd glimpsed in those few tense moments, and he made a mental note to speak with Kian about this later.

If Ell-rom posed a greater threat than they'd been led to believe, the council needed to know.

Despite the jarring experience, he maintained his outward composure. Years in the entertainment industry had honed his ability to project calm and warmth even when he felt anything but.

He smiled pleasantly at Ell-rom, still working on winning the prince over. Given his wish to stay with Morelle, it was crucial to stay in Ell-rom's good graces.

"I believe that I can change enough of your story so it would be unrecognizable. Of course, it would need to be handled with care, combining the right balance of truth and fiction, just enough detail to make it feel real without risking exposure."

Ell-rom chuckled, the sound at odds with the fearsome creature Brandon had glimpsed earlier. "I wish I remembered more about my sister's personality. I don't know if she would love the idea of our story being turned into a fairy tale or hate it."

Brandon recognized the deflection for what it was. What Ell-rom was really trying to say was that he didn't know if he hated the idea or loved it. Brandon had a feeling that deep down the prince was intrigued by the concept, but he wasn't willing to take even the smallest risk.

It was understandable, given their precarious situation.

Truthfully, Brandon had no intention of turning the twins' story into a script. The idea had merely been a tool to make Ell-rom shift his attention away from his initial suspicions and focus it on something else. It had worked beautifully, perhaps too well. Now, Brandon found himself trapped in his own web and needed to untangle it with all the grace and elegance he had honed over the years.

"I didn't mean to overwhelm you, Ell-rom. It's just an idea, one of many I spout nonstop throughout my waking and slumbering hours." He gave a self-depre-cating laugh. "I am cursed with an overactive mind that sees everything in movie format. I really need to shift gears to social media productions, but as the saying goes, teaching an old dog new tricks is difficult."

Ell-rom's brow furrowed in confusion, his head tilting slightly to the side. "I'm sorry, but some things get lost in translation. What does a house pet have to do with movies?"

The prince's genuine bewilderment caught Brandon off guard, reminding him of just how much of Earth's culture and idioms were foreign to Ell-rom.

Brandon laughed, feeling some of the tension leave his shoulders. "It's just a saying. It means that it's difficult to teach new things to those who are entrenched in their old ways."

"Oh." Ell-rom's face cleared, and he smiled. "Now it makes sense." He turned to look at Morelle, his expression softening with concern. "I should get back to Jasmine. I didn't mean to be away from her for so long."

Brandon rose to his feet. "I hope it's okay with you

that I stay a little longer. I was in the middle of telling Morelle a story."

To his surprise, Ell-rom extended his hand. "Stay as long as you wish. If it helps draw Morelle out of her coma, I will be forever in your debt."

Brandon shook the offered hand. "Thank you for allowing me to stay."

Ell-rom nodded, giving Brandon another hesitant smile before turning to leave.

As the door closed behind the prince, Brandon let out a long breath and sank back into his chair beside Morelle's bed.

The glimpse of the power he'd witnessed was terrifying, and he wondered now whether he had imagined it. The prince was half Kra-ell, and the Kra-ell's eye color changed according to their feelings. Brandon didn't remember what all the different colors signified, but red was probably anger and aggression.

Not that Ell-rom's eyes had been red. They'd looked as if they were reflecting the fires of hell.

Brandon chuckled, blaming his overactive dramatic imagination.

His gaze drifted to Morelle's peaceful face. "Your brother certainly knows how to make an entrance." He shook his head. "I have a feeling your story is going to be even more interesting than I initially thought."

He needed to talk to Kian and tell him what he had seen. Kian was a straight shooter, and if there was something he knew about Ell-rom, he might try to hide it, but he wouldn't lie about it when confronted.

It just wasn't how Kian rolled.

If he confirmed Brandon's suspicion, the council needed to be informed about Ell-rom's capabilities.

For now, though, he had a story to finish.

"Where were we?" he asked Morelle, his voice taking on the warm, engaging tone of a storyteller. "Ah yes, I was telling you about the first moon landing and the origins of the conspiracy theories the event provoked."

ANNANI

nnani stood by the large window in her living room, her gaze sweeping over the meticulously maintained greenery outside. The midday sun cast a warm glow over the rose bushes surrounding her front porch and the rows of rosemary growing along the pathway with their woody stems and tiny blue flowers.

Her Odus moved around her, setting the long table for the family lunch in their usual quiet manner.

She looked forward to having her children and grandchildren gathered around her, but she regretted not having Morelle, Ell-rom, and Jasmine join them.

With a sigh, Annani reached into the hidden pocket of her gown, pulled out her phone, and called Bridget.

The doctor usually did not work on weekends, but Annani knew she was in the clinic supervising

Jasmine and Morelle in person because she knew how important they were to her.

"Clan Mother," the physician answered. "What can I do for you?"

"You are already doing a lot by being there and watching over Morelle and Jasmine. How are they?"

"No change. Both are still unconscious, but their vitals are strong. You are not going to lose either of them on my watch."

Annani was taken aback. That was such an odd thing for Bridget to say. "I do not doubt that for a moment. I expect both of them to make it. My concern is *when* they will wake up, not if they will."

"I know." Bridget sighed. "It's just that Ell-rom is panicking, and I've gotten used to repeating those words to calm him down. I wish I could give him a relaxant, but he refuses."

Annani winced. "I did not expect him to react so strongly. Kian and I did our best to downplay the risks of transition, not to worry him."

"Good that you did, or it would have been worse. The two most important people in his life are unconscious, and he does not have enough life experience to have developed the tools to deal with difficult situations."

Annani wondered whether Julian had told Bridget about Ell-rom's potential ability to kill with his thoughts. Probably not, or she would have known that he was more resilient than he seemed.

Jasmine's transition had arrived on the heels of a most jarring incident that had shaken Ell-rom to his core, and that was on top of weeks of worry about Morelle, who was not waking up from stasis.

"Did anyone get Ell-rom something to eat and drink? I am sure he forgot to feed himself."

Annani planned to visit him and Jasmine later in the day, but she should have thought to inquire about her brother's basic needs being met. Yesterday, Kian had asked Ogidu to pack a bag for him, and Okidu delivered it to the clinic, so at least that was taken care of.

"Don't worry," Bridget said. "Hildegard brought him and Brandon coffee and breakfast, and Brandon is getting them lunch."

Annani frowned. "Brandon? What is he doing in the clinic?"

After a moment's hesitation, Bridget chuckled. "Brandon has taken it upon himself to talk Morelle into waking up. He spent the night sitting by her bedside and only went home early this morning to shower and change, and he is back again now."

"That is surprising. I have never known Brandon to volunteer for any community service. He always claims to be too busy."

Bridget snorted. "Forgive me, Clan Mother, but Brandon is not thinking about this as a service to the community. He's smitten with the princess and fancies himself her Prince Charming or at least her knight in shining armor."

"Interesting." Annani turned away from the window, walked over to the couch, and sat down. "Jasmine stayed by Ell-rom's side because she had anticipated his arrival in her life for months if not years, and he was like the fulfillment of a prophecy for her. But why would Brandon feel compelled to help Morelle? Is he so taken with her beauty?"

Brandon was a valuable member of the clan and a councilman for a reason. He was very capable in his field, intelligent, resourceful, and charming. There was a lot to like about Brandon, but Annani was also aware of aspects of his personality that were less desirable. Like his aloofness, his choice to live outside of the village until recently, and his propensity to project an image of himself to fit the situation, whatever it might be, rather than show who he really was.

It was not her choice, though. It was Morelle's, and once she woke up, she would decide what kind of partner she wanted. Perhaps one of the many laid-back artists in the community would appeal to her more than the ambitious and charismatic Brandon.

Then again, being half Kra-ell, Morelle might find a warrior more appealing.

There were many good Guardians to select from, but none of the single ones held leadership positions, and Morelle might want someone who did.

"Perhaps Brandon is answering the Fates' call," Bridget said. "If they decreed that he belonged to Morelle, he would have felt the pull toward her even while she was still unresponsive."

Bridget's words rang true, but Annani reserved judgment. When she saw Brandon with Morelle, she would have more clues to assess the situation.

"Thank you for keeping me informed, Bridget, and thank you again for giving up your weekend to take care of Jasmine and Morelle. Please let me know as soon as there is any change in either of their conditions."

"It's my pleasure and privilege to welcome a new Dormant into immortality and the daughter of Ahn into our clan. I will inform you as soon as there is anything to report, Clan Mother."

"Thank you." Annani ended the call and put her phone back into its hidden pocket.

Morelle was beautiful, and that might be enough to enthrall a male, but there was something else about her, an aura of regality tinged with danger that might have appealed to Brandon.

What talents might her sister possess?

Ell-rom's newly discovered ability to kill with a thought was terrifying, but it might be extremely useful, depending on how it worked and at what distance.

It would be a sweet twist of fate if Ell-rom could eliminate their grandfather and save everyone on Earth from the Eternal King's deadly intentions. It would be a weapon of last resort, of course, but it would be nice to know that they had the option and would not be waiting helplessly for Earth's annihilation.

Should she share the news with all of her children and their mates?

To have it out in the open would be a relief, but she needed to discuss it with Kian first. She trusted everyone who would shortly be sitting around her dining table with her life, but Kian often saw danger and obstacles where she did not, and Annani did not wish to burden her family with news that would put them in danger.

She also did not wish for them to fear Ell-rom.

MORELLE

M orelle drifted in dreamscape at the edge of consciousness, the soothing cadence of the voice that had become her nearly constant companion, a beckoning beacon. The world beyond her closed eyelids remained frustratingly out of reach, but within the confines of her mind, vivid scenes played out with startling clarity.

One moment, she was lost in the fantastical tales spun by the velvet-voiced stranger, his words painting landscapes of wonder and intrigue, peppering her imagination with heroes and villains from Earth's rich history—and the next, she found herself swept away by visions of her mother, so vivid and real that Morelle couldn't be certain if they were memories or elaborate constructs of her subconscious mind.

As if summoned by her thoughts, her mother's face swam into focus, regal and beautiful, her expression soft and dreamy and unlike any Morelle remembered from real life.

"Morelle," her mother's voice echoed in the vast expanse of her mind, "there is so much I never had the chance to tell you."

Morelle felt a surge of longing, an ache to reach out and touch her mother's face. But in this ethereal space, she had no form, no substance. She was thought and feeling, nothing more.

"I'm listening," she said.

Her mother smiled. "In here, I can show you."

The scene shifted, and Morelle found herself observing a younger version of her mother, her face alight with fierce determination. Beside her stood a god, so bright and luminous that he was blinding, his white hair contrasting with the blackness of her mother's. Nevertheless, she didn't need to be told who he was. His features bore a striking resemblance to Ell-rom's and hers.

The god was their father.

"We were young," the younger version of her mother said. "So young and full of hope. Your father and I believed we could change the world, tear down traditions, and bring justice to the Kra-ell."

Morelle watched, fascinated, as the scene unfolded. Her parents huddled in secret meetings with other young gods and Kra-ell, the air around them crackling with possibility and danger in equal measure.

"It started as a friendship," her mother continued. "Shared dreams, shared ideals. We were kindred spirits, both of us chafing against the constraints of our societies and longing for something better."

The young couple in Morelle's vision grew closer, their hands brushing with increasing frequency, their gazes lingering.

"We were thrilled to disregard the old taboos," her mother's voice took on a hint of mischief. "We joined our bodies as we had joined our minds, reveling in the forbidden nature of our union."

The scene shifted again. Morelle caught glimpses of stolen moments, fervent kisses in shadowy corners, tender caresses behind closed doors, tender words that would have never passed the lips of a proud Kra-ell warrior but seemed to spill out of her mother's mouth.

Detached, she watched the young couple with interest as if they were strangers, not her parents, and she was touched by the beauty of their connection and the passion that seemed to ignite the air around them.

But as Morelle witnessed their love story unfold, she sensed a looming shadow on the horizon, and her mother's voice lost its mischievous lightness and grew heavy and sad.

"We thought we were invincible," she said. "We never imagined how quickly it would all fall apart."

The idyllic scenes gave way to chaos—flashes of conflict, angry faces, raised voices, the clash of weapons, robotic beings overpowering gods and Kra-ell alike.

So much blood had been spilled.

"The gods' rebellion was quashed," her mother said. "Your father and the other young gods who joined him in the rebellion were sent into exile. And I was left alone with a precious gift I would always cherish."

Her mother, now adorned with the regalia of the Kra-ell queen, placed a protective hand over her still flat stomach.

"No one knew," she continued. "I had four loyal Kra-ell males in my family unit, and even though they knew none of them had fathered my children, they protected me, and not one of them breathed a word about the true nature of my pregnancy. I was also lucky that my older sister had decided to join the priesthood instead of becoming the next Kra-ell queen, and she helped me protect you."

Suddenly, the head priestess protecting two abominations made more sense. They were blood, and for a Kra-ell, that was sacred. "I did not know that the head priestess was your sister."

Her mother nodded. "As you well know, Kra-ell priestesses relinquish their familial connections upon becoming holy mothers. The moment Jeal-lani put on the robes, she was no longer my sister."

"But she helped you nonetheless."

"Of course. Nothing could change the bonds of blood. Jeal-lani was a formidable female, and she would have made a better queen than me. To this day, I do not know if she chose priesthood out of religious conviction or because she realized that the head priestess was the most powerful among our people, even more powerful than the queen. In any case, I would not have been able to hide and protect you without her. You and Ell-rom looked like gods, not Kra-ell, and putting you in priest robes and veils was the only way to protect you."

Morelle marveled at the complexity of the maneuvering her mother had to come up with to hide the identity of her children from the very moment of their conception.

"Is Jeal-lani with you in the Fields of the Brave?"

Her mother shook her head. "She joined me many years after my passing, but only briefly. She was reborn almost immediately after dying. The Mother of All Life must have needed her to return to serve our people."

The scene dissolved, leaving Morelle once again in

the formless void of her own mind. She called out, wanting to hear more, but her mother was gone.

For now.

Morelle was confident that she would return.

BRANDON

Brandon watched with fascination as Gertrude wheeled in what looked like a cross between exercise equipment and a medieval torture device. The gleaming metal contraption had straps, hinges, and a digital control panel that made him curious and also a little apprehensive.

"What is this thing?" he asked.

Smiling fondly, Gertrude patted the frame as if it was a cherished pet. "This is called a CPM machine. It provides immobile or recuperating patients with continuous passive motion. It helps prevent muscle atrophy and maintain joint flexibility in comatose patients." She began positioning the device near the foot of the bed. "Julian ordered it after his experience with Ell-rom's rehabilitation. The prince's muscles had atrophied completely during the long stasis, and even though his body did a remarkable job of rebuilding them, he still had a hard time recovering.

Hopefully, this will help Morelle get on her feet much faster. Her body has had more time to fix the damage of the stasis, so her starting point will be better than Ell-rom's, and this machine will exercise her muscles to help her further along the way while she is still comatose."

Brandon hadn't known that a device like that was available, but then immortals had no need for such things.

"Is it going to stay on her all day?" he asked.

Gertrude chuckled. "That would be too much even for a half goddess, half Kra-ell. One hour at a time, three times a day."

He watched as the nurse adjusted the straps, noting how careful she was not to pull them too tight. "Is it painful?"

"Morelle can't feel a thing, but even if she could, the movement is very gentle." Gertrude pressed a few buttons on the control panel, and the machine hummed to life, slowly bending and straightening Morelle's knees. "See? It's basically like someone is helping her do very slow, controlled, basic movements."

Brandon pulled his chair closer, fascinated by the smooth mechanical motion. "It's amazing how much thought goes into caring for someone in such a state. I guess our medical staff had no experience with that before the twins' arrival."

Gertrude leaned against the bed and crossed her arms over her chest. "You are right, and it's true, not just for the twins. Now that we have humans living in the village, we need to expand our treatment capabilities." She glanced at the CPM machine doing its thing. "Julian also ordered a Pilates Reformer and tasked me with learning how to use it so I can help Morelle when she wakes up. When it gets here, I will need a volunteer to practice on." She looked at him expectantly.

As someone who had spent the majority of his time in the Hollywood crowd until recently, Brandon knew what a Pilates Reformer was and that it was a favorite among older actresses and some of the actors. It couldn't be too challenging if middle-aged women and men used it to stay in shape.

"I would gladly volunteer, but I think you will get more benefit from training one of the humans."

"Yeah, you are right." Gertrude sighed. "The thing is not built with immortal males in mind."

"Morelle might be very strong," he reminded the nurse. "She is half Kra-ell."

Gertrude shrugged. "Ell-rom was as weak as an old woman when he started his rehabilitation. I'm not worried about the princess breaking the Reformer. When she gets strong enough to do that, she will no longer need it."

Brandon's gaze drifted to Morelle's peaceful face. "I'm glad that Julian thought of those things to make her recovery easier than Ell-rom's."

"We live and learn, right?" Gertrude glanced at her watch.

"You don't have to stay here and monitor the device," he told her. "I'm here."

The nurse hesitated. "I'm supposed to watch her the entire time the CPM is working, but that's three hours out of my day. It would be a great help if you can do that for me."

"No problem. I'm here anyway."

A knowing smile played on her lips. "Actually, talking to the princess while the machine is working will make the treatment more effective. Patient engagement during passive therapy helps maintain neural pathways even if they can't actively respond."

"Really?"

Brandon was knowledgeable about many things, but science wasn't among them.

"Mhmm." Gertrude made one final adjustment to the machine. "It's the body-mind connection. Stimulating the body and the mind at the same time creates an amplified result. It's like a feedback loop. At least in theory. I didn't read any studies on the subject."

Gertrude continued talking about her need for continuing education, but Brandon remained stuck on what she'd said about stimulating the body and mind at the same time. Her words evoked images that were grossly inappropriate for this setting, and Brandon felt ashamed of entertaining such thoughts.

"I don't want to bore you with my chatter." Gertrude pushed away from the bed and headed for the door. "I'll be back in an hour. Let me know if anything seems off with the machine."

"I will."

After she left, Brandon tried to banish thoughts of all the ways he would one day stimulate Morelle's body while engaging her mind, but the harder he tried, the more vivid the images became.

He was cursed with a very vivid visual imagination, which made him a great movie producer, but was giving him a most inappropriate hard-on now.

13

ANNANI

At the sound of the doorbell ringing, Annani schooled her features into a warm, welcoming expression, pushing her worries to the back of her mind. There would be time for heavy discussions later when she revealed Ell-rom's talent to the rest of her children. For now, she would focus on enjoying the presence of her loved ones.

As Kian and Syssi entered, little Allegra squirming in her father's arms, Annani broke into a grin. "Come to Nana, sweetheart." She took the child from Kian.

"Mother." Kian leaned in to kiss her cheek. "How is your day going so far?"

Annani hugged Allegra to her chest and kissed her granddaughter's soft blond curls. "It has just gotten infinitely better." She accepted a slobbery kiss from Allegra. "There is nothing in the universe that can rival the joy of holding my grandchild in my arms."

The girl giggled, a sound of pure joy that seemed to lighten the air around them. "Nana," she said in a tone that sounded like she thought her grandma was being silly.

"It is true." Annani kissed her cheek. "Wait until you are a grandmother, and we will talk then. You will agree with me." She lifted the child so she could look into her eyes. "Children are wonderful, but grandchildren are like the icing on the cake or the cherry on top."

"I bet," Syssi said. "All the fun without all the work."

"Precisely." Annani returned Allegra to her father. "You look troubled, my son. What is amiss now?"

Syssi laughed, stepping forward to kiss Annani's cheek. "He's working too hard, as usual."

Before Annani could respond, the door opened again, admitting Amanda and Dalhu with little Evie in her father's arms.

Evie was not as friendly as her cousin, and she clung to her father, hiding her face in the crook of his neck. At six months old, she was starting to babble a few words, but 'Nana' wasn't one of them.

Annani tried not to be disappointed, but she was. At the same age, Allegra had already been a big fan of her grandmother.

"My sweet little Evie," Annani cooed, pressing a kiss to Evie's back. "Do not be shy. Your Nana loves you."

"She loves you too, Mother." Amanda leaned to kiss Annani's cheek. "She is just shy around people. Put her around animals, though, and she becomes a different girl."

"Oh?" Annani lifted a brow. "How so?"

"She just adores animals," Dalhu said. "I took her on a walk in the stroller yesterday afternoon, and we bumped into Parker walking Scarlet. Evie had a whole conversation with that dog. I recorded some of it." He pulled out his phone. "Would you like to see?"

"Of course." Annani leaned closer.

Dalhu hadn't exaggerated. As Evie babbled happily to the dog, the golden retriever responded with joyful howls and furious wagging of her tail.

"Fascinating," Annani said. "Perhaps she has a special affinity with dogs."

"She might," Amanda said. "Dalhu is trying to convince me to adopt a puppy."

"That's a great idea." Syssi unceremoniously took Evie from her father. "We can adopt two puppies from the same family. Wouldn't that be great?"

"I'd prefer a kitten." Amanda leaned on Dalhu's arm. "They don't bark, and they do their business in a sandbox instead of having to be walked."

Dalhu shrugged. "I don't mind walking a dog. I can do that while taking Evie on a stroll."

As the doorbell rang again, all eyes turned to the door, and when Alena walked in with Orion and little Evander Tellesious sleeping in his carrier, it was hard to believe that he was only two weeks old. So much had happened since he had been born.

David and Sari were the last to join their gathering, even though they were staying in Annani's house. They had gone on a walk around the village and returned just in time for lunch.

"The village is as lovely as ever," Sari said after exchanging hugs and kisses with her siblings and their mates. "The weather is absolutely perfect."

"You can still change your mind." Kian wrapped his arm around his sister's shoulders. "My invitation to you and your people is standing. You can move in any time."

She chuckled. "You gave away the houses you reserved for us to the Kra-ell. There is no more room."

"Nonsense." He kissed the top of her head like he used to do when she was little. "There is enough room for everyone, and I can always build more."

With the room filling with the chatter of her family, Annani felt the tension leave her shoulders. This was what she needed: the chaos and warmth of familial love.

Annani deliberated about how to take Kian aside without anyone noticing. She needed his opinion on whether telling everyone about Ell-rom's potential talent was a good move or not. She trusted her family, but her greatest reservation was about them becoming fearful around Ell-rom.

She caught Kian's eye and, with a subtle nod, indicated that she needed to speak with him privately. Understanding, he transferred Allegra to Syssi and put his hand on Annani's arm. "You wanted to show me that artifact you've seen on the web."

"Oh, yes. The artifact." She smiled. "I forgot about it. Let's see if I can find it again." She walked toward her room, where she had transferred her desk from the spare bedroom to accommodate Ell-rom and Jasmine. The guest quarters had gone to Sari and David.

After closing the door behind her, Annani walked over to her workstation and sat on the chair. "Do we tell them?"

"About Ell-rom's talent?" Kian guessed right away.

She nodded. "I hope Julian kept it a secret from Bridget."

"He did because I asked him to." Kian ran a hand through his hair. "I guess it doesn't make sense to keep it from my sisters and their mates. I just hope they won't start acting weird around him. The guy is barely holding it together as it is."

"That is my concern as well. We need to make them aware of how fragile Ell-rom is at the moment and how important it is to make him feel welcome and loved."

Kian put his hands on her shoulders and leaned to kiss her cheek. "I can deliver the facts. I leave assuaging their fears to you."

She nodded. "I hope I can do that."

MORELLE

I n the wake of her mother's departure, Morelle became aware once more of the voice that had become her constant companion in this twilight state. He was in the middle of a story, his words weaving a tale of star-crossed lovers that seemed to echo her parents' ill-fated relationship.

"...and though they knew their love was doomed, they couldn't bear to part. Each moment together was stolen, precious beyond measure. They lived a life-time in those fleeting encounters, knowing that the world would soon tear them apart."

Morelle was moved by the beauty and tragedy of the tale. Was this a legend? A myth?

The stranger's storytelling was masterful, his voice rising and falling with the rhythm of the narrative. Morelle found herself completely entranced, picturing the scenes he described with vivid clarity.

She could almost feel the desperate passion of the lovers and taste the bittersweet flavor of their stolen moments.

As the tale reached its poignant climax, Morelle felt an overwhelming urge to open her eyes and see the face of her storyteller. She willed her eyelids to lift, her fingers to twitch, anything to show that she was present, that she was listening. But her body remained stubbornly unresponsive, a prison of flesh and bone that kept her isolated from the world.

Frustration welled up within her. She was so close to the surface, so near to breaking through the barrier of unconsciousness. She could feel the world just beyond her reach—the bed beneath her, the cool air on her skin, the presence of the stranger at her bedside. Yet, no matter how hard she tried, she couldn't breach the final barrier.

"Mother of All Life, please help me find a way out of this prison."

Morelle felt like a hypocrite for beseeching a deity she didn't believe in. Asking her own mother for help would make much more sense. After all, she had appeared in this dream state and demanded that Morelle wake up.

"Mother!" she called in her mind. "Come back and help me breach the surface. I'm locked inside."

No one answered her plea.

Her mother had not returned, and the Mother of All Life was not real.

Morelle focused all her will on lifting her eyelids, and when that did not work, she imagined her eyelids fluttering or her fingers twitching, but her body refused to obey.

She remained still, silent, by all appearances lost in the depths of unconsciousness, while on the inside, she was a storm of awareness and emotion.

The voice continued its tale, unaware of her internal struggle. "And so, my dear princess, the lovers were forced to part. But their love lived on, a ray of hope in a world that sought to extinguish it. Some say that even now, centuries later, their spirits seek each other out, destined to find one another in every lifetime."

Despite herself, Morelle felt a pang in her chest at the bittersweet ending. It was beautiful and tragic, even if it was just a myth.

Real life was never as poetic as legends and myths tried to make it. Real life was mostly devoted to the mundane task of maintaining one's physical body, producing the next generation of beings, and for the Kra-ell, dying honorably in battle to gain for their soul admittance to the Fields of the Brave.

As the story came to a close, Morelle sensed a shift in the atmosphere around her. The male sighed, and she imagined him running a hand through his hair.

"I wonder if you can hear me, Princess," he said. "I like to think you can. That somewhere in there, you're listening, maybe even enjoying my tales."

Oh, if only he knew.

Morelle wanted to reach out and grab his hand to assure him that, yes, she was listening, and yes, she was enjoying his stories.

Well, most of them. She preferred the ones about epic battles and great technological achievements. The silly myths and legends about lovers were entertaining, but they also made her angry for some reason.

Still, all his stories served to anchor her, keeping her from drifting too far into the abyss.

"You know," he continued with a hint of amusement in his voice. "I've never had such an attentive audience. It's rather addictive, I must say. I could get used to a captive listener who doesn't interrupt or check their communication device every so often."

He was joking, and Morelle liked that he could do that at his own expense. It took confidence to do so. She wondered what he looked like and what sort of expressions crossed his face as he spun his tales.

"I will step out for a little bit to stretch my legs, but I'll be back soon with more stories. You might think that I have exhausted my repertoire, but I have plenty more. I've lived for a long time and accumulated enough stories to keep talking for years without pause."

Morelle felt a surge of panic at the thought of him leaving. His voice had become her constant, her guide. Without it, she might drift back into the void and get lost again.

Redoubling her efforts to move, to give some sign that she was aware, she focused all her will on her hand, imagining her fingers moving.

For the briefest instant, she thought she felt something, a twitch, a spark of connection between mind and body, but as quickly as it came, it was gone.

She was trapped.

"Dream of happier endings than the one in my tale, Princess. When you wake up, we'll write a new story together, one of hope and new beginnings."

At the sound of retreating footsteps, Morelle felt a wave of exhaustion wash over her. The effort of trying to break free of her body's prison had drained her, leaving her mental landscape fuzzy and indistinct.

She drifted again, caught between the vivid memories of her mother's revelations and the lingering echoes of the storyteller's voice. In this hazy realm, past and present blurred, reality and myth intertwined.

Morelle saw flashes of her childhood, the dark corridors of the temple, the whispered conversations with Ell-rom, and the constant fear of discovery. They had felt so alone, ignored by their mother, but now, armed with new knowledge, she understood the depth of her mother's sacrifice and what it had taken for her to save their lives.

ANNANI

As Kian and Annani returned to the table, Annani wondered how to begin telling her family about Ell-rom's ability. It was not the sort of thing she could just casually drop into the conversation.

Oh, by the way, your uncle might be able to kill with his thoughts. We are still trying to confirm his ability and figure out how it works, but we wanted you to be aware of this.

Now that Annani had verbalized it in her head, it actually did not sound that bad. She and Kian agreed that he would explain what had happened when Jasmine had been mugged, but Annani would introduce the topic at a convenient moment.

She wanted to wait until dessert was served, but the tension was robbing her of enjoying this meal with her family, and she wanted to get it done.

Annani put her fork and knife down, lifted the napkin to dab at her lips, and then put it down. "My dear children, by birth and by mate-hood, there is something I need to share with you. It might be a little premature since Kian and I do not have all the details yet, but I prefer not to keep this from you until we do."

"What is it?" Amanda cast her a worried look.

"It is about Ell-rom and a special ability he might have." She turned to Kian. "Would you like to explain how it came to light?"

Kian nodded. "It's not what you think. So far, Ell-rom hasn't manifested any compulsion ability, but to be perfectly frank with you, I expect him to develop it in the near future. We know that the trait is hereditary and that it usually comes from the father. Our mother inherited it from Ahn, but none of us have it because our fathers were all human and had no paranormal talents. Mother, Ell-rom, and Morelle are all the children of Ahn, so I expect Ell-rom and Morelle to have inherited the ability."

"Shouldn't he have manifested it by now?" Sari asked.

Kian considered the question for a moment. "I assume that for some, the ability starts showing later in life. The perfect example of that is Drova, who inherited Igor's compulsion ability but didn't show signs of having it until she turned seventeen. On the other hand, both Kalugal and Lokan have been able to compel since they were just boys. I don't know why it differs from person to person, but compulsion is not what Mother was alluding to. What Ell-rom can do is more significant than even that." He swept his gaze over everyone seated around the table. "None of what I'm about to tell you leaves this room. Is that clear?"

Amanda chuckled. "We are going to talk about it between ourselves, so obviously, it is going to leave this room. Even as a non-compeller, you need to be more accurate in your phrasing."

He cast her a glare. "Because I am not a compeller, I can phrase it in a way that anyone can understand my meaning without me having to spell it out. But to humor you, please don't discuss this with anyone other than those present here now. Julian also knows because he was involved, and so does Jasmine. I might tell Bridget and Turner, and once we have all the details, I will inform the council."

"Fine." Amanda crossed her arms over her chest. "Just get on with it. I'm dying of curiosity."

"Ell-rom might have the power to kill with a thought," Kian said, as matter-of-fact as if he was reporting a new building project.

The silence that followed was deafening. Annani watched as surprise and disbelief played across the faces of her loved ones.

As always, it was Amanda who first broke the silence. "How is that even possible?"

"We're not sure," Kian said. "I think it is a combination of compulsion that does not need sound to travel and hitches a ride on thralling. When pushed, Ell-rom can focus that thrall like a laser beam and use it to kill, but that's just a hypothesis. As you can imagine, testing his ability is problematic."

"But he seems so harmless," Alena said. "He doesn't seem capable of killing a fly."

"Appearances can be deceptive," Dalhu cut in, his expression grim. "How was his talent revealed?"

Kian told them about the mugger who had Jasmine by her throat with a gun pressed to her temple. "Ell-rom was afraid to move a muscle because the attacker looked unstable, and he feared that he might press the trigger even accidentally, so he just wished him dead, and the mugger complied."

Orion chuckled. "I wish we all had that ability. But it could have been a coincidence. The guy could have died of natural causes."

"It's possible," Kian agreed. "Not likely, though, and I'll tell you why. Julian examined the body very thoroughly and didn't find anything that could have been the cause of death. Secondly, it wasn't the first time that Ell-rom had killed with a thought. He dreamt about killing a guard when he was still a boy in the Kra-ell temple. Separately, neither of those incidents are conclusive, but together they are more than coincidental."

"Ell-rom is not a killer at heart," Annani said. "He is deeply disturbed by what happened, and I don't want any of you to act fearful around him. With both his mate and sister unconscious, he is in a very fragile emotional state right now, and the last thing he needs is his family giving him looks or asking him questions about it. I think it is best if you pretend not to know until further notice."

A murmur of acknowledgments sounded in response.

"Does he have control over it?" Sari asked. "Or is it unpredictable?"

"Ell-rom is terrified of lashing out in anger and killing accidentally," Kian said. "But I don't think he would do that unless someone he cares about is threatened, and he sees no other choice. We also don't know how far his death ray can reach and if it can kill more than one person at a time."

"So, he's dangerous," Sari said flatly. "We just don't know to what extent."

"Ell-rom is first and foremost family." Annani threw Sari a hard look. "And he is struggling to understand his own abilities. I bound his talent with compulsion so he could not use it accidentally, which provided him with great relief. What he needs now is our support, and the best approach is to make him feel loved and welcomed and not mention what he can do."

As a heavy silence fell over the table once more, Annani could almost see the wheels turning in each of her children's minds. It would take time for them to process and reconcile the gentle Ell-rom they had met with this new, potentially lethal version of him.

"What if Morelle has it too?" Amanda asked.

Annani shook her head. "From the dream Ell-rom had, it would seem that he is the only one who has the ability. Nevertheless, once Morelle regains consciousness, we will need to watch her closely, and what I said about Ell-rom applies to her as well. The best approach is to show her love and acceptance."

"How are you going to test Ell-rom's ability?" Dalhu asked Kian.

Kian's smile was feral. "You are going to love it, but I'd rather not discuss it around the dinner table. We can talk about it later over cigars and whiskey in the backyard."

DROVA

rova stood by the window, looking out at the lush greenery that seemed to mock her confinement. The cuff on her wrist wasn't that bad, but it was a constant reminder of her punishment.

House arrest was not the only way she was being punished, though. Her sentencing also included consuming only the vile synthetic blood. Her mother refused to take her out even to drink from the farm animals their former human servants were cultivating at the back of the village.

With a frustrated sigh, she turned from the window and flopped onto the couch. The television had become her only companion, and she was starting to develop what felt like butt sores from sitting all day.

Well, not literally, of course, but it certainly felt that way.

When the front door opened, Drova perked up, hoping it was Phinas. He was much nicer to her than her own mother, and he tried to be more understanding, but regrettably, it was Jade.

"Magnus is coming over," her mother said without preamble. "He's bringing Parker, Lisa, and Cheryl with him."

Drova's gut squeezed uncomfortably. "So?"

She knew perfectly well why they were coming, and it wasn't going to be pretty, but she pretended as if she couldn't care less.

"You will apologize to them," Jade said. "Taking the will of another is a grave offense in the clan's rulebook. When we moved in here, we agreed to abide by their laws. Thralling and compulsion are only allowed to protect lives and hide us from humans. Never for personal gain."

"It might be their way, but it's not ours." Drova crossed her arms over her chest. "In our rulebook, the strongest get to lead. Besides, I don't remember being told that I can't use compulsion."

No one had known that she had the ability, including herself, so of course, no one had told her not to use it.

Jade's expression hardened. "Imagine if it were the other way around, and Parker was the stronger compeller, using his power to make you do things against your will. Would you be okay with that and say it was his right because he was more powerful, or would you complain to whoever would listen?"

Her mother had a point. "I would probably complain," Drova admitted reluctantly. "But the fact remains that both you and my father ruled because you were the strongest compellers in your communities."

Jade sighed, her expression turning pained. "It's true, but being under Igor's control taught me an important lesson. I no longer use my compulsion ability to rule over others. I do the best job I can for them and hope it's enough for them to see me as their leader. You must agree that mine is a better way."

She was right, but she was also wrong, and Drova did not have all the answers.

"I agree that meritocracy is better than dictatorship," she conceded, "but we shouldn't forget our ways and become copies of the immortals either. We need to forge our own identities in a way that preserves our unique traditions, and—"

"Save this debate for another day," Jade cut her off. "Today, you will apologize to Lisa, Cheryl, and Parker and accept whatever retribution your victims demand."

Mother above, they would probably do everything they could to humiliate her. Then again, no one could force her to do anything she didn't want to.

She could always refuse.

She was already under house arrest. What else could they do to her?

Her mother's stern expression prevented her from voicing her pushback, but the knowledge that she could refuse to do anything that was too abhorrent was a comfort.

"When will they be here?" Drova asked instead.

"Soon. I can't stay to supervise, nor do I want to. I trust Magnus to be fair and not let things get out of hand." Jade turned on her heel and went out the door.

Drova resumed her position by the window.

She hated having to apologize when she didn't feel truly remorseful. Well, maybe she was a little sorry about forcing the two human girls to steal for her, but she wasn't sorry for Parker. There was no way he didn't use his own meager compulsion abilities to gain advantages with the girls at the human school he attended, or force his teachers to give him better grades, so if he came up with some horrible thing for her to do as retribution, it would be hypocritical on his part.

Still, he was a decent guy and had never been mean to her. Lisa and Cheryl had been even nicer, welcoming her to the village when she'd first arrived and doing their best to make her feel at home.

She had repaid their kindness with manipulation and betrayal, excusing her actions with the lame adage that it was survival of the fittest. In the Kra-ell society, the weak served the strong, and everyone accepted the pecking order, and that was how it should be, but they weren't Kra-ell, so it hadn't been fair to them.

Whatever.

It didn't matter now.

There was no taking back what had been done.

The question was what potential punishments her former "minions" might demand. Would they try to humiliate her? Make her shovel manure in the barn or herd the animals?

The uncertainty gnawed at her, but she pushed it aside. She was a powerful Kra-ell, and she could handle whatever they threw at her.

What a bloody mess.

Her desire to shake things up, to prove herself, had backfired spectacularly, and instead of gaining respect and power, she'd ended up isolated and punished.

Drova shook her head, trying to clear the troubling thoughts. She couldn't afford to show weakness, not now. Predators smelled fear, and despite the veneer of civility that those immortals wore like a badge of honor, they were predators like her.

Lisa and Cheryl were human, but they possessed immortal genes, so their humanity was a temporary state until they were old enough to hook up with immortal males who would induce their transition.

The thought of hookups led to Pavel's handsome face appearing in her head and warmth spreading over her cheeks.

Would he ever see her as more than a kid?

She was seventeen, which even the immortals considered as the age of consent, but he was a decade or more older, and he never looked at her as he looked at females he desired.

Still, in their tradition, it was her right to invite him to her bed, and it would be very rude of him to refuse. The problem was that she didn't want him to do this out of obligation.

Drova wanted Pavel to want her.

17

ROB

Rob added a few lines of code to the program he was working on and, satisfied with his progress, looked up over the screen of his laptop, hoping to see Margo enter the café, but she was running late and the cappuccino he'd ordered for her was getting cold.

Not her fault.

It wasn't as if she could just get in the car and drive to the village. She had to wait until one of the Guardians on rotation in the keep could give her a ride on his return journey.

Someone waved at him, and he smiled and waved back, but he couldn't remember who the guy was. Perhaps he knew him from the gym.

Rob had been going every day and meeting so many people that it was impossible to remember them all. It didn't help that they were all so freakishly perfect that it was difficult to find things to remember them by, like a bald head, a crooked nose, glasses, or a big-ass mole on the cheek.

When Margo finally appeared, her face lit up with a smile as she spotted him, and she waved while rushing over as if she hadn't seen him in months.

Rob rose to his feet, ready to embrace his sister.

She looked radiant and more beautiful than he remembered her from before her transition, but he wasn't sure that immortality was the only reason she looked so good. She was happy with her guy, who, despite being a freaking god, worshiped the ground she walked on.

"Rob!" Margo weaved her way through the tables. "Sorry I'm late. My ride needed to make a stop on the way."

"No worries." He embraced her tightly. "I've been keeping myself busy with work."

"You know it's the weekend, right?" She sat down on the chair he pulled out for her. "You're not supposed to be working."

He smiled. "I enjoy my work, and it's not like there is much else to do around here other than train in the gym, which I have been doing daily." He flexed his bicep. "Does it show?"

She scrunched her nose. "Give it some more time."

Laughing, he leaned closer to her. "You look good. Happy."

Margo's smile widened. "I am, but I will be even happier when I can move into this incredible place. Don't get me wrong, living in Kian's penthouse is no hardship, but it's difficult to relax when I don't know what the future holds. I don't know if, in a week or two, I will have to pack my bags and trek with Negal and the others through some godforsaken country-side, searching for the missing Kra-ell pods, or if I get to move into the village. I'm crossing my fingers for the experiment to work and for their commander not to notice that the tracker was moved from Dagor to a human host."

"Why does it need a host?"

"Those trackers only work in live bodies. Otherwise, they could've put it in a box and shipped it from place to place."

"Who is the host?" Rob asked.

Margo winced. "A trafficker they captured during one of their raids. They are keeping him locked up in the dungeon below the keep."

He arched a brow. "They have a dungeon?"

"They do," she whispered conspiratorially. "They also have catacombs under the keep. That's where they keep the Doomers they catch and put in stasis and also where they store the Kra-ell in their stasis chambers. The place is huge. It's spread out under an entire city block."

"Now you tell me?" Rob leaned back. "You should have said something while I was still there and taken me on a tour."

"You were in a rush to get to the village, remember?"

"Yeah." He rubbed the back of his neck. "I have no regrets. I love it here. So what now? How long are Aru and the others planning to wait for the commander to notice that the tracker was moved?"

"Aru wants to wait until the end of next week. If they don't hear from their commander, they will find humans willing to carry the trackers for a fee and send them trekking through Tibet, China, or Russia. The idea is to replace the hosts every now and then so they stay young and healthy."

Rob nodded slowly. "What if something goes wrong? I mean, what happens if one of those humans dies for some reason? Things happen, even to young people. It could be days before the gods could reach that person and transfer the tracker to someone else, and their commander will notice that one of the trackers is not transmitting."

Margo's smile faltered. "Oh, shoot. We hadn't thought of that."

"Could they claim it malfunctioned?" Rob asked.

She shook her head. "The gods' tech is supposedly fail-proof, but maybe they can do that. On the other hand, if that was a viable option, don't you think Aru would have thought of it already? There must be a reason he can't just tell the commander that one of the trackers broke down."

"Right." Rob drummed his fingers on the table, thinking of a way to solve the problem.

Margo's shoulders slumped, the excitement draining from her face. "Fates, how did we not think of that? What do you think we should do?"

Rob took a sip of his cappuccino, buying himself a moment to think. "Honestly? I don't know. But I'll keep thinking about it. There's got to be a solution. It's also possible to ignore the risk and hope for the best. It's not that likely that a young, healthy person would die if they are keeping safe and not doing anything stupid."

"True." Margo's mood seemed to have improved instantly. "By the way, did you get to speak to William?"

"Not yet, why?"

She shrugged. "I was just thinking on the way here how great it would be if both of us got to work for Perfect Match. You could work on the code part of it while I come up with amazing ideas for new adventures. My training is almost complete, and I'm ready to start."

He frowned. "I thought you were training to become an operator."

"I'm flexible. The truth is that I will be happy with any position they give me. I'm dying to experience a virtual trip, but I haven't done it yet because I've been waiting to do it with Negal. He's only agreed to do it in the village because he doesn't feel safe doing it outside and risking exposure. I tried to convince him that it was fine, and that Toven did it in one of the outside studios, and nothing happened, well, other than Mia nearly dying, but that had nothing to do with him being a god or someone discovering that he wasn't human. She got overexcited."

Rob knew about the Perfect Match service, of course.

Who didn't?

Advertisements for the studios were everywhere, and Margo had been talking about it ever since Mia had met her fiancé through the service, but somehow, it had never occurred to him to try it himself.

Rob leaned back in his chair. "From what you've told me, participants are monitored by people with medical training. How come no one noticed that Toven didn't react like a human?"

She shrugged. "I don't think the differences are so evident. We still have the same organs in the same places, but gods and immortals have a much better self-healing ability."

"Also better hearing, eyesight, sense of smell, etc."

"True, but that's not something that would become evident from monitoring blood pressure and heart rate. Negal is worried that the interface will tap into his memories, but since memories are nearly indistinguishable whether they are of real events, dreams, or fantasies, how would the AI running the program know what's real, right?"

Rob nodded. "I wonder what it's like to get completely immersed in an adventure and forget who I am in the real world. Frankly, I don't think it's possible."

Margo's eyes lit up. "It is, and it's incredible. People can't tell it is not real. You feel like you are living inside the virtual world. You can do a solo adventure and experience things like piloting a fighter jet or parachuting or any other dangerous activity that you would have never dared in real life, but in my opinion, the best adventures are those you do with a partner. You're sharing the experience with someone else, either a stranger that the algorithm matched you with or the person you are currently with. In both cases, you get to know them in ways you never could in the real world, and since there are two minds involved, the adventures are richer and more full of surprises."

"It's intriguing, but as someone who is intimately familiar with code, I don't think I trust an algorithm to find my perfect match."

She seemed surprised. "You don't? Why?"

"Biases that are introduced by the programmers or the material the AI is trained on. Despite my obviously inadequate judgment, I still prefer to find my partner myself. That being said, I would love to try an adventure and get out of my comfort zone. I can still hear Lynda screeching about how boring I am."

Margo's eyes softened. "Forget that harpy." She put her hand on his arm. "You are embarking on the greatest adventure of your life by just being here."

"That's true." He looked around the café and all the perfect people sitting at the small tables, drinking their coffees and munching on their pastries or sandwiches. "It feels like a movie set here. Everyone is beautiful."

She followed his gaze. "They are, aren't they? Not as perfect as my Negal, though."

Rob laughed. "Who would have thought that my baby sister would snag a god?" He leaned over and kissed her cheek. "So, tell me what you have learned in school today."

He used to ask her that when they were still kids, imitating their father.

"Well, today I wasn't at school, but I can tell you what I've learned over the past weeks."

As Margo talked about the psychological profiling, the customized scenarios, and the extensive questionnaires that were needed to craft the experience, Rob found himself imagining what it might be like to step into one of those virtual worlds. To shed the constraints of reality and explore unknown parts of himself.

"The best part," Margo said, "is that it's not just about romance. Sure, that's a big part of it for many people, but the experiences can be tailored to all kinds of relationships. Friendships, mentorships, even just meeting like-minded individuals who share your interests."

Rob nodded. "It sounds transformative."

Margo beamed. "It is. That's why I'm so excited to be a part of it."

18

DROVA

As Drova opened the door for Magnus, her eyes immediately zeroed in on the earpieces he wore. She'd expected that he would come prepared, and in a way, it was better than him coming in with a gun holstered at his hip, but for some reason it still hurt to see every adult who walked through that door wearing earpieces, including her mother.

"Hello, Drova." Magnus offered her his hand.

"Hello." She shook it reluctantly. "Please, come in."

Since moving into the village, she'd been forced to learn what the immortals considered basic manners, mostly thanks to Phinas, who'd made a point of educating her in Western etiquette.

Behind him walked her former minions, Parker, Lisa, and Cheryl. All three were wearing backpacks as if they were on their way to school, but it was the weekend, so maybe they were planning a joint study session in the café later.

"Hi," Parker murmured.

Cheryl and Lisa only nodded in her direction, both looking very uncomfortable to be there.

Magnus walked over to the dining table and pulled out a chair. "Please, sit down." He motioned to Drova.

Having no choice but to comply, she did as he commanded and watched as the three teenagers sat across from her while Magnus positioned himself at the head of the table.

"Before we begin," he said, looking into Drova's eyes. "I just want to make some things clear. Parker and the girls are not wearing filtering earpieces, and they were nervous about coming here today, but I assured them that you will not try anything because you won't like the consequences." He smiled, but it was a cold smile. "House arrest is not the worst punishment we can mete out. If you try to compel anyone, you will find yourself in a small cell in the keep's dungeon."

The implied threat sent an involuntary shiver down Drova's spine, but she kept her face impassive. "I'm not going to compel anyone," she replied, her tone just shy of insolent as she swept her gaze over the three teenagers. "You have nothing to be afraid of." She added a chilly, threatening smile.

Magnus shook his head. "You'd better change your attitude and fast, Drova. I don't have patience for your games."

"What games?" She leaned back and crossed her arms over her chest.

"It's time to apologize, and you'd better make it sound sincere."

Drova gritted her teeth, the words sticking in her throat. But the thought of being stuck in a tiny cell in the keep's dungeon spurred her on. "I'm sorry," she managed, the words coming out stilted and insincere. "I shouldn't have compelled you to do those things."

Magnus nodded his approval. "That will do, but you need to apologize to each person you harmed by name."

Drova stifled the urge to roll her eyes. The faster she did what he wanted, the sooner this charade would be over, and they would leave her alone.

"Parker." She looked the boy in the eyes. "I'm sorry I made you steal things for me."

"And break things," Parker added.

She nodded. "And break things."

"Apology accepted, but I also want you to give me your vow that you will never compel me again."

As long as he wasn't demanding that she never

compel anyone else, Drova was willing to do it. "I vow to never compel you again."

She had never vowed to do or not do anything before, but she'd always imagined a magical thunderclap would accompany the vow, the Mother of All Life putting her stamp of approval on it.

Of course, nothing like that happened, but Drova still felt the weight of her promise. Parker would never have to worry about her compelling him to do anything.

"Thank you." He smiled at her.

She was forced to repeat the same ritual with Cheryl and Lisa, and once it was done, everyone seemed to calm down, even Magnus.

Drova turned to the boy. "Tell me the truth, Parker, have you never used your abilities on the humans at your school? It must be so tempting, having all that power and not using it."

There was no chance he would admit it in front of his father, but she enjoyed needling him.

"Never," Parker said firmly. "Thralling and compulsion are forbidden unless it's to save a life or keep our existence secret from humans. We don't abuse our powers. When I want to practice my ability, I ask Lisa and Cheryl's permission first."

Well, that was a neat loophole. Maybe she could hone her ability in a similar way. Except Cheryl and Lisa trusted Parker, while no one was going to trust her after the stunt she'd pulled.

Still, she wasn't sure she believed Parker's avowed innocence.

"You expect me to believe that no one ever bends the rules a little?" She looked at Magnus this time. "There's no way to enforce compliance, and you can't expect a rule that can't be enforced to be followed."

"It's true that we can't find out about every infringement," Magnus said. "But it's a matter of character, Drova. Good people don't go around thralling and compelling others to gain an unfair advantage."

"Bullshit," Drova chuckled, shaking her head. "I'm a faster runner than any human or immortal. Should I not use my speed because it gives me an 'unfair advantage'? Where do you draw the line?"

"There's a big difference between natural physical abilities and manipulating someone's free will," Magnus countered. "One is a gift you were born with, the other is a violation of another person's autonomy. Nevertheless, I would not advise running competitions with humans even if you could win great rewards. The risk of exposure is not worth it."

Had he just said great rewards?

"What kind of rewards?" Drova asked.

Magnus laughed. "Competitive sports reward winners with monetary prizes and opportunities to promote sports apparel for financial reward, but as I said, don't even think about it. The money is not worth your life, and this is what you could be forfeiting if you expose yourself."

"What if she wins only by a little?" Lisa asked. "And wears makeup to hide her alien features?"

Magnus shook his head. "Forget I ever said anything about it. No immortals or Kra-ell can compete in human sports, and that's the end of this discussion. I have other commitments to attend to today." He turned to his son. "Parker, why don't you tell Drova what you've decided to ask from her as compensation for the harm she has inflicted on you?"

Drova tensed.

With a glint in his eye, Parker leaned down, reached into his backpack, and pulled out four thick books. *"The condensed history of the universe from the beginning of time."* He slammed one book on the table. *"Humans."* He slammed another on top of the first. *"21st Century Science."* He put it on top of the second. *"Greatest Philosophers of All Time."* He put it on top of the stack. "I want you to read these cover to cover. You have two months, and then I'll test you on what you've learned. If you don't pass with flying colors, I'll give you another two months and test you again, and so on, until you pass."

Drova felt her heart sink. Reading? Studying? It was almost the worst punishment he could have devised for her. She hated books, and she hated sitting on her ass. She was a warrior, and her time was best spent sparring and practicing her moves. "You've got to be kidding me," she groaned.

Parker's smile widened. "My mom's penalties for my bad behavior were always educational. I hated it, but when I got older, I realized how smart her approach was. Instead of diminishing you, this punishment will force your betterment."

Before Drova could protest further, Lisa and Cheryl pulled out more books from their backpacks, and her eyes widened in horror as she took in the growing stack on her dining table. At least Lisa's books seemed thinner—a small mercy.

"My contribution to your education is the greatest works in literature," Cheryl said. "I will give you six months to finish them all, and I suggest that you take notes because my test will be exhaustive. I will check your knowledge of the smallest details."

Lisa grinned. "Mine are math workbooks. You are to complete one every two months and bring it to me to check."

Drova hated math even more than all the other subjects.

"This is insane," she sputtered. "There are enough words in these books to fill years of schooling!"

The three teenagers laughed, the sound grating on Drova's nerves.

"That's the whole point," Cheryl said.

"Don't worry," Parker added in an infuriatingly patronizing tone. "You can call me anytime you have trouble understanding something. I'd be happy to tutor you for a fee, of course. I'm sure your mother would gladly pay me for helping you with your education."

Drova felt her cheeks burn with humiliation. The idea of needing help from a fourteen-year-old boy was humiliating. Or was he fifteen? Did it matter?

"Fine," she said through gritted teeth. "I'll read your books, and I'm sure I won't need any help. The fact that I hate studying doesn't mean that I can't do it." She leaned toward Parker. "Let's see either one of you in the training ring able to follow my most basic moves."

Parker's eyes started glowing. "Challenge accepted. I'll help you with your studies, and in exchange, you will train me."

Magnus cleared his throat. "Perhaps once you get your own earpieces. Until then, your visits with Drova will have to be supervised."

"For how long?" Drova asked.

He gave her a sad smile. "I don't know. You will have to earn back our trust, but frankly, I don't know how you will be able to do that nor how long it will take."

ROB

"Oh, look." Margo's eyes lit up. "That's Gertrude."

Rob followed her line of sight and felt his breath catch in his throat.

The woman approaching their table was strikingly beautiful, with long dark hair that fell in soft waves around her shoulders and piercing green eyes. Even among all these perfect immortals, something about her stood out.

It was like an aura.

Was she a goddess?

No, there was only one goddess in the clan, and she was a tiny redhead who looked like an angel.

Rob straightened in his chair, suddenly very aware of his appearance. Had he made sure to wear a clean shirt this morning? He hadn't done laundry since arriving at the village and was recycling the few clothing items he had bought at Walmart on the way.

He really should have gotten better clothes by now. What would this perfect beauty think of a human guy dressed in a Walmart T-shirt and jeans?

"Gertrude!" Margo waved the woman over. "Come join us!"

As the woman reached their table, Rob stood, feeling awkward but determined to make a good impression.

Margo rose to her feet as well and made the introductions. "Rob, this is Gertrude. She's one of the nurses here in the village. Gertrude, this is my brother Rob."

"It's a pleasure to meet you," Rob said, extending his hand.

"Likewise." Gertrude's grip was firm and warm, and her smile was genuine. "Welcome to the village, Rob. I hope you will be happy here."

"I'm sure I will be." He pulled out a chair for her. "I don't think I've seen you around before. I would have remembered you."

It sounded like a cheesy line even to his own ears, but it was the truth. A face like hers wasn't easy to forget.

Gertrude smiled. "I've been at the keep, taking care of Ell-rom and Morelle. I just got back to the village after the experiment was completed." She turned to Margo. "Did you tell Rob about it?"

Margo nodded. "I did."

"There's no reason for the doctors or me to stay there until we are needed again when it's time to put the trackers in other hosts."

"Do you know what they are going to do with the trafficker after he's no longer needed?" Rob asked.

Gertrude's brow furrowed. "I'm not sure, to be honest. That's not really my area. I'm just there to perform nursing duties."

As she spoke, Rob found himself drawn in by her animated expressions. She was lovely, with a hint of shyness that he found endearing.

She was the opposite of Lynda, he realized with a start.

Where Lynda had all golden hair, sharp angles, and almost boastful confidence, Gertrude had dark hair, soft curves, and an inner strength tinged with a touch of awkwardness.

It was a refreshing change.

"So, Rob, what do you think of the village so far? It must be overwhelming."

Rob chuckled. "It is, but it's also refreshing and wonderful."

He proceeded to tell the lovely nurse about Arwel volunteering to be his inducer and how he'd been training to prepare for the induction fight. "I don't want to embarrass myself or Margo," he admitted with a self-deprecating smile.

Gertrude nodded. "That's great that you're taking it so seriously. I try to visit the gym at least four times a week. When are you usually there?"

"I was planning to go tonight, actually. Around seven."

"Oh!" Gertrude smiled. "I might see you there. I want to do some weightlifting this evening. I could use a spotter."

She didn't look like someone who pumped iron, but Rob had learned that looks were more deceptive in the village than in the human world. The other problem was that the soft-looking nurse was probably stronger than he was, and he wouldn't be able to spot for her.

There was no way he was admitting that, though. He would just have to find a way to get out of spotting for her.

"I usually train with the punching bag," he said. "Would you like to join me there?"

"Sure." She gave him a bright smile. "I've never trained with those before, so you will have to show me how to do it."

Rob felt a flutter in his stomach. Was she flirting with him? It had been so long since he'd been in this situation he wasn't sure he could trust his instincts. But there was something in the way she held his gaze, the slight tilt of her head, that made him think maybe she was interested.

"I'd be delighted."

Gertrude grinned. "Thank you. I've always wanted to try boxing." She pretended to punch the air in quick succession. "I don't work in human facilities, but Merlin does, and he tells me that sometimes they bring in patients who are high on drugs and attack the staff. If I ever decide to work with humans, I should probably work on my fighting skills."

"I've heard stories from the ER," Rob said. "The sister of one of the guys I work with is a PA in an ER, and she told him that it's like a war zone in there."

"Oh, my." Gertrude pretended to be scared, but the slight twitching of her lips betrayed that she wasn't. "Perhaps I should stay away from human hospitals. It's not like my duties here leave me with a lot of free time." She seemed thoughtful. "On a completely different subject, have you ever done Pilates?"

"No, but maybe Margo has. Why?"

"We are getting a Pilates Reformer tomorrow, and I'm supposed to learn how to train people on it. I can watch instructional videos, but I need someone to practice on who will not break the device. As long as you are still human…"

The implication was obvious. Rob was weak, and she

wasn't afraid of him breaking her new toy. But if it meant having her hands on him, he didn't mind.

"I'll gladly let you train on me."

She grinned. "Awesome. Thank you for helping me."

He returned her grin. "Any time."

As they chatted for a few more minutes, Rob was becoming increasingly aware of how easy it was to talk to Gertrude. She was knowledgeable and passionate about her work, and he found himself genuinely interested in her stories about the medical herb garden she cultivated in her backyard, and her work with the other village physician who used her herbs to create elixirs and potions for various ailments, and most importantly helping immortals conceive, which was a major problem given their low fertility rate.

Margo found the subject exceedingly fascinating and asked a lot of questions, making Rob suspect that she wanted a child with Negal sooner rather than later.

"The potions taste really bad." Gertrude's lips twisted in distaste. "We haven't had much success yet, and I'm wondering if it's because the couples are not using them consistently because of that. I tried to convince Merlin to mix in some agave nectar to improve compliance, but he thinks it will be detrimental to the potions' potency."

Margo continued asking questions about who got pregnant using the potions and who was still working on it, but Gertrude wasn't forthcoming with information.

Rob waited for a lull in the conversation to ask, "Can I get you a cappuccino?"

"Oh, no. I have to go." Gertrude rose to her feet. "I was just passing by on my way to the clinic."

"Will I see you at the gym later?" he asked.

She gave him a bright smile. "Definitely. I'm looking forward to it."

As she walked away, Rob turned back to Margo, only to find his sister watching him with a knowing grin. "What?" he asked.

Margo laughed. "Oh, nothing. Just enjoying the show."

Rob felt his cheeks warm. "I don't know what you're talking about," he mumbled, but he couldn't quite keep the smile off his face.

Margo's expression softened. "You know, there's something I should probably tell you about Gertrude."

Rob's stomach dropped. "Is she seeing someone?"

"Not that I know of." Margo took a deep breath. "She and Negal used to have a thing."

Rob blinked. "When?"

"During the cruise before he saved me. It wasn't serious, from what I understand, but it ended when Gertrude realized that Negal was losing interest in her, and it was because of me."

"Wow. That must be awkward."

"It is, but it gets worse," Margo admitted, looking a bit sheepish. "I was kind of jealous of Gertrude when I first arrived on the ship and heard Negal promise to see her later. I wanted him for myself. I still feel bad about it. Gertrude is a really great woman, and she didn't deserve to be treated like that by Negal. But you know, when the Fates decide to match you with someone, they don't care whose toes they need to step on to get their way."

"Yeah, tell me about it. It would seem that the Fates thought Lynda would be better off with her ex."

"You've got it all wrong." Margo smiled and leaned closer to him. "The Fates thought that you would be better off with someone else and used Lynda's ex to get you to see that."

"I like your version better." He looked into his sister's eyes. "Would it bother you or Negal if I asked Gertrude out?"

Margo's face broke into a wide grin. "Are you kidding? I think it would be fantastic. Gertrude is wonderful, and you deserve someone who can make you smile like that. In fact, I think you two would be great together. And it would make me feel a lot better about the whole situation with Negal."

"Well, let's not get ahead of ourselves. We've only just met."

"True," Margo conceded. "But I saw the way you were looking at each other. There's definitely a spark."

Rob felt a flutter of excitement in his chest.

He'd enjoyed spending time with Lusha, but this was the first time since his life had imploded that he saw a potential connection.

"So," Margo said, a mischievous glint in her eye, "what are you going to wear to the gym tonight?"

Rob groaned. "Come on, Margo. It's just a workout, and everything I have with me is from Walmart. Nothing I have will impress even a down-to-earth girl like Gertrude."

Well, calling her a girl was probably wrong. "How old is she? Do you know?"

"No clue. Does it matter?"

He shrugged. "Not really. If Toven, a seven-thousand-year-old god, can be happy with Mia, a twenty-seven-year-old woman, then age is truly irrelevant."

20

KIAN

As Kian stood next to the limo, watching Okidu load Sari and David's luggage into the trunk, he felt a twinge of sadness at his sister's departure. A weekend was not enough time, and telling himself that the entire family had recently spent ten days together on the wedding cruise wasn't helping.

Syssi and Amanda had already said their goodbyes on their way out to work this morning, and their mother had bid farewell to Sari and David at her home. Now, it was Kian's turn to see them off, which always left him feeling a bit melancholy.

It would pass, drowned out by the demands of his job and the joys of being with the rest of his family, but from time to time, he would think of the one sister who did not attend most of their family dinners, and he would get peeved at her refusal to move into the village. In that respect, he was much more of a

129

mother hen than their actual mother, who had only recently started spending the majority of her time in the village.

He wanted to take credit for creating the utopia that drew her in, but the truth was that as idyllic and safe as the village was, it was far from perfect, and that was his doing as well.

He shouldn't have invited the Kra-ell to live with them.

Kalugal's men had integrated better, but even they hadn't become true members of the community yet.

Kalugal had, though, maybe because he was family or maybe by the power of his personality, and perhaps the leader's position was what mattered.

Following that logic, though, Jade had become a pillar of the community as well, so maybe the rest of her people would integrate better in time.

Sari leaned in, pressing a soft kiss to his cheek. "It's always a pleasure to visit your village. You have truly made it a haven for the clan."

He lifted a brow. "Then what's stopping you from joining us?"

She sighed. "We've had this talk so many times before, and my reasons haven't changed. It is not smart for us to all congregate in one location, not in light of the constant threats from enemies who wish to annihilate us, and also, it is not good for us as a society."

She was right about them having had the same argument many times before, and her points were valid but not conclusive. In his opinion, the advantages of the entire clan living in one location outweighed the disadvantages.

"Keep me posted about testing Ell-rom's talent." Sari patted his arm.

Kian raised an eyebrow, a mischievous glint in his eye. "Why? Are you eager to find out how far Ell-rom's talent can reach because you have someone you need to be assassinated?"

Sari's lips quirked into a smirk. "Several someones, actually."

Kian chuckled, but a part of him wondered if there was a kernel of truth in her jest. His sister always had a sharp edge to her humor. "I won't ask who."

"Good, because my list is long, and we need to go. Keep me posted about Morelle and Jasmine's status as well."

David extended his hand. Kian grasped it firmly, then pulled his sister's mate into a brief but heartfelt hug, complete with the obligatory back-slapping. "Take care of her. Don't let her work herself to the bone."

David chuckled. "I keep trying, but you know Sari. She doesn't listen to me or anyone else."

"Yeah, I know." Kian kissed his sister one last time before she climbed into the limousine.

He watched for a moment as the limo pulled away, waved for the final time, and turned around.

He was halfway to the office building when his phone rang.

Pulling it out of his pocket, he glanced at the screen. "Good morning, Aru."

"Good morning, Kian. I just wanted to give you an update. The commander hasn't called yet. The stress of waiting for him to make contact is driving me up the wall, and I'm tempted to call him myself, but I have nothing to report."

"It might be a good idea to prepare a story either way. Something about your ongoing research into potential pod landing sites."

"Of course," Aru said. "I've got a detailed report ready to go, filled with enough technical jargon and dead ends to keep him satisfied for a while, but nothing that justifies a call from me."

"I understand. Then don't call. It would just make your commander suspicious."

"I know." Aru sighed. "I will wait until the end of the week to transfer the other trackers, but we should start searching for human hosts so we have them ready by then. I was hoping that you could help us find the right candidates. We need people who are young, healthy and love to travel. Preferably with extensive hiking experience. Any ideas where we could find such people?"

"Not off the top of my head. I'll get Shai working on it."

"Thank you. Should I consider it taken care of?"

"Of course. Don't worry about it. By Friday, you will have three strapping humans ready to embark on an all-expenses-paid trip to wherever."

After ending the call, Kian entered the office building and took the stairs up to the second floor while his mind worked on Aru's problem.

Young, healthy men who loved to travel. Former soldiers, perhaps? Those who had just been discharged from active duty and were looking for a little adventure before settling down.

Or maybe mercenaries.

They were used to high-risk situations, comfortable with travel, and often operated outside normal societal constraints. Better yet, he knew just the person who could help him find the right people.

Walking over to his desk, he sat on his swivel chair, turned it toward the windows, and called Turner.

"Good morning, Kian," the guy answered. "Trouble in the village?"

He chuckled. "Always, but nothing that requires your particular talents. Are you at your city office or still here?"

"I'm on my way out."

"Can you stop by my office for a few minutes? We haven't talked in a while, and I have a bunch of updates."

Turner snorted. "Do you really think that there is anything going on in the village that I don't know about?"

"Bridget?" Kian asked.

"Naturally. She tells me everything. But I'll stop by anyway. You are right about the two of us not having a one-on-one in a while."

"Do you want me to get you coffee from the café?" Kian asked.

"Naturally. And a pastry to go with it."

21

BRANDON

B randon's eyes drifted between Morelle's serene face and the open door that led to the waiting room. The sounds of hushed conversations filtered in, creating a backdrop of quiet activity. He'd left the door open deliberately, both to stay connected to the goings-on outside and to encourage others to check in on Morelle.

The more visitors she had, the better.

Earlier, Alena had arrived to keep Ell-rom company by Jasmine's bedside. She had listened to the prince express his worry for his mate and had said all the right things to encourage him, but there was a note of tension in her voice that only someone who knew her well would detect.

Was she worried about Jasmine? Had Bridget told her something that she had kept from Ell-rom?

135

Brandon hadn't heard anything that would indicate that Jasmine was experiencing difficulties, but he planned to ask Gertrude or Hildegard later. The nurses were much more likely to spill the beans than the physicians.

"Poor guy is losing his marbles," he told Morelle. "And no amount of talking and reassurances are helping him. I just hope that he's worrying for nothing. I wish you would wake up, not just because I want to see the color of your eyes and hear your voice. Your brother is falling apart."

Brandon kept his voice low as he narrated his observations, and the device he was using to translate his words into Kra-ell adjusted seamlessly.

At least to his ears.

"It's been days now, and Jasmine is showing no signs of waking. We were hoping she would be one of those who recuperated fast, but she's not. Still, this is considered normal for a transition. Some were out for weeks like you are. Only you are not transitioning. You are just healing. Although I have to tell you, you look as good as healed. Your color is good, and your face has filled out. The docs are taking good care of you."

Brandon's eyes traced the contours of Morelle's face, her hands that were resting by her sides, searching for any hint of response, but as usual, there was none.

He sighed and shifted his gaze to the lap desk balanced across his knees. He'd brought a laptop and a tablet to work on his ideas for the InstaTock project, but he hadn't made much progress. Every time he tried to focus on the screen, his attention was drawn back to Morelle.

What if he missed something?

A flicker of an eyelid, a twitch of a finger?

"I'm trying to work on this project," he told her, gesturing to his laptop even though she couldn't see it. "The idea is to create content that promotes critical thinking, something that will help young people distinguish fact from fiction. But I've got to admit, Princess, it's hard to concentrate with you lying there looking so..." He trailed off, searching for the right word. Beautiful? Vulnerable? Fascinating? All of the above, if he was being honest with himself.

As the sound of familiar voices from the waiting room drew Brandon's attention, he recognized Kalugal's melodic timbre mixing with Ell-rom's softer tones, and a few moments later, Kalugal appeared in the doorway, his figure filling the frame.

"Can I come in?" Kalugal asked, his eyes fixed on Morelle.

Brandon straightened in his chair. "Of course. Please join us. Morelle needs as many different visitors as we can get in here. The more stimulation, the better."

Damn. He really should avoid saying that word.

Kalugal walked in and stood at the foot of the bed, studying her for a long moment. "She looks like Ell-rom, but not as much as I expected. There's a softness to her features. She seems younger than him, although they are the same age. Sweet. Innocent, almost."

Brandon disagreed with that assessment, but he held his tongue. Sweet and innocent weren't the words he'd use to describe Morelle, even in her unconscious state. There was a regality to her, a hint of something fierce lurking beneath the surface. But then, he was basing this on nothing more than intuition and the fragments of her past he'd pieced together from conversations with her brother.

"She's beautiful," Brandon said instead, the words slipping out before he could stop them.

A knowing smile tugged on one corner of Kalugal's mouth. "That she is." His gaze shifted to Brandon's laptop. "What are you working on?"

He angled the screen towards Kalugal. "I'm still working on ideas for the game on InstaTock we talked about. I wrote outlines for a series of short videos designed to promote critical thinking and fact-checking skills." He pulled up a few sketches on his tablet, showing Kalugal the rough storyboards he'd been working on.

Kalugal studied the images, nodding slowly. "It's a good concept, but I'm not sure it's enough to entice young humans. From what I've observed, they have very short attention spans. And seeking the truth, as noble as it is, might seem too time-consuming and boring to them. They like to be told what to believe by influencers they trust, and influencers say whatever you want them to say in exchange for money."

Kalugal had a point. "So, what would you suggest?"

"You should talk to your target audience. Parker, Lisa, and Cheryl are in that age group, and I know that Cheryl is active on the platform. She might have some insights that could help you come up with the right approach."

Brandon nodded. "That's brilliant, actually. Thank you, Kalugal. I'll definitely reach out to Cheryl and maybe use the other two as my sounding board."

Kalugal smiled, clapping Brandon on the shoulder. "Happy to help."

As Kalugal turned to leave, Ell-rom appeared in the doorway.

The prince looked tired, worry etched into his face. He nodded to Kalugal as they passed each other, and he then approached Morelle's bedside.

Brandon watched as Ell-rom leaned down and pressed a gentle kiss to his sister's cheek. "Hello, Morelle," he murmured.

A surge of irrational jealousy coursed through him.

He envied Ell-rom for kissing Morelle, something he couldn't do.

As his eyes fixed on her lips, he was struck by an overwhelming urge to kiss her. Not passionately, not romantically, but just as a connection, to feel her skin on his lips.

Maybe he could kiss her hand? Would that be crossing a line? He glanced at Ell-rom, wondering if he should ask his permission. But no, that wouldn't be right. Ell-rom didn't have the authority to grant such permission. Only Morelle did, and she was in no position to give it.

Brandon sighed quietly, forcing himself to focus on Ell-rom instead. "How's Jasmine doing?" he asked, even though he knew the answer to that.

Ell-rom's shoulders slumped. "No change," he said, his voice heavy with fatigue as if he hadn't slept at all during the night. "Julian says that her vitals are strong, that this is normal for a transition, but..." He trailed off, shaking his head.

"It's hard to see someone you love like that," Brandon finished for him. "I can't imagine how difficult this must be for you."

Ell-rom nodded, his gaze fixed on his sister's face. "I keep thinking about the small glimpses of memories I got in my dreams going back to when we were children. Morelle seemed like the strong one between us. But she was also disillusioned..." He stopped as if realizing he had said too much. "Perhaps in my dreams, I let the other side of me speak through my sister. She might be an upbeat and optimistic person. All I know is that I miss her."

"I'm sure you do. Morelle used to be your other half in your previous lives, your anchor, and then you woke up on Earth, met Jasmine, and she became that for you, but now she is unconscious as well."

When Ell-rom sighed, Brandon got to his feet and put his hand on the prince's shoulder. "You are not alone, Ell-rom. You have a big and loving family here, and we are all rooting for you and Morelle."

The prince nodded. "I know. Perhaps I need to remind myself of that more often."

22

KIAN

Kian hadn't expected to be excited about the prospect of meeting with Turner. He only got the strategist involved when something major was happening and his expertise was needed, and he missed the guy's cold, analytical mind. A mind not swayed by emotions.

There were downsides to Turner's emotional detachment, but they were too few to mention and by no means had any impact on his brilliance.

As he waited for the coffees to be delivered and Turner to arrive, Kian's thoughts drifted to Ell-rom and his newly discovered ability. The power to kill with a thought was both terrifying and awe-inspiring, and he knew Turner would find ways not only to test it but also to use it. He hadn't planned on sharing the information with the guy, but he trusted Turner implicitly, and the same was true for Bridget, with whom he would no doubt share the information.

Mates did not keep secrets from each other.

He thought of Sari's joke about the assassinations she had in mind, wondering again if there had been a hint of truth behind her words. The world of international politics was full of threats, both overt and hidden, and taking out key players could bring peace and stability to the world.

On the other hand, there was the undeniable fact of unforeseen consequences. Taking out a bad player without guaranteeing that his successor was any better was foolish. It was like playing whack-a-mole, and it had been done too many times to count. Sometimes, it was better to leave a mostly bad player in power as long as he kept even worse ones from taking over, especially when everyone knew who would suffer the most.

In those hellholes, it was always the women.

It boiled Kian's blood to witness women's complete dehumanization.

But what would taking out the leaders achieve?

Nothing.

More of the same would take their place, and the female population would remain in shackles for the crime of being born into the utterly devalued gender.

Kian shook his head, banishing the disturbing thoughts.

The only thing the clan could do was continue driving innovation forward while promoting their core values of equality irrespective of gender, ethnicity, or origin, and assigning merit based solely on strength of character, ability, and tenacity. By spreading these ideals as far and wide as possible, they would hopefully inspire other societies to follow, creating ripples of change that would gradually transform the world.

It wasn't a quick solution, but it was the only sustainable one.

A knock at the door pulled Kian from his musings. "Enter," he called out.

Shai walked in with a cardboard tray and a paper bag. "It's only me." He walked over and deposited his purchases on the conference table. "Is there something I should be aware of that necessitates Turner's expertise?"

"You know everything that I do." Kian walked over to the conference table and took one of the paper cups. "I just haven't spoken with Turner in a while, and I thought this would be a good opportunity. We need to locate good human hosts for the gods' trackers, and if he can help us with that, it would save us the trouble."

"I see." Shai released a relieved breath. "I thought some new threat was on the horizon."

"I'm sure there is." Kian removed the cover and took a sip of his soy cappuccino. "And I don't mean the Eternal King. Something is always brewing whether we are aware of it or not."

Shai nodded. "Ain't that the truth." He walked toward the door.

When he opened it, Turner was on its other side with his hand raised, poised to knock.

"Now, that's service. The door opens even before I get to knock on it."

"I aim to please." Shai moved aside, letting the strategist pass by him.

Turner strode in, his eyes zeroing in on the coffee and the paper bag next to it.

"Thank you, Shai," he said as he took a seat next to Kian.

"You are most welcome." Shai dipped his head before stepping outside and closing the door behind him.

Turner opened the paper bag first, pulled out a Danish, and only then removed the remaining coffee cup from the cardboard tray. "So, what do you need my help with this time?"

"I need mercenaries," Kian said without preamble. "Three of them. Young, healthy, with a love for travel and lots of discretion."

Turner's eyebrows rose. "That's an interesting shopping list. May I ask what you need them for?"

"To take the gods' place in the search for the missing pods so that Aru, Negal, and Dagor will be free to join their mates in the village, and by taking the gods' place, I mean to host their trackers. As long as the gods have the trackers in them, I can't risk them joining us here even though their commander and everyone else on that ship are rebels. They need to maintain the charade and report to the Eternal King, and we don't want them to have anything to report that can lead to us. We need to send those men on a very long trip, naturally, all expenses paid."

Turner nodded. "I can find a few candidates who fit the bill and would be thrilled to fill the position with no questions asked. Ex-special forces. Good men who need some time off to clear their heads."

"Perfect," Kian said. "How soon can you have dossiers on potential candidates?"

Turner tore off a piece of the Danish. "I'll have Brian make some calls and verify a few things. I should have a list for you in three days or so."

"Brian is your assistant, and I know that you trust him, but he can't know what we need these men for."

Turner regarded him with a small smile. "I will tell him only what he needs to know. All I will tell him is that three operatives need to follow a certain trek for a long-term operation."

Kian nodded. "Excellent. Are you going to interview them, or just give us their contact information?"

"That's up to you. I don't mind interviewing them for you." Turner stuffed the piece of Danish in his mouth.

"Thank you. I appreciate your help."

"Of course. I'm always at your service."

As Turner washed down the pastry with his coffee, Kian considered sharing the information about Ellrom, but he decided to save it for another day.

23

ROB

As Rob stepped into the elevator in the glass pavilion, he gazed at the panel of floor buttons, realizing that he didn't know which level the lab was on. He'd been so eager to meet with William about potential work opportunities that he'd forgotten to stop by the café and ask someone for directions to his lab.

He scanned the panel again, hoping for some clue. Every floor had some symbol next to it, but the only one he recognized was the one for the gym level. He could stop there and ask for directions.

As the elevator descended, his mind drifted to the previous evening, and a smile tugged at his lips as he remembered his time with Gertrude. She'd been so eager to learn how to use the punching bag, her eyes sparkling with enthusiasm as he'd shown her the proper stance and technique.

"Like this?" she'd asked, throwing a tentative punch at the bag.

Rob had gently corrected her stance, trying to ignore the warmth that spread through him at their proximity. "Almost. Try to rotate your hips more as you punch. It'll give you more power."

She'd nodded, a look of determination crossing her face as she tried again. The bag had barely moved.

"That's okay," Rob had assured her. "It takes practice to build up the strength and technique."

Now, as the elevator doors opened on the gym level, Rob couldn't help but wonder if Gertrude had been holding back. She was an immortal, after all. Surely she was stronger than she'd let on. It was a disconcerting thought that she might have been pretending, letting him play the role of the knowledgeable instructor so he wouldn't be embarrassed when she punched harder than he could. It sent a conflicting wave of emotions through him.

On one hand, it was sweet of her to consider his feelings. On the other, he'd had enough of pretense with Lynda.

He preferred the naked, unadorned truth, no matter how uncomfortable it might be.

As he stepped out of the elevator, the familiar scent of cleaning products filled his nostrils. The gym was busy. Immortals and a few hybrid Kra-ell were scattered across various machines and workout areas. He scanned the room, looking for a familiar face or someone who seemed approachable.

He spotted a guy working with free weights who gave him a friendly smile and decided to ask him. As Rob approached, the man set down his dumbbells and looked up expectantly.

"I'm trying to find William's lab. Would you happen to know which floor his lab is located on?"

The guy nodded. "Of course. William's lab isn't on a specific floor. Not anymore, that is. It has turned into a complex that spans multiple levels. I can take you there if you'd like." He extended his hand. "I'm Randel."

Rob shook it. "I'm Rob."

"I know," Randel said. "You are Margo's brother."

He was surprised at how many people knew his sister, but then she had become a celebrity when she'd been rescued from the cartel boss's yacht and brought to the clan's cruise ship.

Still, how did everyone know that he was her brother?

"That's right. If you point me in the right direction, I'm sure I can find the place myself. I don't want to interrupt your workout."

Randel waved off his concern. "It's no trouble. I was about done anyway. I heard that you are a programmer." He started toward the door.

Rob chuckled. "I was warned that the village is a small community and that everyone knows everything about everyone else, but I've just gotten here. How come you know that I'm a programmer?"

Randel shrugged. "Rumors travel fast through the village." He called the elevator. "And we are always strapped for programmers and tech people. William is going to welcome you with open arms."

"Do you work in his department?" Rob asked.

"I do." Randel entered the elevator, and Rob followed. "But I'm not a programmer. I'm an engineer, and I'm currently working on the Perfect Match machines."

"Those are fascinating. Margo is interested in a position on the Perfect Match team, and she doesn't even care in what capacity. She will take any job."

Randel smiled. "I get it. We have a list a mile long of people who want to go on an adventure, so we are trying to put together two more machines. We had a problem with some parts that were difficult to get, but we finally got them."

As they traveled up, Rob's mind wandered back to Gertrude and their time in the gym. He turned to Randel, curiosity getting the better of him. "Can I ask you something pretty mundane about immortals?"

"Sure, shoot."

"I was working out with an immortal female yesterday, showing her how to use the punching bag. But I couldn't help wondering if she was holding back. I mean, aren't immortals significantly stronger than humans?"

"It depends. Immortal females are generally much stronger than human females and even many human males, but the difference isn't as drastic as it is for immortal males. If she hasn't trained with the punching bag before, she might have been doing her best."

The relief Rob felt was disproportionate for what had been at stake. It wouldn't have been a big deal if Gertrude had held back a little. He just needed to make it clear to her that he appreciated honesty and didn't need coddling. He believed she was a good woman, and she would understand.

When the elevator came to a stop and the doors slid open, the sight that greeted him was somewhat chaotic, but the sprawling wonderland of advanced tech had his mouth watering.

Sleek workstations were arranged in clusters, each surrounded by screens displaying all kinds of schematics and lines of code, and in one corner, a group of people were gathered around what looked like a partially disassembled humanoid robot. In another, someone was manipulating what appeared to be a multi-armed type of robotic device that was mounted on a wide base with wheels and was twirling around like a ballerina.

"Welcome to William's domain," Randel said with a grin.

He led Rob into an office that occupied a corner of the large hall. "Where is William?" he asked a beautiful blond woman who was peering over a table covered with scattered pieces of paper. "He stepped out for a moment." She turned to look at the door. "Oh, here he is. William, you have visitors."

"Hello." The slightly chubby guy approached with a bright smile on his face and an energetic stride. "You must be Rob," he said, extending his hand. "I'm William. I've been looking forward to meeting you."

Rob shook his hand. "It's an honor to meet you and get to see this place. For me, it's like Wonderland."

William's smile widened. "Just wait until you see what we're working on. But first, let's chat in my office. Thank you for showing him the way, Randal."

Randel nodded and gave Rob an encouraging pat on the back before heading back to the elevator.

William led Rob to a messy desk at the back of the room. "Excuse the mess." He pointed to a dust-covered chair. "Please, sit down."

Rob stifled the impulse to clear the dust first and sat down. It was better to wash his jeans later than to embarrass his future employer.

William sat behind his desk and leaned forward, his bright blue eyes sparkling. "So, Rob, tell me about your experience. What kind of projects have you worked on?"

Rob took a deep breath, trying to organize his thoughts. "Well, I've been in software development for over a decade now. My focus has mainly been on creating efficient algorithms for data processing and analysis. I've worked on projects ranging from financial modeling software to predictive analytics for marketing campaigns."

William nodded, looking not particularly impressed. "Excellent. And how comfortable are you with adapting to new programming languages or paradigms?"

"Very comfortable," Rob replied with confidence. "In fact, it's one of the things I enjoy most about the field. There's always something new to learn, new problems to solve in innovative ways."

"That's exactly the kind of attitude we value here." William gestured toward the lab. "Much of what we do here requires thinking outside conventional paradigms."

Rob's curiosity was piqued. "Can you tell me more about it?"

"Oh, where to begin? We're working on so many exciting things. Our robotics department and the Perfect Match systems are where we are focusing our efforts currently, but there are dozens of smaller projects that we are working on in addition to that.

We're constantly refining our algorithms, improving the AI's ability to adapt to user responses in real time. And that's just scratching the surface." He paused, studying Rob intently. "Are you ready to join our team? You can start right away, this afternoon if you want."

He chuckled. "I wish I could, but I can't just drop everything immediately. I have a project I'm in the middle of for my current employer. I wouldn't feel right leaving them in the lurch."

William's smile grew warmer. "I appreciate your loyalty and integrity, Rob. Give your employer notice, finish your project, and join us whenever you are ready."

24

KIAN

Kian was midway through reviewing a stack of reports when a sharp knock on his office door interrupted his concentration. Before he could respond, the door swung open, revealing Jade.

Had he forgotten that they had a meeting?

"Jade," Kian greeted her, setting aside the document he'd been going over. "This is unexpected. Is everything alright?"

Jade strode into the office, her posture tense. "I need to speak with you about Drova. It won't take long."

Kian glanced at his watch. "I have a few minutes before I'm due to meet with Onegus. Please, sit down." He indicated one of the chairs in front of his desk.

She looked nervous, which was uncommon for the

Kra-ell leader, but then this was about her daughter. He hoped she didn't have bad news.

Jade sat down, her large dark eyes blazing with determination. "Parker, Lisa, and Cheryl came up with an ingenious punishment for Drova. They assigned her a bunch of books on various topics that she needed not only to read but also to learn well enough to pass tests that they would administer. Drova hates studying, but she needs the education, so the punishment is most fitting. It also gave me an idea."

Kian smiled. "I love this. Do you know who came up with it?"

She shrugged. "I don't, but I suspect Cheryl. Out of the three, she is the most cunning."

"I agree. So, what's your idea?"

"I want Drova to shadow me," Jade said. "To observe my work and learn from me. But to do that, I need control over her movements. Is it possible to adjust her cuff so that I can control it with a remote?"

Kian lifted an eyebrow. "That's quite a leap from having her read books, Jade. And it's risky. Drova can compel anyone not wearing earpieces with just her voice, and it's not as if we can or should muzzle her."

"Of course not." Jade shifted in her chair. "But I can demand her silence, and if she disobeys..." She trailed off, but the implication was clear.

"You zap her into obedience," Kian finished. "She is a young female, Jade, not a dog. I don't think that's the right approach."

Jade's expression hardened. "It's better than keeping her locked in the house with only books for company. She'll go mad. At least this gives her a chance to learn and broaden her horizons. The first thing a leader needs to learn is that nothing is black and white, and the necessity of navigating the shades of gray."

Kian stifled a chuckle at the reference Jade had inadvertently made to the popular book.

He drummed his fingers on the desk, weighing the proposal. On the one hand, it did offer a more active form of rehabilitation for Drova. On the other, it walked a fine line between punishment and humiliation.

"She will not disobey," Jade said. "I will never have to actually zap her. It's just a precaution, more for your sake than mine, so you would allow it."

Now, that made much more sense. "So, you want to make me the bad guy?"

Jade tilted her head. "Does it bother you?"

"Not really," he admitted. "You can tell her that it was my demand before agreeing to let her out of the house and that you hope never to have to use it. I think that can work quite well."

"Thank you." Jade dipped her head. "How do I get Drova's cuff modified?"

He liked how assertive Jade was and that once she decided on something, she implemented it. She didn't waste time.

"You can go to William's lab and explain what you need. He or one of his techs will modify the cuff for you and give you a remote. It's possible that they will have to give you a different cuff, though, and if it needs modifications, it might take a day or two."

Given her sour expression, Jade didn't like his answer. She wanted to take Drova out of the house right away.

"Is there somewhere you want to take her that you are in such a rush?"

Jade nodded. "Ell-rom called me and asked that I come to the clinic so he can ask me questions about his past on Anumati. I thought it would be a great opportunity for Drova to learn about her origins without it seeming as if I'm shoving it down her throat."

"I see." Kian agreed that her plan had merit. "I hope William can accommodate your request."

"I hope so, too." She rose to her feet. "I'll let you know when I'm taking her out of the house. I assume that you will want to inform Onegus so he can notify the Guardians."

The truth was that it hadn't occurred to him to put the Guardians on alert because Drova was let out of the house, but perhaps he should. As he liked to remind everyone, it was better to be safe than sorry, right?

"Please do."

As Jade left the office, Kian found himself hoping he hadn't just made a big mistake. If Drova did something stupid, they would have no choice but to put her in the dungeon, and he really did not want to do that.

It would devastate Jade and cause unrest in the Kra-ell community.

He also didn't want to collect scumbags for Ell-rom to test his talent on, but he was going to do that anyway.

25

GERTRUDE

"Excuse me, Brandon." Gertrude cast him an apologetic glance. "I need a few moments alone with the princess."

"Of course." He set his lap desk on the floor and rose to his feet. "I'll be in the waiting room." The councilman had been through this routine often enough to not ask why she needed him to leave.

Once the door closed behind him, the only sound was the steady beeping of Morelle's heart monitor. The princess lay still under the blanket, her face pale and serene but no longer as gaunt as it had been in the beginning. Gertrude had been there for the transformation, and it was truly miraculous.

It would have taken a mere immortal weeks longer to rebuild such shriveled organs and muscles. The princess was part goddess, but instead of the other half being human, it was Kra-ell, and it had given her an advantage.

Gertrude approached the IV stand and eyed the nearly empty fluid bag. It was time to replace it. She reached into the cabinet and retrieved a fresh bag of saline, feeling the weight in her hands. After clamping the line, she disconnected the old bag, hung up the new one, and watched as the new fluid began to drip into Morelle's veins.

After that she scanned the vitals on the screen—heart rate, oxygen saturation, blood pressure. All were stable.

Gertrude let out a slow breath and turned her attention to the catheter bag at the foot of the bed. It had almost filled since she had last checked it, so she clamped the rubber drainage tube from the Foley catheter and unhooked the filled bag to empty it. That done, she reconnected the collection bag and then unclamped the rubber drainage tube.

It was a repeat of what she had done in Jasmine's room only moments ago, a routine task she had performed many times and hoped to continue doing for many other transitioning Dormants or long-lost relatives recovering from comas. Not that it was common to find people who had been in stasis for thousands of years, but every life recovered was a miracle.

The work was a far cry from her earlier days when she'd mainly treated injured Guardians, patching them up while their accelerated healing did most of the work. Occasionally, she'd assisted with birthing an immortal's child, but those joyous occasions were regrettably rare, even rarer than transitions.

Gertrude knew that firsthand.

She had been taking Merlin's potions for months and hooking up with human males whenever her schedule had allowed it, but nothing had happened yet. Still, she wasn't giving up. She just had to persist and keep on going, and one day, the Fates would answer her prayers and give her a child.

When everything was in place, Gertrude glanced at Morelle's face, watching for some flicker of movement, some sign of awareness. But there was nothing. Just the steady hum of the machines.

"Until next time, Princess," she murmured as she opened the door.

Someone was in the waiting room, talking with Brandon while holding a cardboard tray with two coffees. He was standing with his back to her, so she couldn't see who he was, but she assumed he was another visitor for Ell-rom. The prince had had many well-wishers come since Jasmine arrived at the clinic unconscious. On a second listen, though, the voice sounded familiar, and she realized it was Rob.

A flutter went through her stomach, which she firmly quashed. She shouldn't read too much into their recent interactions. He wasn't there for her but for Ell-rom. Margo had probably asked her brother to check on the prince.

After all, they'd all shared the penthouse, and bonds formed quickly in close quarters.

The dinner Gertrude had had to endure with Negal and Margo still made her cringe. She liked Margo, and she was over her infatuation with Negal, but it was still an uncomfortable situation. The god had dropped her like a stone into deep water, swiftly and without hesitation, leaving no trace of the warmth he had shown her before.

It was never a good feeling to be passed over for someone else.

It was also a lesson to be learned.

She shouldn't get involved with anyone who lived in the village because it was awkward as hell to deal with a former lover in such a small place. Some of the clan ladies hooked up with the former Doomers, but they were smart enough to keep it casual and switch partners often so it wouldn't become an issue.

Gertrude preferred to have her fun away from where she lived.

It used to be that clan females hunted for one-night stands in bars, but in recent years the internet, with its endless parade of dating apps, was the way to go. It was even less personal than meeting a guy in a club, but that was how it was done these days.

As if sensing her scrutiny, Rob turned, his face lighting up with a smile that did funny things to her insides. "I brought you coffee." He held up the tray.

Then uncertainty crept into his expression. "I hope that's okay. Are you allowed to have coffee on the job?"

He looked like a shy boy trying to do something nice for the girl he liked, and the wall Gertrude tried to keep up around her heart crumbled a little. "Yes, I'm allowed to have coffee, and I'm also allowed to take breaks." She glanced toward Bridget's office, where the doctor sat working at her desk with the door open as usual. "Dr. Bridget, I'm done with both patients. Can I take my break now?"

"Of course," Bridget replied without looking up from her computer. "Enjoy your break."

Gertrude turned to Brandon. "Can I get you something from the café?"

"No, thank you. I'm meeting Kalugal there later, so I'll grab something then."

She didn't have to ask Ell-rom because his vegan meals were being delivered to the clinic now, and she knew he had eaten lunch already.

Rob said goodbye to Brandon, and as they stepped outside, he cast her an apologetic look. "I didn't bring you anything to eat. I assumed that coffee would be fine, but I wasn't sure about food in a hospital setting."

"It's fine." Gertrude placed her hand on his arm, then quickly withdrew it. Professional. She could be friendly but needed to stay professional. "We can get sandwiches from the vending machine. It'll save us the time of standing in line at the counter."

"Great idea."

After selecting sandwiches from the machine, they found a table and sat down.

"I've met William." Rob unwrapped his sandwich. "His lab is like a fortress and a factory all in one. The place is insane. It looks like every person in the clan is working down there."

Gertrude smiled at his enthusiasm. "Not everyone, but many. William is constantly recruiting. He's convinced several people to study mechanical engineering and software development. Some of those working at his lab are still students."

Rob nodded. "I can see how such a limited pool of people might hamper his hiring progress. Maybe that's why they are working on robots, not that robots can do what people can. They can be good for menial jobs, and artificial intelligence is advancing at a frightening rate, but I still believe that humans are much better at generating fresh ideas. They can literarily think outside the box, while AI is limited to what's inside the box." He tilted his head. "Do you get what I mean?"

"I think so."

He grinned. "It's such a pleasure to talk with an intelligent person." Rob launched into a detailed explanation about some interface that went mostly over her head, but his passion was infectious. His hands moved animatedly as he spoke, his eyes bright with excitement.

Gertrude couldn't help but smile when his face lit up while he described particularly interesting aspects of technology, or when his voice rose slightly when he got to something that really impressed him. It was endearing, and dangerous territory for her thoughts to wander into.

"Sorry," he said suddenly, cutting himself off mid-sentence. "I'm probably boring you with all the technical details."

"Not at all," Gertrude assured him, and it wasn't entirely a lie. While she might not understand everything he had been talking about, his enthusiasm made it interesting. "It's nice to see someone so passionate about their work."

Rob ducked his head. "My former fiancée accused me of being unable to talk about anything other than my work, and she wasn't wrong. I tend to get carried away."

Gertrude had heard about Rob's canceled wedding and the betrayal he'd experienced.

"We are all like that. I used to freak people out talking about the things I did in nursing school and later when I worked for a human doctor to improve my skills. I loved describing the open wounds and the puss I cleaned—" His horrified expression stopped her, and she laughed. "Yeah, that face you just made is what usually happened, so I learned to only talk shop with other medical practitioners."

Looking slightly green, Rob let out a breath. "You should teach me that trick. I need something to talk about that inspires me, but that is easy for everyone to understand. Any suggestions?"

Gertrude laughed again. "That's why men talk about sports. Religion and politics are a no-no in polite company so that leaves sports, food, and kids, if you are lucky enough to have them."

26

KIAN

K ian had managed to go over two more contracts when another knock sounded on the door.

Onegus was right on time for their meeting.

"Chief," Kian greeted him, rising to his feet. "Perfect timing." He reached into his drawer and pulled out his box of cigarillos. "I've been waiting for you to get here to go on the roof and indulge in a smoke. You don't mind, right?" He pulled a small bottle of fine whiskey from another drawer and put it in the pocket of his jacket. Two shot glasses went into the other.

Onegus chuckled. "You should get yourself a bar up there. Somewhere you could store your vices without having to carry them in your pockets."

"Good advice." Kian started toward the door. "I'll tell

Shai you suggested that." He headed toward the stairs.

The fleeting levity of the moment eased some of the weight of what he needed to talk to Onegus about. What he was about to propose wasn't conventional, and it was morally gray, but it had to be done.

The rooftop of the office building offered a panoramic view of the village, the lush greenery stretching out in all directions.

Kian sat down on one of the lounge chairs and pulled the box of cigarillos out of his pocket. He flipped it open and offered it to Onegus.

The bottle of whiskey went on the table, followed by the two shot glasses.

As they lit up, Kian poured each of them a finger of whiskey. The ritual gave him a moment to gather his thoughts and find the right words for what he needed to tell the chief.

Onegus took an appreciative sip of the whiskey and put his glass on the side table between the two lounges. "Are we here just because you wanted to smoke or because you wanted this conversation to be confidential?"

Kian took a long drag on his cigarillo, letting the smoke curl around him before exhaling slowly. "You know me well, Onegus. I don't like keeping secrets from Shai, but for now, I would like to limit the number of people who know about this. Although, given what I'm about to propose, I don't know how long we are going to keep it from the Guardians, especially those directly involved in the mission."

Onegus regarded him with amusement in his eyes. "This must be huge for you to talk in circles. You are usually as direct as a bullet."

Kian took another puff of his cigarillo. "Ell-rom might be able to kill with a mere thought." He narrowed his eyes at Onegus. "Is that direct enough for you?"

"What do you mean, 'might be'? Can he kill with a thought or not?"

Kian explained what had happened with the junkie who had attacked Jasmine, Ell-rom wishing him dead, and the guy obliging.

"Julian couldn't find anything that pointed to the cause of death. The vagrant's heart might have stopped for no reason, or maybe his brain short-circuited when he saw Ell-rom's fangs and glowing eyes, but since Ell-rom dreamt about using this ability as a boy, we should assume that it was he who killed the attacker."

"That's quite something," Onegus said. "He could be useful to us if he is willing to be used in that capacity."

Kian took another sip of whiskey. "Right now, he is terrified of his ability and relieved that my mother bound it with her compulsion so he won't misfire accidentally. Nevertheless, he's agreed to test the extent of his talent. We need to understand what he's capable of and to help him learn control."

"How?" Onegus asked. "Hunting animals?"

That was actually not a bad idea, but Ell-rom would have almost as much trouble with that as killing humans. The guy was incredibly softhearted for a born killer.

"No, not animals. Even if he can enter their minds somehow, and I'm not sure his talent would work on them, we need to test him on humans, or rather subhumans." He leveled his eyes on Onegus's. "Remember your comment about going after the end users? Pedophiles in particular? The scum of the earth who prey on the most vulnerable, those who subject children to such suffering do not deserve mercy. Not from us. We can enter their minds and verify their crimes. I want a team of Guardians dedicated to tracking them down and bringing them to the keep. I want several such demons in human skin to test Ell-rom's ability on."

Onegus was silent for a long moment, his cigarillo forgotten, burning between his fingers. "Let's ignore for a moment the morally gray area, which is a complete departure from our normal mode of operations. Do you have any idea what it would do to Ell-rom? It would destroy him."

"I'm not sure it would." Kian puffed on his cigarillo. "Our Guardians had no problem tearing apart the monsters in Mexico with their bare fangs. No one needed to talk with Vanessa to ease their conscience after that, because they knew what those demons had done to defenseless people. I think Ell-rom will develop a taste for it despite being a vegan."

Onegus burst out laughing. "Now, that was funny."

Kian smirked. "I know. As a vegan, I can empathize with Ell-rom. But, after all, I don't avoid animal flesh for health reasons or because of an aversion to killing. I just prefer not to end the lives of animals unless I have to in order to avoid starvation. Nevertheless, I have absolutely no qualms about ending the lives of monsters. On the contrary, it's my duty to do so whenever I can. Every monster we kill means less suffering in the world." He took another sip of his whiskey. "Ell-rom agreed to the testing on the condition that we wait until he learns to thrall so he can verify the guilt of his targets. I promised him that it would be done in accordance with his wishes."

The silence that followed was thick with tension. Kian could see the conflict playing out on Onegus's face—the Guardian's law-abiding moral compass warring with his deep-seated desire to protect the innocent.

Onegus sighed. "That might be even worse for Ell-rom. What he will see in the heads of those abusers of children is horrific."

Kian hadn't considered that. "You are probably right, and Ell-rom is like a kid in a lot of ways. Because he doesn't remember his life before entering the settler ship, he hasn't developed emotional resilience yet."

Onegus took another puff of his cigarillo. "You mean apathy?"

"No, not really. We wouldn't want him to be totally lacking in feeling or indifferent. He just needs to learn to take that anger and rage that he'll feel and channel it toward a positive result. So, let's call it resilience. Ell-rom will have to grow up sooner or later, and given that he is terrified of his ability, he is eager to learn to harness it." Kian stubbed out his cigarillo and pulled out a new one from the box. "Besides, every monster we take off the streets means potentially dozens of children saved from a lifetime of trauma. We should do that regardless of Ell-rom's testing requirements. And if it helps him to learn control and enables him to use his ability for good rather than letting it consume him, it's just the cherry on top."

Onegus let out a heavy sigh. "You are right, and even if you weren't, you're the boss, and I take my orders from you. I'll put together a team."

"What are you going to tell them? Only a handful of people know about Ell-rom's ability, and I want to keep it that way."

Onegus shrugged. "As far as anyone else is concerned, we're simply expanding our efforts to combat child exploitation."

"That's good." Kian lit up his second cigarillo. "Do you have anyone in mind to head up this new unit?"

"That depends on how large you want the operation to be. We have our hands full with the traffickers. This will take away from those efforts."

"Not necessarily." Kian emptied what was left in his glass. "We can involve more of the Kra-ell in the rescue operations and gradually move some of the Guardians to teams that will combat the buyer side of the equation. That being said, we should start small to test the waters, and once we get the hang of it, increase our efforts."

Onegus nodded, stubbing out his cigarillo. "I'll start working on selecting the first team. We'll need individuals with strong stomachs and even stronger moral compasses. This kind of work can eat away at a person's soul if they're not careful."

"I trust your judgment," Kian said. "This isn't just another mission. It's a whole new frontier."

ELL-ROM

Ell-rom couldn't tear his eyes away from Jasmine's face. Four days had passed since she'd lost consciousness, and despite Bridget's reassurances about her strong vitals, he could see the changes happening to his mate's body. Her cheekbones were more pronounced now, her face thinner, and her already tall frame had somehow grown even longer—half an inch in just four days, according to the doctors' measurements.

He ran his thumb across the back of her hand, noting how hot her skin felt to the touch. The fever hadn't broken yet, and though Bridget insisted this was normal for transitioning Dormants, every hour that passed felt like torture.

"Your body is working so hard," he whispered in Kra-ell, the earpieces in Jasmine's ears automatically converting his words to English. "Bridget says you're using an enormous amount of energy to transform."

He wondered how Jasmine would feel about growing even taller. She was already tall for a human female, and she liked wearing those ridiculous shoes with spiky heels. Would she give them up if she grew a few more inches?

A knock at the door startled him.

He hadn't been expecting visitors, but then people had popped in at all hours of the day to check up on him, bring him food and drink, and show their support.

It was heartwarming, but it was also exhausting.

He wasn't used to dealing with people all day long, having to smile and make polite conversation while his heart was breaking, and his mind was melting from worry.

When he opened the door, he found himself face to face with Jade, her familiar features set in their usual stern expression. A young female stood beside her, a teenager with distinctive Kra-ell features.

"Good afternoon, Prince Ell-rom," Jade said, inclining her head. "I hope we're not disturbing you. This is my daughter, Drova."

The girl extended her hand in the human greeting gesture. "Hello, Prince."

Ell-rom shook her hand, noting how her eyes fixed on his ears. "Please, just Ell-rom is fine."

"Why are you wearing earpieces?" Drova asked bluntly, earning a sharp look from her mother.

"For translation," he explained, finding her directness refreshing. "My English skills are not sufficient for conversation yet." His gaze drifted back to Jasmine's still form. "I should be studying while I sit by my mate's side, but I can't seem to focus. My mind is scattered."

"Then perhaps this isn't a good time," Jade said. "You asked me to come talk to you about life on Anumati, and I thought that Drova might benefit from the history lesson as well, but we can return another day."

Ell-rom considered the offer. He'd been consumed with worry for days, his thoughts cycling endlessly through the same fears. Maybe a distraction would help.

"No, please stay," he said. "It might be good to focus on something else for a change."

Drova was staring at Jasmine now, her head tilted thoughtfully. "Will Jasmine's earpieces still work while she's unconscious?"

"They should," Jade said. "The devices don't require conscious interaction to function. As long as they're activated, they will translate for her what we are saying."

"I will bring two more chairs." Ell-rom rose to his feet.

Jade lifted a hand to stop him. "We can sit on the floor. We are Kra-ell, and chairs were not part of our culture. We usually sit on floor cushions, but in their absence, we can sit on the floor."

Her words stirred a hazy memory in Ell-rom. His and Morelle's room had two bedding platforms and two short-legged desks but no chairs. They had sat cross-legged on large square cushions, with the tables in front of them, and copied texts.

Still, he had been using chairs to sit since he had recovered from stasis, and sitting on the bare, cold floor did not appeal to him. Reluctantly, he lowered himself to the floor, watching as Jade and Drova did the same with practiced ease.

"What can you tell me about my sister and me?" he asked. "What kind of a relationship did we have?"

Jade's expression grew thoughtful. "I know very little of you. I served in the queen's guard, and the palace was in the same compound as the main temple, but I only saw you and your sister when you were strolling through the palace gardens, and it was from afar. You were always covered in ceremonial robes from head to toe and veils were hiding your faces, and while you were enjoying the gardens, no one else was allowed to enter. But you were always together." She smiled tightly. "No one knew your names, but that wasn't unusual for clergy and acolytes."

"We weren't really clergy," Ell-rom said. "It was just a cover."

Drova leaned forward, her eyes bright with interest. "A cover for what?"

"Drova," Jade warned. "You are here to listen and stay silent."

"It's alright," Ell-rom said. "Our very existence was forbidden, and our mother was hiding who and what we were in plain sight. She made up a great story of why we should become priests because then she could keep us secluded and protected."

Jade nodded. "The head priestess was your mother's older sister, and there were rumors that she was hiding you from view because you were born deformed. Without her, you wouldn't be here today."

He hadn't known that. Had the head priestess ever told him and Morelle that she was their aunt, and he had forgotten? Or had she kept it a secret from them?

"I did not know that you were hybrids," Jade said. "No one did."

"Anumatians are bigoted and savages," Drova murmured under her breath. "Why do they despise hybrids so much?"

Jade regarded her daughter for a long time before answering. "I guess that the gods just don't want anyone undermining their genetic hegemony, and the Kra-ell are purists who want to keep their blood clean. On Earth, we bred with humans because we had no choice. We hoped to keep our kind from extinction, but I admit that I used to think of hybrids as inferior. The fact that the children born to hybrids with humans were human themselves made them useless for propagating our species."

"Prince Ell-rom is not half-human," Drova pointed out. "He is half god, half Kra-ell. That's kind of cool."

Ell-rom smiled. "Thank you. I don't know what temperature has to do with anything, but being called cool sounds much better than being called an abomination."

Drova returned his smile. "Cool means that you are okay and that I like you."

"I like you, too, Drova."

Jade dipped her head. "That's very gracious of you, Prince Ell-rom."

Drova fidgeted with the odd-looking bracelet on her wrist. "Yeah, I'm not liked by many people. Not after the stunt I pulled." She looked at him from under lowered lashes. "I'm sure you heard about the thefts and the sabotage."

He nodded. "I did."

"It was me. I compelled three kids to steal things for me and break things."

She sounded more proud than remorseful, and he didn't know what to say, so he opted to respond with a question. "Does the bracelet you are wearing have anything to do with that?"

Drova nodded. "It's not a bracelet. It's a cuff. It transmits my location, and if I misbehave, my mother can zap me with a remote."

Jade didn't look perturbed by the accusation, so Ell-rom assumed it was true. "You must be deemed dangerous."

"I am," Drova said with resignation rather than pride.

He leaned closer to her. "Having a dangerous ability does not make you dangerous. It's what you do with it. You get to choose if you want to be the hero or the villain of the story, the protector or the abuser. It's up to you."

The girl's cheeks reddened. "I was an abuser. I abused these kids, forcing them to do things they hated. But they got me back. Now they are forcing me to do things that I hate."

Ell-rom lifted a brow. "Oh, yeah? Like what?"

"Reading." She groaned. "A stack of books as tall as this bed. It's much worse than what I did to them."

"Did they compel you to read those books?"

She squared her shoulders, the look of defiance returning to her eyes. "No one can compel me. I'm the strongest compeller in the village. I'm stronger than Toven and probably even stronger than the Clan Mother."

"We don't know that," Jade said. "The Clan Mother hasn't tried to compel you."

Drova's eyes blazed red for a moment, reminding Ell-rom of the fire he felt behind his eyes every time his death ray was activated.

"Of course not. They would never try because they don't want me to be proven the strongest, but the fact that I can defy her compulsion says it all."

"It says nothing," Jade countered without much conviction.

Ell-rom was intrigued and also a little worried.

If Drova was indeed a more powerful compeller than Annani, she might release his death ray, which meant that she must never find out about it.

"What about you?" Drova asked. "Do you have compulsion power?"

"I don't think so. I can thrall, but just a little. I'm still learning."

Her eyes returned to their natural black as she looked at him. "Maybe you should practice compulsion and see if it works for you. I can help you."

Jade shot her daughter a glare. "You've done enough. Ell-rom will not remove his earpieces for you."

He frowned. "Drova speaks Kra-ell. I don't need the earpieces to communicate with her."

Jade let out a breath. "I forgot that your earpieces are for translation only. They don't filter compulsion like these do." She pointed to the ones she had in her ears.

Had Drova thought that his earpieces were of that kind?

Oh, the girl was clever and cunning. He really should be careful around her.

"I have no wish to learn compulsion." Ell-rom smiled at her. "I think its use should be severely restricted to extreme cases only."

"Yeah, you are right." Drova's shoulders slumped a little.

He turned to Jade. "What can you tell me about our mother? The queen?"

Jade's expression softened. "I was just a junior guard commander, but I vowed to protect my queen and her family, which included you. I would like to believe that the queen rigged the lottery so I would be chosen for the settler ship and offer my protection to you. There were others from the guard who got selected, but their pods haven't been found. I assume that they are all dead."

"That's regrettable. What was she like as a person, though?"

"She was formidable. Not just physically and mentally powerful but politically brilliant. She maintained order among the Kra-ell, pretending to be a traditionalist while secretly fostering progressive ideas."

"Like what?" Drova asked.

"Like questioning the rigid structure of our society," Jade explained. "The queen never openly challenged our traditions, but she had ways of rewarding those who showed independent thinking." She turned to Ell-rom. "Your mother was playing a very long game, trying to gradually change our culture from within. Regrettably, her life was cut short, but according to Aru, her successor continued her work, so not all was lost. The Kra-ell of today are doing much better than the Kra-ell of our time, but it is still a far cry from where the gods are."

He tilted his head. "Do the Kra-ell want to be like the gods?"

"Good question." Drova nodded. "What's good for the gods is not necessarily good for the Kra-ell."

"Education is critical for everyone," Jade said. "And that's what the Kra-ell are missing. Without it, they will always remain a primitive society."

As mother and daughter continued to argue, Ell-rom tried to reconcile what Jade had told him with his fragmented memories of his mother. He remembered her as distant and formal, yet there had been moments, brief flashes of tenderness when no one else was watching.

"Did you ever suspect what we were?" he asked.

Jade was quiet for a moment, considering her answer. "There were whispers, mostly of deformities that you were hiding under your robes and your veils. No one suspected that you were half gods even though everyone had heard the rumors about the queen's affair with the son of the Eternal King when she was still just the princess, but many assumed that she used him to gain information that helped her with the rebellion."

Drova's eyes widened. "The son of the Eternal King was your father?"

He glanced at Jade. "I thought that it was obvious to everyone by now."

"Drova wasn't paying attention." She smiled coldly at her daughter. "She was too busy concocting plots to undermine the relationship between the clan and the Kra-ell."

"I had my reasons," Drova said under her breath.

28

MORELLE

The storyteller painted pictures in Morelle's mind of a world different from anything she had known. She had listened to many of his tales over the past few days, but this one captured her imagination in a unique way.

"The founding fathers knew they were creating something unprecedented." The storyteller's voice carried the passion she had come to associate with his most engaging tales. "They gathered nearly two and a half centuries ago to design a framework for governing that would stand the test of time."

She was fascinated by the concept.

Two and a half centuries were less than a blink of an eye in the lifespans of societies. How had a document written not too long ago effected such a change so quickly?

On Anumati, laws were handed down by the monarchy, and they had been established for many thousands of years.

"Most of them were young men, but Benjamin Franklin was not young at the time of the crafting of this document, and he wasn't healthy either, suffering from a number of different ailments, but he was a brilliant human and my favorite. He knew how crucial this document would be for future generations."

Morelle wondered why there were no women in that group. Had it been by chance, or had women been intentionally excluded?

In either case, she did not approve.

"They debated every word, every concept," the storyteller went on. "Some wanted a stronger central government. Others feared centralized power. The small states worried about being overwhelmed by the larger ones. It took compromise and wisdom to find solutions that would work for everyone."

Questions burned in Morelle's mind. What were those states that the storyteller was talking about, and why did they want to combine into one large country?

Had they faced a common enemy and needed to unite to defeat it?

How had they enforced those compromises?

What happened when some of the states disagreed and refused to comply with the document?

She wanted to ask all these questions with a burning passion, but her body remained frustratingly unresponsive.

"The Constitution they created wasn't perfect, but it was revolutionary for its time. It established checks and balances, divided power between three branches of government, and most importantly, it allowed for amendments as society evolved."

The gods' laws were absolute and unchanging, and the Kra-ell were equally stubborn in their ways.

Had been, Morelle reminded herself.

Everything might have changed over the thousands of years she had spent in stasis. For all she knew, Anumati could have been destroyed by either a natural disaster or an enemy more powerful than the gods.

It was also possible that another rebellion had obliterated the old ways and established a new order.

"They believed in the power of reason and discourse," the storyteller continued. "The ability of people to govern themselves through representation and the rule of law rather than the whims of a monarch or tyrant."

That one energized Morelle's blood. On Anumati, everything was up to the Eternal King. Her mother supposedly had autonomy over the Kra-ell, but she couldn't do anything without the king's approval. Even the settler ship had belonged to the gods and was loaned to the Kra-ell.

No wonder it had exploded.

They had probably given her mother the oldest clunker they had.

"Of course, they didn't get everything right." The storyteller's voice took on a warm tinge. "The original document had serious flaws, particularly regarding slavery and voting rights. But they built in mechanisms for future generations to correct those mistakes through amendments."

Slavery?

The gods were slavers, and in the past, they had enslaved the Kra-ell, but that was a very long time ago. Hadn't they abolished the abhorrent practice on Earth?

She had to know how such a thing had been allowed and whether it was still practiced.

Focusing all her will on opening her eyes, she pushed against the weight that seemed to press her lids down.

"The First Amendment, for example, protects freedom of speech, religion, and assembly," he was saying. "These weren't just abstract concepts. They were hard-won rights that the founders knew were essential for a free society."

Of course they were. Even when they were still slaves to the gods, the Kra-ell had been allowed to practice their own religion, and they could speak freely, even against the gods. The two things they had not been allowed were access to advanced technology and higher education, which would enable them to create their own advanced technology.

Although, to be fair, even if the gods had not limited the Kra-ell's access to education, she doubted there would have been many takers. The Kra-ell liked to roam free, hunt, and quarrel among themselves.

They were not studious people.

Did the storyteller know all that?

Oh, how she wished to discuss those things with him, to see what he looked like, and maybe indulge in some of those things her mother had told her she should.

He was such an interesting male.

Concentrating all her will on lifting her eyelids, Morelle didn't really expect them to respond, and when they did so, she was euphoric even though she managed to lift them only a fraction. Light pierced her vision, but all she could make out was a wall. She didn't see her fascinating storyteller, and the effort drained her, but she felt triumphant.

It was the first voluntary movement she'd managed since becoming aware of her surroundings, and if she could do that, she could do more once she gathered her energy again.

"The Second Amendment was about maintaining militia for the common defense," he continued, unaware of her small victory. "Though its interpretation has been debated ever since..."

He hadn't seen her crack her eyes open, hadn't witnessed her victory.

Disappointment washed over Morelle.

She wanted to see his face, to match a physical presence to the voice that had become her companion in this twilight state.

Was he young or old?

Did his features reflect the wisdom and knowledge he shared so eloquently?

Did his eyes light up with passion when he spoke of human history and progress?

"The Constitution became a model for democratic governments around the world," he said. "Even today, it continues to guide and shape our society."

Drained by the effort of lifting her eyelids, even for that tiny fraction of a moment, she was starting to drift away. Morelle wanted to fight it and keep listening to the fascinating story, but exhaustion was pulling her under.

Perhaps after she'd rested and gathered her strength, she could try again.

BRANDON

Brandon took a sip of water from his personal *Star Wars* bottle and put it back down on the floor. "I wish you could tell me what you think about my stories, Princess. I don't know which ones you like more and which ones you like less. History or fiction, politics or romance, I can talk about any subject on the face of the planet, not expertly, but well enough to be entertaining."

That was a slight exaggeration since his knowledge of the sciences was limited, and he lacked even the terminology to describe them. Brandon was a humanities guy, so to speak. He was well versed in history, and his love of stories had made him a life-long reader. He read everything from abstract philosophy to raunchy romances, and his memory for stories seemed almost limitless. He wasn't like Shai, and he didn't remember all the details, but he remembered the essence of the drama.

A good, memorable story always had drama, even if it strived to be funny.

His voice, filtered through the teardrop device and translated into Kra-ell, filled the silence as he finished his explanation about the Constitution.

Why had he chosen that seemingly boring subject? It had been on a hunch that the daughter of a queen who had once started a rebellion would be interested in political structures. He might be wrong, of course, and perhaps Morelle detested everything that had to do with politics. He wouldn't know until she woke, and he could ask her in person.

"I'll keep telling you stories until you're ready to join the conversation and tell me what you want to listen to. There's so much more to share just about American history, and then there is world history, of which I have only told you bits and pieces..."

He trailed off as a strange sensation washed over him. The air in the room suddenly felt different somehow, charged with energy he couldn't explain. The medical equipment continued its steady rhythm of beeps and whirs, and Morelle lay as still as ever, only the rise and fall of her chest providing visual proof of her being alive.

If he listened intently, he could hear her heartbeat and the soft sound of her breathing. Maybe that was what had alerted him?

Brandon glanced at the monitors to see if there had been any changes, any spikes that would indicate that something was going on, but it didn't seem like anything had changed significantly. The graphs were moving up and down all the time, and unless they went haywire, he assumed that nothing out of the ordinary was happening.

Yet something had shifted. He could feel it.

Brandon stood and moved to lean over Morelle's bed. Her features were serene, almost luminescent in the soft lighting. She was pale, but her lips had good color, and they almost looked like someone had painted them with rouge. Without conscious thought, he reached for her hand.

Her skin felt cool against his palm, her fingers delicate and unresponsive.

"Hey, Princess," he said softly, "would you be offended if I kissed your hand?"

Was that the ghost of a smile touching her lips? No, it had to be his imagination, a trick of the light, or his own desperate wishful thinking. And yet...

"If you can hear me, and if you're willing to grant me that small liberty, could you give me a sign? Just a twitch of a finger or a flutter of your beautiful eyelashes?"

For a moment, nothing happened. Then...

Was that movement?

The faintest pressure against his palm?

Brandon held his breath, afraid to trust his own senses.

"I would love to take that as an invitation to kiss your hand, but could you do it again so I know it's real?"

This time, when he felt the light flutter against his palm, there was no doubt. One of her fingers definitely moved.

His heart leaped into his throat.

Brandon lifted Morelle's hand to his lips and pressed a gentle kiss to the nearly translucent skin on the back of it.

"I need to tell Bridget about this," he told her, still holding her hand.

As if to confirm she'd heard him or maybe to stop him from leaving, her finger twitched again.

Brandon's chest felt too tight to contain the hope swelling within it.

"Bridget!" he called out, eyes fixed on the security camera in the corner. "Bridget, please come in quickly!" He then remembered to deactivate the device hanging around his neck and repeated what he'd said.

The doctor entered the room a moment later. "What's going on?"

"Morelle moved her finger," he said, trying to keep his voice steady despite his excitement.

"Involuntary movements are common in coma patients."

"She hasn't moved anything before, and she only did it after I asked her to give me a sign."

Bridget lifted one red eyebrow. "A sign for what?"

He was embarrassed to admit what he had asked for, but the doctor needed to know. "Permission to kiss her hand."

Bridget smiled. "That's sweet. I didn't know you were such a romantic."

"Given what I've been doing for a living for the past seventy years or so, it should have been obvious."

She chuckled. "You were promoting the clan's agenda, and sometimes you included the message we wanted to promote in romantic movies because it was easier for the public to swallow when delivered with a spoonful of sugar. That does not make you a romantic. I would say it makes you pragmatic."

That was a nice way to describe what most of his fellow council members thought of him. He had a reputation for being a shark, and it was well deserved.

"I'm many things."

Bridget smiled. "Aren't we all? So, you asked her to give you permission to kiss her hand by moving her finger?"

He nodded. "I asked for any physical sign. When I first felt it, I thought I had imagined it, so I asked her to do it again, and she did. If you take her hand, you will feel it too." He reluctantly let go so the doctor could take his place.

Looking skeptical, Bridget clasped Morelle's hand.

He activated the device before speaking to Morelle. "Can you move your finger for the physician?"

He held his breath, watching Bridget's face for a sign that she felt something as well and that he hadn't imagined it.

"I felt it." Bridget's professional demeanor couldn't quite hide her excitement. "This is very encouraging." She glanced at the monitors. "Her brain activity has been increasing over the past few days as you were talking." She nodded at him. "Good job, Brandon." She put Morelle's hand back on her bed. "I think we can help her along."

"How?"

"I'm going to give her a small amount of amantadine. It's sometimes used to accelerate emergence from coma states by increasing dopamine activity in the brain." She turned to the door. "I will be back in a moment."

When she left, Brandon lifted Morelle's hand to his lips again. "I might be overstepping my kissing allowance, so I'm apologizing in advance." He gently kissed the back of her hand. "I'm so excited. Soon, I might be able to see your eyes, maybe even your smile."

When Bridget returned with a syringe already filled with the medicine, he put Morelle's hand down and took a step back to give the physician room to work.

Brandon watched as she injected the medication into Morelle's upper arm "How long before we know if it's working?"

"It varies from patient to patient," Bridget said. "The key is to watch for any signs of increased awareness or movement."

He took hold of Morelle's hand again, his thumb stroking the back of it as he waited.

The seconds stretched into minutes, each one feeling like an eternity. The steady beeping of the heart monitor seemed to grow louder in the tense silence.

"Come on, sweetheart," he murmured, remembering that the device was off only after he had spoken.

"I'm activating my earpieces," Bridget said. "You can keep the teardrop on."

He was also wearing his earpieces, but not for the same reason Bridget had activated hers.

He was doing it so he could understand Morelle the moment she woke up, provided that she said anything to him. Bridget was doing so because they were still afraid of the princess's powerful compulsion ability, and her lashing out the moment she woke up.

He thought about all the stories he'd shared with her over the past days, all those tales of human achievement, of progress and change, of hope in the face of overwhelming odds. Had they reached her in that twilight realm between sleeping and waking?

Had they given her something to hold on to, a reason to fight her way back to consciousness?

Bridget moved quietly around the bed, checking readings and making notes on her tablet. But Brandon barely noticed, his attention completely focused on Morelle's face, watching for any sign of change.

Was it his imagination, or had her color improved slightly? Did her breathing seem different? He'd spent so many hours by her bedside that he felt attuned to the smallest variations in her condition, yet he didn't trust his own observations.

Hope could play tricks on the mind, making him see what he desperately wanted to see.

But that finger movement had been real. He hadn't imagined that.

"The medication should give her a boost," Bridget said quietly. "But it will need time to take effect. Keep talking to her. It seems to be helping." She gave him a reassuring smile before leaving the room.

Brandon kept on holding Morelle's hand, afraid to let go and miss another twitch. "There are so many more stories I can tell you about the brave people who fought for equal rights and made the promise of freedom real for everyone. Would you like to hear more about it?"

He felt another slight pressure against his palm—stronger this time. His breath caught.

"That's it," he encouraged. "You're doing great. Can you try to open your eyes? I'd love to finally see what color they are."

The minutes ticked by with agonizing slowness. Brandon held on to Morelle's hand, hoping that a small point of contact might serve as an anchor, helping to guide her back to the waking world. He continued talking, his voice growing hoarse, but he didn't care.

He would talk until his voice gave out completely, if it helped bring his princess back.

30

MORELLE

Vitality was gently seeping back into Morelle's body, slowly burning through the lethargy that had dragged her back under after her earlier triumph. She'd managed to move her finger not just once but three times, and what had made it possible was the excitement of feeling the storyteller's hand in hers.

It had felt like being zapped with a bolt of energy, and it had given her the strength to force her body to move, to show him that she had been listening and that she wanted to feel his lips on her hand.

The contact had been too brief because he called the medic.

By then, Morelle had been exhausted, but she'd managed to move her finger one more time to prove to the medic that the storyteller hadn't imagined it. She needed these people to know that she was in there, aware, awake, and locked inside a body that refused to cooperate.

It would cooperate now, though. The vitality coursing through her veins wasn't in her imagination, and this time, when she attempted to open her eyes they responded, and bright light flooded her vision.

The assault on her retinas was as jarring as it had been the first time she'd managed to lift her eyelids, but she refused to let her lids close again. Instead, she waited for her eyes to adjust, watching as the blurry shapes around her slowly gained definition.

Just like before, the only thing in front of her was a wall, and her storyteller couldn't see that her eyes were open. He was talking, but he wasn't holding her hand like he had before. If he had been, she would have moved a finger to alert him.

Instead, she forced her head to turn, and there he was, sitting in a chair beside her bed with his head bowed as he looked at a device balanced on his lap.

He wasn't Kra-ell. That much was immediately obvious from his features, which lacked the distinctive markers of her mother's people. But he wasn't human either. His beauty was too perfect, too sculpted. He was a god, and an exceptionally handsome one at that.

Morelle had seen gods before, mostly in vids but also during that nerve-racking trip to the spaceport where the settler ship had been docked. Many gods had worked there, and she couldn't understand how she and Ell-rom had walked past them without being noticed.

The elaborate makeup they'd worn wouldn't have been enough on its own, and their shrouding shouldn't have worked on the gods.

Perhaps her mother had bribed the few techs they'd encountered?

That wasn't likely. What must have happened was that the gods had been too preoccupied with their work to pay much attention to what appeared to be a pair of unremarkable Kra-ell.

However, the one in charge of their pod had known for sure. She remembered how nervous he'd appeared.

The storyteller must have sensed her scrutiny because he suddenly lifted his head, his eyes widening as they met hers. They were a striking blue and held warmth and intelligence in equal measure.

"Morelle!" He jumped to his feet, nearly dropping the device he'd been holding to the floor. "You are awake!"

She tried to smile for him, wanting to show him how much his presence had meant to her during her long twilight state, how his stories had anchored her and given her something to hold on to, but her facial muscles refused to cooperate.

All she could do was look at him, hoping he could read in her eyes what she couldn't express in any other way.

He took her hand, and the sensation was even more intense than before. His skin was warm against hers, the touch sending little sparks of awareness through her, but it was his eyes that truly captured her attention. The joy in them matched the warmth she'd heard in his voice and the optimism she'd heard in his stories.

He was so different from her.

"Bridget!" he called out, his gaze darting to the ceiling for some reason. "The princess is awake!"

The title made her want to roll her eyes.

He'd called her that many times before, and she liked it despite it not being true. She was the first-born daughter of the Kra-ell queen, and therefore her successor, but the matter of her conception invalidated her claim.

Her very existence was a violation of both societies' most sacred laws. Still, she didn't mind it if he used it as a term of endearment.

Morelle tried to open her mouth to tell him that she didn't need or want titles, but her throat felt dry and unused, and no sound emerged.

The frustration must have shown in her eyes because

he immediately moved away from her, and she heard him fill a container with water.

"Here," he said, producing a small cup with a straw. "Small sips only. Your throat hasn't been used in a very long time."

As the door opened, the storyteller looked in that direction. "I hope it's okay to give Morelle a small sip of water?"

The medic answered in a foreign language that Morelle had heard spoken around her before.

The medic must have approved because the story-teller held the straw to her lips.

Morelle managed a small sip, and the water felt wonderful on her parched throat. She wanted more, but he pulled it away after that first taste.

"I'm sorry, Princess. I know that you want more, but we need to wait a moment to make sure that stays down."

She wanted to tell him that she felt fine and that she needed more water, but she still couldn't talk. She wasn't sure whether it was the muscles of her face that were not working properly, or that the signals from her brain were not interpreted correctly by her body. Hopefully, that would pass soon.

Instead, she focused on his face, mapping all the details. Brown, lustrous hair, high cheekbones, strong jaw, and a straight nose that was a little on the longish side but fit his face perfectly. His most striking features were his beautiful eyes and what she saw in them.

He didn't shy away from her intense scrutiny. In fact, he seemed pleased by it. "My name is Bran-don, in case you are wondering."

Bran-don. Her storyteller's name was Bran-don.

It wasn't a Kra-ell name, but it did not sound foreign to her ears either.

She liked it.

31

BRANDON

"I need you to step out," Bridget told Brandon in her usual no-nonsense tone. "I have to perform a few cognitive tests on Morelle." She pulled out a teardrop just like his from her pocket and activated it.

Reluctantly, Brandon released Morelle's hand, his body and soul both protesting the necessity to step away from her. "I'll be right outside," he promised, trying to catch her eye one last time, but Bridget was already positioning herself between them.

"Go," the doctor commanded. "I'll call you back when I'm done."

Forcing himself to walk away from her, Brandon cast one last glance over his shoulder.

Morelle's eyes were still open, still as mesmerizing as the moment she'd first looked at him, and they were trained on him. Her gaze was so intense, so aware, that he had no doubt she'd heard him during all those long hours he had been talking to her and that she had understood everything.

As he opened the door, Gertrude was there, grinning happily. "This is a good day."

"It is." He let her slip by him. "Take good care of her."

"Of course." The nurse closed the door behind her.

Brandon sat down on one of the chairs in the waiting room, but he was too restless to remain seated, so he got up and started pacing from one end of the room to the other. Excitement and worry were mixing together to create a volatile compound in his gut that could only be quieted when he returned to Morelle's side.

Those eyes. Dear Fates, he hadn't expected them to be quite so striking. The instant they'd met his, he'd felt like Morelle could see straight into his soul. There had been recognition there, understanding, and something else he couldn't quite define.

Curiosity? Determination? Courage?

Had she retained some of her memories from life on Anumati, or had she lost them all like her brother had?

Ell-rom.

No one had told him that Morelle was awake, or he would be out of Jasmine's room and demanding to see his sister.

Brandon knocked on the door, trying not to make it sound too urgent and scare the prince.

After a moment, the door opened. "What is it?" Ell-rom asked.

Brandon couldn't keep the smile off his face. "Morelle woke up, Ell-rom. She opened her eyes and looked right at me. Bridget and Gertrude are with her, conducting some tests or examinations, so they kicked me out, and it has just occurred to me that no one has told you…"

Before he could finish the sentence, Ell-rom stepped forward and wrapped his arms around him in a fierce embrace, a sound somewhere between a laugh and a sob escaping the prince's throat.

"Thank the Mother of All Life, and thank you," he half sobbed, half whispered. "You brought her back to me."

Getting over the initial awkwardness, Brandon returned the hug just as tightly and clapped Ell-rom on his back. They were virtual strangers, but they were bound by their care for Morelle.

"I just talked," Brandon said, his voice thick with emotion. "Morelle is a fighter. She found her own way back."

Ell-rom pulled back just enough to look at him, his eyes bright with unshed tears. "She was revived from stasis weeks ago, and there was no change in her condition until you started your vigil and refused to leave her side." He chuckled. "I think that your instant infatuation with my sister is a little odd, but I welcome it. Perhaps the Mother of All Life used you as a tool to revive my sister."

Brandon nodded even though he did not believe in the Kra-ell's harsh deity, and he didn't like being called a tool, but he wasn't going to get upset about something an emotional alien prince had said. Perhaps his meaning had been lost in translation.

"Maybe it was the Fates," Ell-rom added. "They must have known that my sister needed a storyteller to help her find her way back to the world of the living."

As the door to Morelle's room opened and Gertrude stepped out, he and Ell-rom turned to her expectantly, still half-embracing.

"She's doing remarkably well," the nurse said, smiling at their emotional display. "The doctor says that you can come back in now." She glanced at Ell-rom. "I'll pretend that Bridget meant that both of you can come in. Just remember that Morelle is still very weak and confused. Don't overwhelm her."

Brandon and Ell-rom exchanged glances, sharing a moment before stepping apart. They were both aware of the shift between them. No longer just mere acquaintances, they had become entangled by their feelings for Morelle.

32

ELL-ROM

A
s Ell-rom entered Morelle's room, his heart nearly stopped when his sister's eyes found his. His other half was finally awake and looking at him with recognition and love.

Tears slid down her cheeks in twin rivulets.

He rushed to her bedside, gathering her in his arms carefully, mindful of the tubes and wires still attached to her. "Morelle," he whispered, his voice breaking with emotion. "You came back to me." He pressed his cheek to hers, his own tears mingling with hers.

He was vaguely aware of Brandon, Bridget, and Gertrude quietly leaving the room, giving them privacy for this reunion.

"Morelle, Morelle, Morelle," he kept whispering her name like a prayer, holding her close, overwhelmed by the reality of having her truly present and aware in his arms.

When he realized that she wasn't moving, he loosened his hold and lowered her head back to the thin pillow.

"Was I squeezing you too tightly?"

He hoped for a smile, but all he got was a double blink of her eyes, and somehow, he knew it was her way of saying no.

Was it a memory?

Had they developed a language of silent communications?

She was looking up at him, and as another tear slid down her cheek, she lifted her hand shakily toward his head but then dropped it back down.

Understanding what she wanted, he took her hand, leaned down, and helped guide it to his mostly bald scalp, where only a light fuzz of new growth had started to appear.

The question in her eyes was clear, and he managed a small laugh through the mist in his eyes. "The stasis chambers malfunctioned, and the only thing that kept us alive was our godly genes that allowed us to enter unaided stasis. We were found completely emaciated, with only clumps of long strands of dry, matted hair remaining. It wasn't a pretty sight, so the medics shaved off what was left." He saw her eyes drift upward, clearly wondering about her own head. "Yes, yours too. The trauma to our bodies must have slowed down the growth because I should have more by now, but it will come."

Gently, he guided her hand to her own scalp, letting her feel the similar fuzzy growth there. Her fingers moved slowly over the unfamiliar texture, and another tear slipped down her cheek.

"It's okay," he assured her. "Our bodies were too busy rebuilding our organs and muscles to worry about something as trivial as hair. Julian, one of the medics, explained that our bodies were prioritizing the most important repairs." He smiled at her. "I promise that it will all grow back, just as full and beautiful as I remember it." He paused. "I have to admit that I don't remember much of our lives on Anumati. My memories were lost during the long stasis." He cupped her cheek. "I hope you've retained your memories and can help me understand who I was, who we both were as people."

Morelle blinked once, deliberately, and somehow, he knew this was her way of saying yes. Relief flooded through him. At least one of them remembered their shared history.

"Why aren't you speaking?" he asked gently. "Is it too difficult?"

One blinks. Yes, then. It was too difficult for her to speak.

"That's alright," he said. "Your voice will come back. I'm certain of it." He hugged her again, pressing kisses to her tear-stained cheeks. "I love you so much, and I've missed you terribly, even when I couldn't remember exactly what I was missing. There was just this huge hole in my chest. Jasmine filled some of it, but it would never mend completely unless I had you back in my life."

Settling more comfortably on the edge of her bed, he kept hold of her hand. "I have so much to tell you. Jasmine is the one who helped our sister's people find us. We would have died if they hadn't reached us when they did. The stasis chambers had stopped working long ago, and they were sealed, so we couldn't absorb nutrients from the environment. We were nearing our end."

When Morelle's eyes widened, he realized that he was jumping ahead of the story. "We have a half-sister here on Earth, the daughter of our father. She is the leader of this community that shelters us, and she is incredible. Her name is Annani, and she is a full-blooded goddess. She is as magnificent as our father was, and maybe more. She is also loving and warm and has welcomed us into her clan with open arms." He lifted her hand to his lips and kissed her fingertips. "I wonder how much Brandon has told you. Did he tell you about Annani?"

Morelle blinked twice.

"That's odd. I was sure he was telling you about the gods and immortals and their history on Earth." He chuckled. "Now I wonder what he has been telling you through the long hours he sat with you. Jasmine also sat by my bedside for days, talking to me, singing to me, pulling me back to consciousness. She did the same for you, just not as often, but it didn't work. I guess you needed a different kind of voice to reach you."

A small smile curled Morelle's lips, the first expression she'd managed other than the widening and narrowing of her eyes.

"Brandon has barely left your side since we moved to the village." Ell-rom put Morelle's hand down on her chest. "I think he fell in love with you at first sight." He chuckled. "As Kra-ell, we are not supposed to believe in love, let alone love at first sight. But the humans believe it, and I've learned that it can be very real. It happened to me with Jasmine."

He noticed Morelle's eyelashes starting to flutter, her eyes fighting to stay open. "You're tired," he said softly. "You should rest." Leaning down, he pressed another kiss to her forehead. When her eyes popped wide open, he quickly added, "Don't worry. I'm in the room next to yours, and I'll come back as soon as you wake up again. I'm not leaving you. I promise."

Morelle's eyes closed, and she let out a sigh.

He stayed for a moment longer until her breathing evened out into the rhythm of sleep that seemed frighteningly similar to a coma, but he had to trust that this was natural rest.

Morelle was back. His other half returned to him.

33

ANNANI

When Annani's phone rang, displaying Kian's name, her heart skipped a beat. Her son rarely called during work hours unless something significant had happened.

"Hello, Kian," she greeted. "Is everything okay?"

"Morelle woke up," he said, matter-of-fact. "She's resting now, but she was fully conscious and responsive, and Bridget says that she seems of sound mind and fully cognizant."

Joy surged through Annani's chest. "Thank the merciful Fates. I want to see her as soon as possible."

"I thought you would. I'll come get you with the golf cart as soon as Bridget lets me know that Morelle is awake again."

"I want to go now. Ell-rom must be overwhelmed with emotion, and I should be there with him to support him."

There was a brief pause before Kian responded. "You're right. I'll be there in a few minutes. Anandur is getting the golf cart."

After ending the call, Annani walked into her bedroom and examined her reflection in front of her full-length mirror.

Should she change into a different gown for her first meeting with her sister? It was a most special occasion, a heralding of a monumental shift in their family dynamic, but did it really require a different gown?

It was a silly thought since all of her gowns were equally beautiful and appropriate, designed for both comfort and elegance, but while she waited for Kian, she needed to do something to release the excited energy coursing through her.

Looking through her wardrobe, she chose a purple gown that complemented her red hair and exchanged it for the blue one she had put on that morning. The gowns were almost identical in their design and type of fabric, so the improvement in her looks was not significant. Living as long as she had and never changing, Annani had figured out a long time ago what made her look the best with the least amount of effort on her part.

Annani did not wear makeup or style her hair, which prompted complaints from her youngest daughter. Amanda often teased her about her low-maintenance style, but Kian, on the other hand, claimed that she was high maintenance, always requiring his time and attention.

Nonsense. She hardly ever called on him for anything.

Children.

No matter how old they were, they always found a reason to complain about their mothers.

Annani brushed her hair more out of habit than necessity, dabbed a touch of her favorite perfume behind her ears, and then pulled out a pair of earpieces from her jewelry box and put them in.

She did not need them to filter compulsion, even though Kian insisted that she always wear them around Ell-rom and Morelle, but she did need them to translate. She also needed the teardrop to communicate with Morelle if she got a chance.

The device was stored in the drawer of her night table, and she pulled it out and hung it around her neck.

"The marvels of technology," she murmured as she headed back to the living room.

Through the windows, she saw the golf cart stop in front of the house, and a moment later, Kian stepped down and walked up to the front door.

Without waiting for her son to ring the bell and then one of her Odus to open the door, Annani opened it herself.

Kian's eyebrows shot up in surprise, and then he laughed. "Now I know that you're truly excited about meeting Morelle. You never come out when I arrive to pick you up."

It was true. A lady, let alone a goddess and a leader of her clan, never rushed to the door, but today, Annani was making an exception.

"I admit, I am excited."

"Of course, Mother." Kian helped her into the passenger seat at the back and climbed up to sit with her.

"Hello, Anandur," she greeted the Guardian.

"Clan Mother." He dipped his head. "Today, we celebrate."

"Indeed, we do. I am ready to welcome my sister into our clan."

As they drove through the village, Annani's mind raced with questions. What would Morelle be like? Would she be like their brother, gentle and mellow, or more like their father? Would she recognize traces of Ahn in Morelle's character?

"The princess doesn't speak yet," Kian said. "Bridget says that there is nothing physically preventing her from talking, but she might be afraid to use her voice because she hasn't used it in so long, or maybe it hurts to talk. She believes that she will say something soon."

Annani nodded, remembering how Ell-rom had struggled at first. "The important thing is that she is aware and is not cognitively impaired. We were all afraid of that when she was not waking up."

"Bridget performed a few basic tests, and then Ell-rom walked in, and Morelle immediately recognized him. According to Bridget, they had a very emotional reunion."

Annani could just imagine the state Ell-rom was in. Her brother needed someone to hug him right now.

As Anandur stopped in front of the clinic, Kian jumped down and then offered Annani a hand to help her down.

When they entered the clinic's waiting room, Ell-rom rushed toward her and embraced her, having to bend nearly in half to wrap his arms around her tiny frame.

"Annani," he whispered, and the emotion in his voice brought tears to her eyes. "I'm so relieved, so happy."

She hugged him back fiercely. "How is Morelle?"

He chuckled. "Concerned about her lack of hair." Ell-rom straightened up but kept hold of her hand. "She can't speak yet, but she communicates with her eyes. She was even able to lift her hand." His voice cracked slightly. "She remembers, Annani. She'll be able to tell me about our past."

Annani squeezed his hand. "That is wonderful news."

As they settled into the waiting room chairs, Ell-rom held on to her hand, and Kian took a seat on her other side.

"While we wait, we might as well discuss arrangements," Kian said. "Bridget told me that Morelle won't need to stay in the clinic much longer. As soon as she is able to hold food down and is stable enough to go to the bathroom by herself, she can go home and just come in for checkups and rehab."

Ell-rom leaned over Annani to look at Kian. "Gertrude mentioned that Morelle will need to come for regular sessions on some special rehabilitation device."

"The Pilates Reformer," Kian said. "It will help her get on her feet faster. After that, we will probably move the device to the gym, where it belongs."

"I would like to see it." Annani rearranged the folds of her gown.

Kian arched a brow. "Are you considering exercising, Mother?"

"Fates forbid." She huffed in indignation. "My morning walks are all I need to maintain my physique."

Kian chuckled. "That's what I thought. But back to the living arrangements. I assume that you will want Morelle to stay with you?"

"Of course."

Annani wanted Morelle to stay with her so they would get to know each other and develop their sisterly bond. The problem was Brandon.

He would want to spend as much time as possible with Morelle because he was very obviously in love with her sister, or at least infatuated with her, but since they were not a couple yet and needed time to court and really get to know each other, they might not be comfortable sharing a bedroom, and Annani did not have another bedroom in her house where he could stay.

The solution was for him to visit during the day, spend time with Morelle while she was awake, and leave for the night.

Then again, if things progressed between them—and Annani strongly suspected they would—Brandon could simply move into Morelle's room. However, it was more likely that Morelle would prefer to move in with Brandon rather than have him join her at Annani's house.

It was natural for a grown female to want her own space, but Annani hoped that her sister would choose to stay, at least for a little while. They needed time to bond and make up for all the years they had not even known of each other's existence.

What would she have done in Morelle's place?

Annani was not sure. If she was to choose between her Khiann and her sister, it would have been

Khiann. She would have tried to spend as much time as possible with her sister, but she would have chosen to live with her mate.

"Where's Brandon?" Annani asked, noticing his absence.

Ell-rom smiled. "He's in with her now, waiting for her to wake up again. I'm afraid I monopolized her attention earlier and talked to her until I exhausted her, and she fell asleep again."

"It is your right, so do not feel bad about it." Annani patted his hand. "Once Jasmine transitions and is ready to go home as well, we will have a grand time, all of us living together under one roof and getting to know each other."

"I would love that." Ell-rom looked at the closed door longingly. "But I have a feeling that you and I will have to fight Brandon for scraps of Morelle's time."

Annani laughed. "You might be right."

34

MORELLE

onsciousness returned gradually this time, feeling natural rather than strained. Morelle's eyelids felt lighter and easier to lift, and when she opened them, she found her storyteller sitting beside her bed instead of Ell-rom.

Had she dreamt of her brother's visit?

No. She remembered touching Ell-rom's similarly fuzzy scalp and remembering him explaining the stasis chambers and their effect on their bodies.

That had been real.

Her hand drifted to her head, feeling the soft fuzz of new growth there.

Such a trivial thing, losing one's hair. She shouldn't be so upset about it, not when she had survived thousands of years in stasis and found her brother alive and well on the other end. But given that this came on top of everything else, the years she'd lost, her mother's death, the uncertainty of where she had found herself, it felt devastating.

She felt a tear slide down her cheek.

"Morelle," the storyteller whispered. "You're awake."

He stood and leaned over her, his blue eyes conveying a depth of feeling she couldn't understand. Why did he care to dedicate so much time to her?

Was he a healer? Someone who Ell-rom had hired to coax her back to the world of the living?

What had Ell-rom paid him with?

She hoped her brother had been smart enough to hide his ability from these people, or they would turn him into a tool of death. It wasn't that she had a fundamental issue with that; some individuals needed killing, but Ell-rom was not an assassin, and if he was forced to kill, it would maim his soul.

If she were a believer, Morelle would pray to the Mother of All Life to keep Ell-rom from ever bartering his soul for goods or services on her behalf or on behalf of anyone else.

The storyteller took her hand, cradling it against his chest. "The medics said that there is nothing wrong with your vocal cords or your facial muscles. You should be able to talk."

She could feel his heartbeat accelerating through the thin fabric of his shirt. He wanted her to speak to him, and she would if she could, but her previous attempts had been futile.

It was as if her mouth had forgotten how to form words.

Then she remembered him telling her his name.

Bran-don. Perhaps she could start with that. Just saying his name.

Hesitantly, she extended her tongue and licked her lips. They felt sticky, coated with something that the medics must have applied to soften them.

The taste was unpleasant.

She swallowed, trying to bring more moisture into her dry mouth, and then formed the syllables of his name. "Bran-don," she said slowly, and the triumph felt even greater than her earlier victory of opening her eyes.

"You said my name." He gently squeezed the hand that was still pressed against his chest. "You can talk. Oh, Princess. You have no idea how happy that makes me."

Something struck her as odd about his response. His lips hadn't moved in synch with the words she'd heard, and she realized that the sound had come from a small device hanging from a cord around his neck.

Curious, she reached for it, and to her surprise, her hand responded to her command.

He allowed her to hold it, watching as she examined it with questioning eyes. She wanted to ask what it was, but forming her earlier words had drained what little energy she had for speech.

"It's a translation device," he explained, seeming to understand her unspoken question. "It translates my native language to Kra-ell."

Morelle managed to lift her head slightly, looking down at her own chest, but she found nothing similar there. How would he understand her when she didn't have a similar device?

Not that she'd said much, just his name, and now she felt too exhausted to say more. Perhaps he could understand her, or maybe the device worked in both directions?

Brandon smiled, touching something in his ear. "I have earpieces that translate what you're saying in Kra-ell to my language. When you feel well enough, you'll get a pair of these so you can understand those who don't have a teardrop." His hand dropped to the translator hanging from his neck, which was indeed shaped like a teardrop.

Morelle had so many questions about the technology, about this new world she'd awakened to, but one concern pressed more urgently than all others. "Ell-rom?" she managed to ask.

"Ell-rom has them, too," Brandon replied.

He'd misunderstood. "Here?" she clarified, condensing the inquiry after her brother into one word.

Understanding dawned in Brandon's eyes, followed by what looked like disappointment, and she realized that he thought she was dismissing him in favor of her brother.

Didn't he understand that she'd listened to him for so many hours and felt like she knew him well already, while she'd only had a few precious moments with Ell-rom before exhaustion had pulled her under again?

"I'll tell him you're awake," Brandon said, releasing her hand and turning toward the door.

"Bran-don," she said softly, waiting until he looked back over his shoulder. "Thank you."

His smile returned, and he nodded before opening the door.

35

ELL-ROM

hen Brandon emerged from Morelle's room, Ell-rom rose to his feet. "Is she awake?"

Brandon nodded. "She's asking for you."

Ell-rom's heart skipped a beat. "She spoke?"

"Not much. She said my name, which was nice to hear, your name, and here, which I understood to mean that she wants you there. She then said my name again and added thank you. I'd say that's absolutely spectacular progress in one hour since waking up after thousands of years in stasis."

The words had Ell-rom's chest expanding by a few inches.

"My sister is a fighter." He turned to Annani, who was practically vibrating with anticipation beside him. "Both my sisters are fighters. Would you like to come meet her?"

"Are you sure?" Annani asked. "I do not want to rob you of your time with her."

"I have already told her about you in the few moments she was awake. I think she will want to see who I was talking about."

"Wait," Kian said as Annani stood up. "I don't want you going in there without me." He pulled a teardrop from his pocket and hung it around his neck.

Ell-rom barely managed to suppress an eye roll. It seemed ridiculous to be concerned about Morelle harming anyone in her current state, let alone someone as powerful as Annani.

Then again, maybe Kian was just curious and wanted to meet Morelle.

Seeing Ell-rom's hesitation, Kian softened his tone. "I'll just introduce myself and welcome her to the clan. Then I'll leave you three to talk."

"I cannot wait to meet my sister." Annani reached up and activated her translator.

Ell-rom couldn't contain his excitement either. He was eager to introduce Morelle to the half-sister they hadn't known they had on Earth.

As he opened the door and let Annani go in first, Morelle's eyes widened when she saw their sister. His twin's lips parted, probably to ask who she was, but before she could form the words, Annani had crossed to her bedside and enveloped her in a gentle embrace.

"Welcome to my clan, sister of mine," Annani said in her melodic voice. "My name is Annani, and we share a father. I hope we will become the best of friends."

Morelle looked stunned even though Ell-rom had already told her about Annani being their half-sister, the daughter of their father, and a goddess who had been born on Earth. Perhaps it wasn't the information itself that had shocked her, but rather Annani's affection.

Should he feel hurt that Annani hadn't made such an explicit offer of friendship to him?

But then, she hadn't needed to, had she? She'd shown her love and acceptance through her actions, supporting him through his recovery, taking him into her home, and helping him control his ability. Words paled in comparison to everything she'd done for him.

Kian cleared his throat, reminding them that he was still waiting to be introduced to Morelle.

Annani turned and smiled, waving her hand and inviting him over. "This is my son, Kian. He leads the local community, which is comprised mostly of my descendants. My daughter Sari leads another segment of my clan, which resides on another continent. I have two more daughters who are here in the village and would love to meet you. Amanda, my youngest, and Alena, my oldest."

As Morelle's expressive eyes showed her confusion, Kian chuckled. "After seven thousand years in stasis, we should probably drip the information to you instead of dumping everything at once." He kept his voice much softer than usual, and the teardrop provided a pretty accurate rendition of it. "All you need to know right now is that you're with your family who cares about you and your brother and welcomes you into our community. You're safe, and you can take as long as you need to recuperate and learn about your new world."

"Thank you." Morelle's voice was barely above a whisper as she reached out her hand toward Kian.

Ell-rom watched as his nephew—and wasn't that a strange concept?—clasped Morelle's hand and leaned down to kiss her cheek.

"Welcome home, Aunt Morelle," he said.

The words hit Ell-rom like a physical force. Home. They had a home now, a real one, not just a hiding place in a temple. They had family, not just each other, but a sister who loved them, a nephew and nieces who welcomed them, and an entire community that accepted them into its fold.

It was incredible.

"That's all I wanted to say." Kian let go of Morelle's hand. "I'll let you three talk in private." He turned to his mother. "Try not to overload your sister with seven thousand years of history all at once."

Annani laughed, the sound so beautiful that it brought tears to Ell-rom's eyes.

He was too emotional right now, and he had to get a hold of himself. Morelle needed him to lend her his strength.

When Kian left the room, Ell-rom moved to Morelle's other side and took her hand. She responded by shifting her luminous eyes to him and squeezing his fingers weakly.

Annani sighed dramatically and sat down on the single chair in the room. "I thought about where I would like to start my story, and I think I should begin by telling you about our father. Would you like that?"

Morelle nodded.

Ell-rom sat on the edge of the bed with Morelle's hand clasped in his. He would have liked to start with what he had learned about Annani, the clan, and the world around them, but perhaps Annani was right, and they should start at the beginning and how the three of them came to be.

BRANDON

E ll-rom and Annani had been with Morelle for an awfully long time, or at least it felt like that to Brandon. Each minute seemed to stretch endlessly, and he filled the time by committing to memory her beautiful face and those huge blue eyes, an image so perfect it seemed borrowed from a fairy tale.

Next to him, Kian was reading through his emails, frowning and occasionally cursing under his breath.

"Trouble?" Brandon finally asked.

"Incompetence," Kian spat. "I must be really bad at hiring managers. The only good ones are clan members. I know there are competent humans out there, but I can't seem to be able to spot them."

"Perhaps you should use a human headhunter to find managers for you, someone who specializes in the particular industry you need."

Kian regarded him with appreciation. "That's good advice. I'll do that."

"Glad to help." Brandon leaned back in his chair. "Why are you still here, Kian? I don't mind the company, but you are a busy guy. I'm sure you have better things to do than sit out here and wait for your mother. Are you afraid of Morelle attacking the Clan Mother?"

Kian shook his head. "She is in no condition to harm anyone right now, but that's because she has just woken up and is completely overwhelmed." He turned toward Bridget's office, where the doctor sat working with her door open. "Is it good for her to have so many visitors so soon after waking up?"

Bridget looked up from her computer, shrugging. "Could you have kept your mother from visiting her sister until tomorrow?"

"Good point," Kian conceded. "I keep thinking of her as I do of transitioning Dormants, but Morelle is half goddess, half Kra-ell, and she's much more resilient. It's probably okay."

Bridget's smile held a knowing edge. "Your guess is as good as mine." She shifted her gaze to Brandon. "After the Clan Mother and Ell-rom leave, you'll need to wait for Gertrude to put the CPM machine on Morelle's legs to exercise them. You can sit with her while that's being done, but after that, Gertrude will wash her and change her hospital gown, so you will have to leave again." Her expression turned thoughtful. "Perhaps you can utilize the time to get Morelle some things. I can ask Amanda to take care of getting her what she needs, and she'd be glad to do so, but Amanda is already busy organizing Peter and Marina's wedding, so I don't know if she can do it right away. She might delegate it to someone else, but if you're up to it, that could be you."

Brandon's heart leaped at the opportunity. "I'm definitely up to it, but I don't want to leave her side. I'll contact a personal shopper I know to handle everything and deliver the purchases to the reception at the keep."

He could get her an entire wardrobe fit for a princess or a supermodel. Should he order her high heels? How tall was she?

Most of the Kra-ell females were over six feet tall, but Morelle was half goddess, so she might be much shorter than that. Come to think of it, she probably had to wear platform shoes under her priestly robes to compensate for her more diminutive size.

"It's good to have connections." Kian cast him a sidelong glance. "It would never have occurred to me to hire a personal shopper."

"It's standard practice in the movie industry," Brandon said. "Usually, the service is used to provide wardrobes for actors based on the costumer's wish list, but many use it for their personal needs as well." He turned to Bridget. "Did you take any of Morelle's measurements?"

"I took some, but not as many as I do for transitioning Dormants. Once the Clan Mother and Ellrom are out of her room, I can quickly assemble a measurements list for you, and I'll also text you what you need to order." She swiveled her chair, so her monitor was no longer obstructing half of her face. "Remember, she needs everything—underwear, sleepwear, everyday clothes, evening wear, toiletries. Maybe even makeup and hairbrushes will be needed when her hair grows back. Perhaps a wig if she's self-conscious about being bald."

"Morelle is beautiful the way she is." Brandon felt offended on her behalf. "She doesn't need a wig."

Bridget smiled knowingly. "I agree, but does she think so?"

"Good point," he murmured. "I'll get her a wig, but I won't give it to her unless she indicates that she is upset about her baldness."

"Smart male." Kian patted his arm.

Brandon smirked. "After decades of dealing with actresses, I've learned a thing or two about females."

"I'm sure the experience will come in handy." Kian closed his phone and put it in his pocket. "That being said, Morelle is a sample of one. There is no one like her in the entire universe."

"Except for her brother." Brandon pulled out his phone and searched his contacts for his most trusted personal shopper.

"It's not the same." Kian rose to his feet. "He is a male, and his sensitivities and insecurities come from a different place." He walked over to the water dispenser and filled up a small paper cup. "We all want to look appealing and be perceived as strong and capable people, but for males, the ability to protect and provide is what makes us feel good about ourselves, and for females, it's the ability to nurture and create. Naturally, there is a lot of overlapping, and some males are better at nurturing and creating than they are at providing and protecting. The same is true for females who are better at providing and protecting than they are at nurturing and creating, but generally, I believe that's universally true."

"You forget that she is half Kra-ell," Bridget said. "Morelle was raised as a Kra-ell, and some of the roles are reversed in their society."

Kian chuckled. "Their males still provide and protect, and their females are not very nurturing, but they are still in charge of raising the children."

"You are old-fashioned," Brandon said. "Not that I don't agree with you. I'm old-fashioned, too. We are dinosaurs."

Kian laughed. "I hope not. The dinosaurs went extinct. I hope immortals roam the Earth for eternity."

MORELLE

After Annani and Ell-rom left, exhaustion washed over Morelle, and the need to close her eyes and surrender to it was overwhelming, but she fought it. She wanted Bran-don, her storyteller, to return, and she wanted to be awake for him. His presence made her feel safe for some reason.

Was he a warrior?

He didn't move like the Kra-ell warriors from back home, but there was something about him that suggested he could hold his own on the battlefield.

When the door opened, Morelle was disappointed when, instead of Bran-don, one of the medics entered, wheeling in a strange contraption.

"Look what I just got." The woman touched the teardrop hanging from a cord tied around her neck. "Now that you are awake, you need to understand what I'm saying. I'm Gertrude, by the way, if you have forgotten my name."

She remembered the medic introducing herself before, but she hadn't remembered her name until she'd said it again.

Morelle wanted to make a comment, maybe congratulate Gertrude on receiving the new device, but her throat felt painfully dry, and her lips were cracked despite the sticky paste that the medic had smeared on them before.

When she licked her lips, Gertrude reached for a cup and filled it with water.

"Here." She held it to her lips.

This time, unlike earlier with Brandon, she didn't stop Morelle from drinking the entire cup. The cool liquid felt wonderful, sliding down her throat, making speech easier.

"Thank you. That was wonderful."

"You are welcome. Is your stomach okay? Not queasy?"

"I'm okay." Morelle nodded. "What is that device for?" she asked, eyeing the contraption Gertrude was positioning near her legs.

"It's a machine to exercise your muscles without you having to do anything," Gertrude explained as she carefully arranged Morelle's legs. "So that when you're ready to walk, it won't be as difficult. After your brother woke up from stasis, his muscles weren't rebuilt yet, and he could have made use of one, too, but Julian only thought of ordering it after his experience with Ell-rom. It was different for your brother because he was much weaker when he woke up than you were, so we are expecting your recovery to be much faster."

Shame washed over Morelle when she realized that she hadn't even asked Ell-rom how long he had been awake or why he had woken up before her. Had it been voluntary? Or had their newly discovered relative decided to wake them up one at a time?

If she were in their position and did not know what to expect, she would have woken up just one as well to see if they were dangerous, but she had a feeling that was not what had happened.

For some reason, Ell-rom had awakened first on his own.

Well, she suspected what the reason was. She hadn't wanted to wake up, and if not for her mother speaking to her from the Fields of the Brave and Bran-don talking to her, she would be sleeping still.

As the nurse worked to secure the straps, Morelle became aware of all the tubes and wires attached to her body. Some led to bags of clear liquid, others to machines that beeped steadily. "What are all these for?"

"The IV line here," Gertrude touched a tube, "provides fluids and nutrition. This one," she indicated another, "is a catheter for waste removal. The wires connect to monitors that track your vital signs— heart rate, blood pressure, oxygen levels."

Morelle studied the various attachments. "Can they be removed?"

Gertrude hesitated. "I need to check with Bridget about that."

"I want to get out of this bed." The words came out more forceful than Morelle had intended, but they felt right.

The nurse chuckled. "The tubes will have to come out first."

"Then take them out." Morelle met her eyes steadily.

Gertrude studied her face. "You're serious, aren't you?"

"I've been asleep for thousands of years," Morelle said. "I don't want to spend a minute longer than I have to in this bed."

The nurse nodded slowly. "I get it. I would feel the same if I were in your place. I'll get Bridget."

After Gertrude left, Morelle tested her strength by lifting both arms. The movement was shaky but possible, and she was reassured that she wasn't making a mistake by insisting that she didn't need to stay in bed.

At least, she hoped not.

Her mind drifted to Annani and the stories her newfound sister had shared about their father's arrival on Earth, and his mission of a new start for his people and for the humans who had looked up to the gods for leadership. When Morelle asked what had happened to him, Annani was saddened and said that this part of the tale could wait for another time.

Ell-rom seemed to know the rest of the story, but he'd left with Annani, claiming that Morelle needed rest. He hadn't been wrong, and she'd felt the effect of her prolonged wakefulness and how it drained the small reservoir of energy she had, but she'd had enough rest for several lifetimes, and she needed to push through the lethargy that was dragging her down.

Her mother's words echoed in her mind; it was time to wake up.

"I'm trying, Mother," she said to the empty room. "Although I don't know what you expect me to do in this world. It would be nice if you visited me again during sleep and gave me some concrete advice. I'm lost here."

The door opened, and Bridget walked in. "Were you talking to someone?"

"Myself." Morelle shifted her gaze toward the medic. "I want out of this bed. What do I need to do?"

Bridget chuckled. "You are truly a princess, not a spoiled one, but you expect your commands to be followed."

Had she stepped out of line? Perhaps the medic was someone important in Annani's community, and she needed to be addressed with more deference.

For all Morelle knew, medics were regarded like priestesses in her world and were to be addressed with utmost respect.

"Forgive me. I did not wish to be rude. If I spoke too forcefully, I apologize."

"It's okay," Bridget said. "I like assertive people who know what they want. Since you are taking liquids well and holding them down, we can take you off the intravenous line. We can also remove the other line that disposes of the fluids, and if you have trouble getting to the bathroom, we can provide a basin, or Gertrude can carry you."

"I want to walk." Morelle glanced at the machine, still gently bending and straightening her legs. "This is supposed to strengthen my leg muscles, which means that my legs should be able to hold my weight."

Bridget regarded her for a long moment, and Morelle held her breath, hoping she hadn't pushed too far.

Finally, the medic nodded. "We can try. If what you want doesn't work, we can always do it my way."

Relief flooded through Morelle. Bridget was a reasonable person, willing to let her try rather than forcing compliance. "Thank you. I appreciate your willingness to accommodate my wishes."

The medic nodded. "After the device is done, Gertrude will disconnect you from all the tubes and wires, take you to the bathroom, and after you complete your business in the toilet, she will give you a proper washing. How does that sound?"

Morelle couldn't wait.

"Wonderful. Thank you."

BRANDON

As a flurry of activity swirled around Morelle's door, Brandon paced the waiting room, trying to stay out of the way of the medical staff and not worry too much.

Every time Bridget or Gertrude emerged, they offered brief updates about what was going on that only increased his anxiety.

Morelle wanted the tubes removed.

Morelle insisted on getting up.

Morelle was demanding independence mere hours after opening her eyes.

He ran his hands through his hair for what felt like the hundredth time. If the medical staff hadn't been wearing filtering earpieces, he would have suspected compulsion at work. But no, this had to be just Morelle's force of personality bending the formidable

Bridget to her will. Somehow, she'd convinced the physician to disconnect her from everything.

It made no sense.

Bridget was not the type to cave to capricious demands. She was notorious for being unmoved by anyone's demands unless she saw merit in them. So why was she yielding to Morelle's wishes?

She couldn't possibly think that this was a good idea.

When the doctor emerged once again, Brandon intercepted Bridget before she could disappear into the restricted area where the lab and diagnostic equipment were housed. "What's going on, Bridget? Why are you agreeing to Morelle's unreasonable demands?"

One of the doctor's red eyebrows shot up. "Why would you think that they are unreasonable?"

"Because she's not ready to get out of bed on her own and have all the monitoring equipment disconnected. She just woke up." Brandon glanced toward Jasmine's room, lowering his voice so Ell-rom wouldn't hear him. "What if she has a relapse? She can't be ready when she couldn't even speak when she first woke up. Ell-rom had to help her when she wanted to touch his head because she lacked the strength to lift her arm on her own. What could have changed in the span of a few hours?"

Bridget shifted her weight, hand finding her hip in a stance he recognized as her 'teaching moment' pose.

"Morelle is half goddess, and her healing ability is phenomenal. Think of your own body and what it can fix in minutes, let alone hours. Unlike Ell-rom, who woke up when he was still emaciated, she woke up after her body had finished rebuilding her organs and her muscles. At first, she was stiff and unaccustomed to moving, but she has improved rapidly. She walked to the bathroom, leaning on Gertrude, of course, but she did it without falling or needing to be carried. She also showered, with Gertrude's help, brushed her teeth, and is now resting in a fresh gown on fresh sheets." Her voice softened. "When a patient is so determined to move forward, I prefer to take a risk and let them push themselves rather than hold them back. Never underestimate the power of the spirit."

"Wow." Brandon pressed a hand to his chest, feeling genuinely chastened. "I stand corrected. How is she doing now?"

A knowing smile curved Bridget's lip. "Clinging on like the fighter she is. I took blood samples and a few measurements, so that kept her awake, but she stayed alert even after I was done. She's holding on to wakefulness by her fingernails. I'm getting her something to eat."

That was another surprise, but Brandon wasn't going to repeat his mistake and ask if it wasn't too early for Morelle to consume real food. If she was no longer being fed intravenously, she needed to get nutrients some other way.

"Can I see her now? Do you think she wants me there?" The words tumbled out before he could stop them.

"Definitely." Bridget patted his arm. "I think you are the reason she is pushing herself so hard."

That caught him off guard. "Really? What makes you think that?"

"Simple. Imagine the roles were reversed, and you were in that bed while an attractive woman was keeping you company. You are grateful and intrigued by the stranger who dedicates so much time to you, but you feel insecure and unkempt about your appearance. All your hair has fallen out, and it feels like your mouth is chewing on dirt. Wouldn't you want to get all the tubes taken out, get clean, and maybe put some cologne on before you let her see you again?"

He rubbed the back of his neck. "I guess I would."

She chuckled. "I know you would. Now get in there and put on the charm."

"Yes, ma'am." He offered her a playful salute.

As Brandon approached Morelle's door, he remembered at the last moment that he should knock before entering.

"Who is it?"

Wow, her voice was so strong and confident now.

He opened the door ajar so he wouldn't have to shout. "It's me, Brandon. Can I come in?"

"Yes."

When he stepped in, he was struck by the transformation. The mechanical chorus of monitors was gone, replaced by peaceful quiet; the bed had been adjusted to a semi-reclining position, and the slightly lemony smell he had gotten accustomed to had been replaced by the clean scent of soap and laundry detergent.

Most remarkable, though, was Morelle herself. She was alert, upright, and more present than before. Her big blue eyes were clear and shining with intelligence and resolve.

"Hello, beautiful." He flashed her one of his practiced smiles, the kind that had charmed countless Hollywood executives and starlets alike. "Do you feel better now?"

Her lack of an answering smile sent a tendril of worry through him.

"Yes. Thank you," she said, sounding formal.

"Is something wrong?" He moved closer to the bed, studying her face for clues.

"I don't think so." Her eyes fixed on his mouth. "I just remembered something you said when I was still locked inside my body and couldn't respond."

The phrasing sent a chill down his spine. "What do you mean by locked inside your body?"

"I was aware for a long time," she said. "I could hear you talking and understand all the stories you told me, and I could hear the medics talking, but I couldn't understand them because they didn't have teardrops to translate what they were saying. I couldn't respond, I thought. My body did not obey my commands."

He took her hand. "I'm so sorry. It must have been terrifying."

She didn't pull her hand out of his, and he hoped it wasn't because she lacked the strength to do so, but because she enjoyed his touch.

"It was," Morelle admitted.

His mind was reeling. All those hours he'd spent talking to her, telling stories, sharing his thoughts, she'd heard everything. Every confession, every musing, she'd been present for all of it.

"But I knew I would get free," she said quietly. "I was trying so hard to break to the surface. It was exhausting, but I kept trying."

"You are so brave." He lifted her hand and brushed his lips over her knuckles.

When her breath hitched, he let go of her hand. "I'm sorry. I shouldn't have taken the liberty."

"No, it's fine. I've already given you permission to kiss my hand, remember?"

Relief washed over him, and he clasped her hand again, holding it against his chest. "How much do you remember?" he asked. "I mean, from before you gave me permission to kiss your hand."

Her eyes bored into his with an intensity that made his heart skip. "Everything, I suspect. Your voice was my anchor when I was lost in the darkness. Your stories sparked my curiosity and energized me. They gave me a reason to wake up so I could ask you all the questions I had." She looked at the teardrop hanging from his neck. "But it is not your voice I heard, though." She sounded disappointed. "It was the voice of this device."

"It provides a pretty accurate rendition," he quickly said. "Or so I am told."

Her lips lifted in a smile. "Good. I kept thinking that your voice sounded velvety, and it was disappointing to believe that I had been infatuated with a machine voice."

Infatuated?

Perhaps she meant something else, and that was how his earpieces translated it from Kra-ell?

Not sure what to do, Brandon turned off the device and said the only thing he knew how to say in Kra-ell: "Good day, Morelle." He activated the device and added, "Now you know how I really sound."

Her smile was beautiful and heartwarming. "Your voice sounded almost the same through the device, but your real voice is nicer. Is that all you know how to say in my language?"

He nodded. "I haven't lived in the village long, so I wasn't here to learn Kra-ell from those who joined our community recently."

When she just looked at him with those big eyes of hers, he realized that she had no clue what he was talking about. "What did Annani and Ell-rom tell you so far?"

"Annani told Ell-rom and me about our father. Ahn was a great leader who wanted to create a new way of life for the exiled gods and the humans who looked up to them. He wanted everyone to be treated with dignity and justice. Annani didn't tell me what happened to him, though. Could you?"

He closed his eyes briefly and sighed. "I don't think I should. I'd rather leave it to the Clan Mother. I have a feeling that she wants to be the one to tell you of his fate and how it came about. It's a deeply personal story. What else did she tell you?"

"She told me about her children being fathered by humans. Our father was a progressive thinker, and he allowed the gods to take human lovers. That was how the immortals came to be. She did not tell me why she chose humans to father her children, though. It was also one of the things she was saving for another time. Do you know why?"

Brandon nodded. "Of course I do, but this tale also belongs to Annani. I'm sorry that I can't be more forthcoming, but she is our Clan Mother, the head of our clan. I cannot and will not go against her wishes." He lifted her hand to his lips and kissed it softly, reverently. "Not even for a beautiful princess with the most amazing eyes."

39

MORELLE

Bran-don had called her beautiful, and he thought that her eyes were amazing. After growing up fearing that anyone would see the color of her eyes and realize that she was an abomination, hearing that tugged at Morelle's heart.

The compliments smoothed out the edge of her disappointment over Bran-don's deflection of her questions, especially the one about her father's fate. Very few things could kill a god, and she needed to know what had happened to Ahn. Still, Morelle accepted that Brandon's reluctance to share the information was born of respect for Annani's wishes and not his desire to keep her in the dark.

More questions burned in her chest, though, demanding attention. Chief among them was the mystery of Bran-don himself. Or rather Brandon, which was how the medics said his name. The pronunciation sounded less Kra-ell, but then there was no reason for him to have a Kra-ell name.

She wanted to ask him about the Kra-ell living among the gods, or rather the immortals who were the majority of this village's residents. Annani had explained that the gods had been too few to survive after contact was lost with Anumati, which was the main reason for Ahn's approval of gods having children with humans.

It had been a shocking revelation to learn that Brandon, Bridget, and Gertrude were not gods but hybrids like her and Ell-rom, half god and half human, or rather mostly human because some of them were the result of many generations of breeding with humans.

Annani had told her that she had birthed five children who had all been fathered by different human males, but she had only mentioned four by name, and Morelle had not wanted to ask what had happened to the fifth. She had a feeling it was nothing good, and she didn't want to make Annani sad. Her sister seemed even more emotional than Ell-rom, and that was an achievement since their brother used to shed tears over the head priestess's more moving sermons.

"What are you smiling about?" Brandon asked.

"Your compliment." She lifted her hand to her head and smoothed it over the soft fuzz. "I don't feel beautiful without my hair. I used to have long, wavy hair, not straight like the Kra-ell, and not black either. It was a rich brown color. The head priestess used to grimace while helping me braid it when I was little, and she often suggested chopping it off. I refused, of course."

He smiled. "Were you always strong-willed?"

"That's putting it mildly. I was lucky that the head priestess was my aunt, and deep down she felt sorry for Ell-rom and me. Otherwise, my obstinacy would not have been tolerated."

"I'm glad that you retained your memories. Ell-rom remembers next to nothing."

"I know. He told me."

She hoped that Ell-rom had forgotten about his ability, but even if he had, she needed to warn him to keep from getting angry. He could harm people who did not really deserve it.

Morelle brushed her fingers over the fuzz on her head. "I hope it will grow fast now that I'm awake."

"As I said, to me, you look gorgeous just as you are." He looked at her with heat in his eyes that made her feel the kind of things that her mother had talked about. "I wouldn't mind if you wanted to keep it like that."

She chuckled nervously. "Don't be silly. I don't want to be known as the hairless princess."

He laughed, the sound rich and throaty. "Beautiful and funny. What a rare find you are, Princess Morelle."

She felt heat rise to her cheeks.

During her twilight state, Morelle had heard Brandon speak of wanting to kiss her. Was he truly attracted to her? Or was he just being charming?

It must be the latter.

She had seen her reflection in the mirror, and she was far from attractive. Her head was nearly bald, and after thousands of years without sunlight, her complexion was so pale that it was nearly transparent.

Then again, she hadn't looked much better on Anumati. Always hidden behind veils when outside her room, she'd never felt the sun's warmth on her face or breathed truly fresh air. Everything had been filtered through layers of fabric, muting even those simplest and most basic pleasures.

Anumati's volatile climate hadn't helped. Their home had been hot and humid, and if not for the constant strong winds, wearing the ceremonial robes would have been unbearable. After even brief outings in the palace gardens, her and Ell-rom's bodies had been drenched in sweat beneath the heavy garments. Still, they'd seized those precious moments, treasuring the few minutes they could spend outside each day.

"You seem a thousand leagues away." Brandon's voice drew her from her memories. "Where did you go?"

"Anumati," she said. "My face was always pale because I couldn't expose it to the sun, not even by sitting near the window in our room. Ell-rom and I could only remove our veils when the curtains were drawn tight. No one could ever see us. We lived in constant fear."

Something fierce flashed in Brandon's eyes. "Those days are forever gone. You'll never have to wear a veil again." A smile lightened his expression. "Tomorrow, I'll get a vehicle and take you on a trip around the village. It's not a large place, but it's beautiful, green and vibrant. There's even a lookout point where you can see the ocean."

Morelle had never seen a lake, let alone an ocean.

Excitement surged through her. "Why not today?"

He laughed. "Because it's already getting dark, and the village is not as pretty at night. Besides, you need proper clothing." He gestured to the light blue garment that covered her body. It lacked proper buttons or clasps and was open at the back. "I could wrap you in a blanket, but I think you'd prefer to be dressed properly for your first outing."

He was correct, but she had nothing. "Where can I get clothing?"

"It's all arranged." He patted her hand. "Everything will be delivered tomorrow."

Delivered by whom? And who made those clothes? Did they have someone in their village who made clothing?

"How do things like that work here?" she asked. "I mean, how does one obtain clothing on Earth?"

Brandon pulled the chair closer to her bed, his hand still warm around hers. "Well, there are these amazing places with many stores you can stroll through and choose what you like..." He launched into an explanation of how human commerce worked and the money that was used to purchase things.

He also told her about the many places that served food from different cultures, places that played music, and still others that showcased performances of stories.

It all sounded wonderful. The idea of walking freely, choosing what she wanted to wear, eating whatever appealed to her with no veil, no restrictions, no fear.

Morelle couldn't wait to experience it all.

"The village has no shops," Brandon continued, "but it has places where you can eat and drink. The real shopping is in the cities nearby, though. When you're stronger, I'll take you there. I'll also take you to the beach…"

Morelle tried to fight the heaviness of her eyelids, not wanting to miss a word of Brandon's descriptions, but exhaustion was creeping in, making her thoughts fuzzy around the edges.

"It's okay." He rose to his feet and looked at her with a smile. "Get some sleep. I'm not going anywhere. I will be right here when you wake up."

40

MARINA

Marina's stomach fluttered with excitement as Peter guided the car through the city streets. She didn't get to leave the village often, and certainly not in the morning when she was supposed to work, but today was a special day. She was finally going to see the wedding dress that Amanda's designer friend was making for her and get it properly fitted.

Glancing at her fiancé's profile, she marveled for the thousandth time at how she'd gotten so lucky and managed to capture the heart of this incredible immortal.

His chiseled features were softened by a hint of a smile playing at the corners of his lips. "You know," Peter turned to look at her, "I plan on sneaking a peek in the dressing room. Just a little preview."

Marina gasped in horror. "Don't you dare, Peter! It's

bad luck for the groom to see the bride in her wedding dress before the big day."

"Nonsense." He chuckled, reaching over to squeeze her hand. "It's a silly human superstition. I'm an immortal, love."

"Well, I'm still human." Marina entwined her fingers with his. "And I'm not taking any chances. Promise me that you won't peek."

He pouted, pretending disappointment. "Fine. I promise."

Relief washing over her, Marina relaxed back into her seat. As excited as she was to try on the dress, she was also stressed. What if she hated it?

Would she dare criticize Amanda's friend?

It was probably better to pretend she loved it and make everyone happy.

But what about her?

Didn't she deserve to be happy on her special day?

"What are you still frowning about?" Peter asked. "I promised that I wouldn't peek."

"It's not that." She sighed. "I'm worried that I'm not going to like the dress. What am I supposed to do then? I can't tell Amanda's friend that her design is bad."

"No, you can't say that, but you can tell her that you had something else in mind. I want you to have the best wedding dress you can imagine, and I don't want you to compromise because you don't want to step on anyone's toes. If need be, I'll pay for a new gown." He gave her hand a reassuring squeeze.

Was he the best or what?

"I love you." She lifted their conjoined hands and kissed his knuckles.

When they pulled up in front of the boutique, though, Marina was forced to reevaluate Peter's proposal. The place had its own valet parking, and the storefront screamed exclusivity.

Amanda had refused to tell her how much the dress she'd commissioned was costing Peter, and he also had refused to disclose the information, but given this location, it must cost a fortune. There was no way she was letting Peter pay for another one. She would just have to accept anything that Vivienne had come up with.

"Peter," she whispered as he handed the keys to the valet, "how much is this dress costing you? Please tell me."

He wrapped an arm around her waist, guiding her toward the boutique's entrance. "Don't worry about the cost, love. You deserve the dress of your dreams, and I'm more than happy to pay for it."

After Peter rang the bell, it took a few moments until the door swung open, and the woman who greeted them wasn't Vivienne, who Marina had seen on the video call Amanda facilitated on her tablet. That woman had been older and dark-haired, while this one was younger, closer to Marina's age, with light brown hair and a warm smile.

"Welcome," the woman said, ushering them inside after they had given her their names.

The boutique's interior was even more luxurious than the exterior had hinted at, with all soft lighting, sleek leather, and plush fabrics.

"I'm Clarisse, Vivienne's assistant," the woman said. "She's waiting for you in the fitting room, Marina." She turned to Peter. "Would you like something to drink while you wait? We have cappuccino, Perrier..."

"A cappuccino would be lovely, thank you." Peter gave Marina's hand one last encouraging squeeze before walking over to the couch and sitting down.

Marina hadn't been offered a drink, but it made sense, given that she was about to try on a very expensive white dress.

Best not to risk any spills.

"Right this way, Marina," Clarisse said, gesturing toward a doorway draped with a shimmering fabric.

Marina cast Peter one last glance before following Clarisse, and he blew her an air kiss and mouthed, "I love you."

As they entered the fitting room, she was greeted by Vivienne herself. "Marina, darling!" The woman enveloped her in a warm hug. "You're even more beautiful in person than on the screen."

She probably said that to all her clients, but it was still nice to hear. "Thank you. It's a pleasure to finally meet you in person."

Vivienne's eyes sparkled with excitement. "Now, I hope you don't mind, but I made a few modifications to the original design we discussed. I was inspired by your unique coloring." She gestured to Marina's blue hair. "If you don't like the changes, we can always go back to the original, less elaborate design."

Marina's heart skipped a beat, and her hands turned clammy. Changes? Just how fancy had this dress become?

She hadn't wanted anything too elaborate. The design she had chosen was elegant and simple.

"I'm sure it's beautiful," she managed a pathetic whisper.

Vivienne beamed, moving toward a dress form covered by a sheet. "Are you ready for the great reveal, darling?"

Marina nodded, not sure that she was ready for what Vivienne was about to show her, but it wasn't as if she had a choice and could say that, no, she wasn't ready, and ask why her wishes hadn't been followed.

With a flourish Vivienne pulled away the sheet,

revealing the gown beneath, and Marina's breath caught in her throat.

The word 'beautiful' didn't do it justice. This dress was a masterpiece, a work of art that seemed to have sprung from the pages of a fairy tale and belonged in a museum dedicated to royalty.

Marina had chosen the mermaid silhouette, but it flared out dramatically near the bottom. The plunging sweetheart neckline was adorned with sheer off-the-shoulder sleeves that lent an air of romance and elegance to the design. But it was the details that truly took Marina's breath away. The entire dress, from the bodice to the edge of its sweeping train, was covered in intricate embroidery and beadwork. Swirling, ornate patterns danced across the ivory satin, creating a mesmerizing effect.

And then there were the blue accents. Vivienne had incorporated Marina's signature hair color into the design, with blue gemstones and beads strategically placed within the embroidery. It tied everything together, making the dress uniquely, perfectly hers.

"It's... it's..." Marina struggled to find words, her eyes filling with tears. "Perfect."

Vivienne clapped her hands. "Marvelous. I was afraid you would think it was too much, but I just couldn't help it. My hand had a mind of its own as it drew the lines of embroidery and added the blue accents. It was kissed by a muse. I'm sure of it. Now, shall we see how it looks on?"

41

PETER

As Marina stopped to adjust her hair in front of one of the mall's many storefronts, Peter watched her reflection with a smile. Even two hours after the wedding dress fitting, her expression was still glowing.

"I'm starving," she announced, turning away from the window. "Can we stop by the food court? I'm craving a hamburger."

"Actually," he said, taking her hand, "I made reservations for us at a nice restaurant."

Marina's eyes lit up. "Where? Is it the place you took me last time?"

"No, it's not *By Invitation Only,* but it's another very nice place."

"Good." She looked down at herself. "I dressed nicely for the fitting, but it's not elegant enough for that place."

"You look perfect for where I'm taking you." He guided her toward the nearest exit.

As they walked through the parking garage, Peter used the key fob to unlock his car and opened the door for her. "My lady?"

"Thank you," she said as she slid inside, and he closed the door behind her.

As Peter drove through downtown, Marina pressed her face close to the window, trying to guess their destination, but she didn't know the city well enough for that. He'd only taken her out of the village a few times so far.

The late afternoon sun caught her blue hair, creating an ethereal effect that made him smile.

When he pulled up to the sleek glass tower, Marina frowned. "This is it? It looks like an office building."

"The restaurant is on the top floor of the hotel, which occupies the top ten floors of the building." Peter drove down toward the clan's reserved parking spaces. "We need to take an elevator to the lobby, which is on the sixtieth floor, and take another one from there to the restaurant." He parked the car and deliberately left it unlocked.

"How do you even know about this place?" Marina tried to mask her jealousy by looking around the marble-lined elevator lobby.

He chuckled. "I haven't taken any ladies up here if that's what you are worried about. The clan owns the place, and we use the restaurant for business meetings and the like. I've never cared enough for anyone before you to bring her here."

It was true. It had never occurred to him to bring Kagra to the hotel, and it wasn't because of her alien looks or the fact that she couldn't eat anything at the restaurant. A pair of sunglasses and loose clothing would have done most of the heavy lifting of camouflaging her looks, and he might have needed to add a little shroud here and there to smooth out the edges. He just hadn't had the urge to pamper Kagra.

"I wasn't worried." Marina smiled sheepishly.

As the elevator began its rapid ascent, she clutched his arm, her eyes squeezed shut. He wrapped an arm around her waist, steadying her. She wasn't used to fast elevators, and when it came to a gentle stop, she opened her eyes, looking relieved.

She was still holding on to his arm as they stepped out into the hotel lobby.

"Are you okay?" he asked.

"Yeah. That was really fast."

They walked over to the elevator that was marked with the restaurant logo.

"*The Seventy-Second*?" Marina asked.

"That's the restaurant's name and also the floor it is on."

She looked at it with suspicion in her eyes. "Is it going to be as fast as the other one?"

"Probably, but it doesn't have as far to go, so it's not going to be as bad."

When the restaurant elevator doors opened, Peter led Marina to the hostess station. "Peter and Marina MacBain," he said.

"Good evening, Mr. and Mrs. MacBain." The hostess gathered two menus. "Please, follow me."

Marina looked up at him with a raised brow. "Mac-Bain?" she whispered.

"I'll explain in a moment," he whispered back.

Marina's eyes widened as she took in the panoramic view of the city through the restaurant's floor-to-ceiling windows. The sun was setting, painting the sky in brilliant hues that reflected off the glass and steel towers dotting the horizon.

"The whole city looks magical from up here," Marina said.

"Your table, Mr. and Mrs. MacBain," the hostess said, gesturing to a private booth nestled against the windows.

"Thank you." He helped Marina into her seat before sliding in beside her. The leather upholstery was butter-soft, and the table settings gleamed in the warm lighting.

Marina picked up the menu. "So, what's the deal with the last name you gave us? Not that I mind. It sounds nice."

"We always use MacBain to make reservations here. It's a code for the hosts to reserve the best table for us."

"Oh." She sounded a little disappointed.

"We also use the name when dealing with people outside the clan, so if you like it, I can get you documents under this name."

"When we get married, can we choose whatever name we want?"

He nodded. "Perhaps not just any name, but we can pick from a list." He reached for her hand. "Tell me about your dress. It's not bad luck to talk about it, right?"

Marina's eyes sparkled with mischief. "It's beautiful, and it far exceeded my expectations. That's all I'm willing to say about it."

"Oh, come on. You have to tell me more."

"It's mermaid-shaped."

"Mermaid? The top is shaped like a woman, and the bottom is like a fish. What kind of dress is that?"

She laughed. "It's a dress that is form-fitting through the bodice and the hips and then flares out around the knees. Sometimes, it also has a long train."

He tried to imagine it and failed. "Can you show me an example?"

"Sure." She pulled out her phone, did a quick search, and handed him the device.

"Oh, yeah. I've seen the style, and it's going to look great on you." He leaned closer to her. "You have the body for it." His hand closed around her knee and then traveled up, brushing over the soft skin of her inner thigh.

Marina blushed. "Peter. Someone might see."

It was true. *The Seventy-Second* did not offer a fully intimate setting like *By Invitation Only,* and when the server approached with a bottle of wine, Peter removed his hand and leaned back.

He waited until the guy poured it into their glasses, took their order, and retreated before returning his hand to her knee, but he left it there instead of venturing to forbidden places.

The games he and Marina liked to play were for their own entertainment and no one else's. They both liked to skirt the thin line of propriety and danger, but they were also sensible about it. When the chances of getting caught were high, it was exhibitionism, and neither of them was into that.

Marina sipped on her wine, gazing at the cityscape beyond. "I heard the band practicing yesterday. They are not bad."

"I know. They used to perform in clubs when they were still in high school."

She nodded. "Vlad and Jackson can sing, but I was really hoping Jasmine would be the vocalist. That's not going to happen now that she's in a coma. She's not going to be ready to get on stage by next Sunday."

"She might. Transitions are unpredictable. She might wake up tomorrow and be fully recovered in time for our wedding."

Marina cast him a skeptical look. "I'd rather stick with Jackson and Vlad or just get music playing through the loudspeakers. None of the weddings on the cruise had a band performing in them. "

"True. There's also Ray with his piano if we want something classier. I'm sure he would love it if I asked him to play at our wedding."

"Speaking of classy. Now that I've seen my dress, I'm worried that the rest of the wedding won't match up." She laughed nervously. "Now I'm regretting not being more involved in the planning instead of leaving everything to Amanda. It's silly, I want every-thing to be as beautiful and perfect as the dress. It has whetted my appetite, so to speak."

"Why don't you call Amanda and share your thoughts

with her? It's not too late to make changes, you know."

"I'll call her on our way home after dinner," Marina said.

They weren't going home after dinner, but Peter wasn't ready to reveal his plans for tonight yet.

"Call her now. You won't be able to enjoy your meal while stressing over the party not being what you want it to be."

"You're right." She pulled out her phone. "I'll text her. It's rude to talk on the phone in a restaurant."

Peter wondered how she knew that. From watching television, maybe?

As she exchanged messages with Amanda, her expression slowly shifted from concern to relief, and when the appetizers arrived, a plate of perfectly seared scallops for Marina and beef carpaccio for himself, Marina set her phone down with a satisfied smile.

"All sorted out?" he asked.

"I should have known better than to doubt Amanda." Marina's eyes were bright with excitement now. "She'd already seen the dress and made some adjustments to the plans. She's having a wooden walkway installed so my dress won't drag on the grass, and she's ordered bridesmaids dresses in different shades of blue to complement my hair. I totally forgot about the bridesmaids. I didn't even select any, but Amanda did that for me, took their measurements, and sent them to Vivienne." She shook her head. "Amanda is amazing. How can she do all that while working full-time and taking care of a baby?"

"She has lots of help, my love." Peter lifted her hand and kissed her knuckles before returning it to the table. "She has her own Odu, and Dalhu has a studio at home and is always available to fulfill her requests. Not only that, she has a network of volunteers she knows how to mobilize."

"Amanda is one impressive lady. She even remembered to ask about your tux and whether you are having one custom-made for you."

"I have two perfectly good ones from the cruise weddings," he said. "They're practically new, and I've had them cleaned."

Marina looked disappointed. "Okay. They were both very nice," she said without much conviction.

Peter smiled. "On second thought, I should order a brand-new tux. My tailor has my measurements, so all I have to do is call him and ask him to make it blue to match your hair."

42

MARINA

"It was amazing." Marina leaned against Peter's arm as they stood in the hotel lobby, waiting for the second elevator that would take them down to the parking level where they had left their car.

She wasn't looking forward to another bullet ride in the insanely fast elevator, but she was definitely looking forward to getting home and undressing Peter while kissing every inch of skin she exposed.

The pink dress shirt he had on might have looked feminine on another man, but he looked as masculine as ever, his biceps straining the fabric even though he wasn't an iron pumper.

He was just an excellent male specimen.

When they entered the elevator, Peter tapped on the glass screen but not to take them to the parking area. Instead, she saw him selecting the seventieth floor.

Maybe there was an observation deck he wanted to show her?

However, why would it be two floors below the restaurant?

"Where are we going?" she asked.

Peter's eyes sparkled with mischief. "It's a surprise."

Had he arranged for them to spend the night? If so, she needed to call Wonder and let her know she wouldn't be coming to the café in the morning. But maybe he'd planned on using the room just for a few hours?

The thought sent a delicious shiver down her spine.

The problem with that scenario was that she would pass out from his venom bite, and he would have to dress her and carry her to the car afterward.

Not that it was a problem for her mate.

She cast another admiring look at the pink shirt that was stretched across his broad shoulders in a most enticing way and the gray slacks that lovingly hugged his thighs.

Marina still couldn't believe that this gorgeous immortal was all hers, and that in just a little over a week they'd be married.

"You got us a room, didn't you?" she asked as the elevator stopped and the doors opened.

His only response was that signature smirk that never failed to make her weak at the knees. They walked down the corridor until the very end, where Peter pulled out his phone and waved it in front of a double door—the only one of its kind she had seen on this floor.

When one of the panels swung open smoothly, a pleasant, computerized voice announced, "Welcome, Mr. and Mrs. MacBain."

She turned to look at him. "So, that's how it's going to be from now on?"

He shrugged, and before she knew what he was planning, he swung her into his arms and carried her inside. "This is the honeymoon suite, my love."

He was traditional, but that was just one more thing she loved about him.

Not that celebrating a honeymoon before the wedding was a traditional move, but it was a very Peter thing to do.

Winding her arms around his neck, she pressed a kiss to his jaw. "Aren't we supposed to be married first and then go on our honeymoon?"

"There are fittings and rehearsals for everything else before the wedding, so why not for the honeymoon suite as well? I thought we could have some fun away from the village and the stress of the upcoming party."

He carried her through the opulent living-room portion of the suite to the bedroom area, setting her gently on the plush king-sized bed with the enormous heart-shaped pillow. That's when she spotted the duffle bag on the floor beside the closet door.

"Did you pack things for us?" she asked.

He nodded. "I asked the bellhop to bring it up while we were having dinner." His fingers started moving to the buttons of his dress shirt. "I also packed a few accessories for playtime."

Excitement coursed through her as she tried to imagine what toys he had brought and what he had planned for her, but then the buttons started to pop, taut skin was revealed, and all coherent thought fled Marina's mind.

It didn't matter how many times she'd seen Peter naked. Her body still responded to him like it was the first time, her heart racing and her skin flushing with desire.

"You like?" he teased, shrugging the pink fabric off his shoulders.

"Mmm." She wet her lips. "You are magnificent."

He chuckled, the sound low and rich. "Not as magnificent as you." His eyes traveled over her body with obvious appreciation. "That dress has been driving me crazy all evening."

Marina glanced down at her simple knee-length dress, aware of how the fabric clung to her curves. "You were very well-behaved during dinner. I expected you to be much naughtier."

He'd played with her a little when they had first sat down, but after that, he hadn't done anything more daring than put his hand on her exposed knee or kiss the back of her hand.

"It wasn't easy." He stalked toward the bed with predatory grace. "Especially when you kept shifting in your chair, making that skirt ride up."

"I wasn't doing it on purpose."

Well, not all the time. Sometimes, the clingy fabric just rode up.

"No?" He braced his hands on either side of her, caging her with his body. "What about when you were playing footsie under the table?"

"That was definitely on purpose." She grinned.

Marina hadn't done anything overly daring with her foot, just brushing over his calves, but it had been enough to get him hard, probably as he was imagining what she would have done if they were sitting in a more secluded place, like the booth in *By Invitation Only*.

His lips brushed against her ear. "Minx."

Marina shivered at the endearment, tilting her head

to give him better access to her neck. "Are you going to punish me?"

"Hmm." His teeth grazed her skin, not quite hard enough to break it. "I might have packed something special for just that purpose."

Her breath hitched. "Peter..."

He pulled back just enough to look into her eyes, his expression growing serious. "Limits?"

The familiar question grounded her, reminding her that even in their most intense moments, her comfort and consent were his priority. "None," she whispered. "I want to play tonight."

His answering smile was both tender and wicked. "Good girl." He straightened up and walked over to the duffle bag. "Close your eyes."

Marina complied, listening to the sounds of him unzipping the bag and rustling through its contents. The mattress dipped as he sat beside her.

"Keep them closed," he instructed. Something cool and silky brushed against her arm. "Can you guess what this is?"

She concentrated on the sensation. "One of your ties?"

"Very good." The fabric trailed up to her shoulder. "Do you remember the first time we used these?"

How could she forget? It had been in his cabin. She'd been so nervous but excited, too. "The cruise. You blindfolded me and tied my wrists to the headboard," she recalled, heat pooling in her belly at the memory. "Made me beg..."

His fingers traced along her collarbone. "You are so beautiful." There was a pause, then he commanded, "Open your eyes."

Marina's lashes fluttered open.

Peter had removed his shirt completely, and the sight of his bare chest took her breath away. But what really caught her attention was the bunch of ties in his hand, all in various shades of blue.

"I bought those to replace all of my other ties. From now on, I will wear blue ties until you decide to change your hair color and then I'll replace them again to match it. I think that speaks of commitment even louder than rings."

Her heart melted. She couldn't wait to be his wife.

"I love you so much."

"I love you, my Marina." Peter looked at her with as much hunger in his eyes as he'd had the first time they had been together.

"You are so beautiful," he murmured as he removed her dress, kissing her skin as he exposed more of it until she was lying naked in front of him.

He leaned away and gazed at her as if she were a work of art. "Absolutely perfect."

When they had first met, she might have thought that he was flattering her, but now she not only believed that he meant it, but also believed it to be true. In Peter's eyes, she was the most beautiful of them all, and since his eyes were the only ones that mattered, it was true.

"So are you." She reached for him.

He was still partially dressed, but with his speed, it would take a split second for his trousers to disappear. Sometimes he did it so fast that it almost looked like magic.

He chuckled. "You look at me with so much desire that I'm not sure I want to blindfold you."

"Then don't."

She liked it when he took her vision and freedom of movement away, it heightened her pleasure, but if her coveting gaze pleased him, she would gladly sacrifice the game for him.

Peter smiled. "You know me, love. When I have a plan, I stick to it." He wrapped one of the blue silk ties around her head and tied it on the side so the knot wouldn't bother her.

Closing her eyes, Marina let out a breath and centered herself, ready to fully relinquish control to her mate.

He made quick work of looping a tie around each of her wrists, checking if she was comfortable, and only then tying them to the headboard.

Next, she heard his slacks hitting the floor, and a moment later, he was covering her body with his, his lips taking hers in a passionate kiss that didn't last long.

Peter was a man with a plan, and as he slid down her body, she knew what that plan was.

He attacked with no preamble, his tongue lashing at her clit as he penetrated her with two fingers, sliding them in with ease and slowly pumping in and out of her.

It was nothing like his usual slow buildup, and she wondered whether he was so hungry for her that he was impatient or if it was part of his game plan.

Most likely, it was the latter. Peter did not compromise his plans.

As the pressure built, coherent thoughts became nearly impossible, and Marina was turned into a creature of need, moaning and rocking her hips to get more of those talented fingers inside of her.

When Peter's lips captured her clit, his fingers kept pumping, and her arousal gathered momentum. His other hand traced up to her breast, tugging and pinching her nipple.

Mother above, she was so close.

Then when something cold and metallic rubbed against the turgid peak, she sucked in a breath, and when the clamp closed, it stung. Hissing, she sucked in another breath, waiting for the other clamp to even out the torment.

When it finally happened, she screamed her climax at the top of her lungs.

43

PETER

The hotel probably didn't have soundproofing as excellent as the village homes or even the *Silver Swan*, but Peter couldn't care less if the entire floor had heard his mate scream her climax.

He couldn't get enough of her taste, licking every little bit, but he couldn't afford to linger. He had to remove the clamps.

After taking one of them, he immediately put his mouth around the swollen nipple to ease the pain, licking as the blood rushed in, and then he did the same with the other clamp.

Marina was still riding the high of her climax, and when he removed her blindfold, her eyes remained closed.

"Open your eyes, beautiful," he commanded.

She smiled lazily before lifting her eyelids. "Kiss me."

"Gladly." He positioned himself between her legs and kissed her as he pushed inside of her, going only a third of the way and letting her adjust.

Except, his little minx was impatient, and she lifted her bottom, urging him to surge in all the way.

"Mother above." Marina spread her legs wider to accommodate more of him.

"Perfection," he murmured as he looked at her.

Even after all the time they had been together, the sight of her still took his breath away—the blue hair that was spread across the pillow, framing her beautiful face, the blissful expression, the red lips, swollen from kisses—but it wasn't just her physical perfection that enthralled him. It was the light that seemed to radiate from within her.

Marina had no idea how extraordinary she was, how her smile could brighten even his darkest days, how her laugh made his heavy heart feel buoyant. The look of complete trust in her eyes humbled him.

Suddenly wanting her hands on him, Peter reached over Marina's head and released her wrists from their bindings.

"I'm so lucky," he murmured when she wrapped her arms around him.

"So am I." She lifted her head and captured his lips in a kiss before letting her head drop back.

He gazed into her eyes. "You're everything to me, my mate."

The word 'mate' still filled him with wonder. The Fates had chosen perfectly when they'd brought this remarkable woman into his life. She matched him so well.

"I love you," she whispered.

Those three words never failed to fill him with joy. He remembered a time when he'd dreamt of this kind of connection but thought he would never have it.

Marina had changed everything.

In just over a week, she would be his wife, and the thought made his chest tight with emotion. He would spend eternity showing her just how precious she was to him, protecting her, cherishing her, and loving her in all the ways she deserved.

Eternity.

They didn't have it.

But they might have longer than they'd thought possible if Bridget's hunch was right and his venom would prolong Marina's life.

"My beautiful Marina," he breathed against her lips. "My miracle."

As he claimed her mouth, Peter thanked the Fates for bringing them together. He might be immortal, but it wasn't until Marina entered his life that he truly began to live.

As he kept gently rocking his hips, enjoying the connection and not in a rush to bring this moment to an end, Marina cupped her breasts and then gently stroked her swollen nipples.

"Peter," she murmured. "I want more."

He pushed his hands under her bottom and squeezed her butt cheeks hard. "So bossy."

She smiled. "You can punish me for my bossiness later."

"Oh, I will." He pushed all the way in, retracted, and then surged inside of her again. Soon, he was pounding into her just like she wanted him to.

As her climax shook her body, his own reached critical velocity, and he gripped the top of her head, tilting it to the side and licking his favorite spot.

Marina's lips parted as she waited for the strike, not in fear but in panting anticipation, and as he sank his fangs into the smooth column of her neck, she screamed and climaxed again.

Her sheath tightening around his shaft forced his own release.

As always after the bite, Marina was out, soaring on the blissful clouds of euphoria, and he knew it would take a while for her to come down from the high. She didn't black out for as many hours as she used to when they had been a new couple, but it had been a long day, and she would probably sleep until morning.

He'd already spoken with Wonder, letting her know that Marina was taking tomorrow off as well.

Peter still had plenty of fun stuff planned for the next day.

44

BRANDON

B randon stood in front of the mailroom's long desk and stared at the mountain of boxes and bags that had been delivered from the keep. Given the long list of charges on his credit card, he had expected it would be a lot, but somehow he'd failed to visualize it.

He picked up several bags and boxes and carried them to the golf cart outside. The clinic was next door to the office building, but he couldn't just bring everything in. There just wasn't enough room. He would have to choose a few items for her to wear today and take the rest to his house.

Now that was an idea. After the tour of the village he had promised Morelle, he could take her to his place. He had a house to himself in the newest portion of the village, which was an indulgence for one person, but he was too set in his ways to live with a roommate. Besides, as a council member Brandon enjoyed certain privileges, like not having to share a residence.

It was too much to hope that Morelle would want to live in his house even if he offered her the primary bedroom to herself, but it would be wonderful if she did.

He sighed and looked at the sky.

The weather was perfect for Morelle's first time outdoors. It was sunny but not too warm, and the gentle breeze would caress her face.

His princess deserved to experience everything beautiful about this world, starting with the simple pleasure of feeling sunshine on her skin and continuing with a luxury wardrobe fit for an A-lister.

"Need some help with those?"

Brandon turned to find Kian watching him with amusement in his eyes.

He adjusted his grip on the boxes. "There are many more inside, and yes, I would appreciate some help."

Kian followed him to the mailroom and whistled. "Are all those yours?"

"Yes. Well, they are for Morelle, but they have my name on them."

"You may have gone a bit overboard." Kian clapped him on the back before picking up a couple of boxes in one hand and a garment bag in the other. "This looks like you bought out an entire department store."

"Morelle needs everything." Brandon picked up two garment bags in each hand and followed Kian outside. "She's never had normal clothes before. All she'd ever worn were ceremonial robes and the suit she wore in stasis."

"True." Kian waited for him to arrange things on the cart before handing him the boxes he'd carried out. "She wouldn't have even known what to get. It was a smart move on your part to hire a personal shopper for the task."

"Yes. I've worked with Melinda in the past, and she is not only very good but also knows what I like. I just hope that Morelle approves."

If Kian had known how much everything had cost he would have rolled his eyes, but Brandon wasn't going to share that information, and he didn't regret spending a small fortune on his princess.

He wanted Morelle to feel like royalty every day.

Not that she was his, but he hoped she would be. He had no idea how to court a virgin half Kra-ell half goddess who had grown up in a temple, so the only thing he could do was to be sincere and let her know how he felt.

That wasn't easy after leading a carefully crafted lie in Hollywood for as long as he had, but it was refreshing to be authentic for a change. He wasn't sure who the authentic Brandon was, though.

Trying it with Morelle would be a journey of self-discovery.

"You know," Kian said as they headed back for more, "Morelle won't know the difference between Chanel and Walmart."

Brandon snorted. "Maybe not, but I will." He paused in the doorway, suddenly serious. "I want her to have beautiful things and feel like a princess instead of someone who had to be hidden away and cover her face whenever she stepped outside her room."

Kian nodded. "So, what's the plan after surprising her with this fashion show? Taking her back to my mother's house?"

Brandon froze mid-reach for another box. "I hadn't thought that far ahead," he admitted. "I was just going to take Morelle on a tour of the village. Let her feel the sun on her face and see the ocean from the lookout point. She's never felt the wind in her hair or watched a sunset without layers of veils between her and the world."

"A tour of the village sounds like a lovely idea." Kian rubbed his hand on the back of his neck. "But since there is no reason for her to stay in the clinic after being disconnected from all the equipment, the tour should end at the Clan Mother's home. I will call my mother and inform her that Morelle is coming so she can instruct her Odus to prepare the room for her if she hasn't done so already."

Brandon's heart clenched. He'd gotten used to spending every possible moment with Morelle, reading to her, talking to her, and just being near her, and the thought of being forced to be apart from her made his chest ache.

Would he be allowed to visit?

Kian must have seen the worry in his eyes because he put his hand on his arm. "The Clan Mother expects you to be with Morelle throughout the day, and she's happy to host you. But since you are not officially a couple, I don't think Morelle will be comfortable with you sitting by her bedside or sleeping on the floor next to her. You'll need to go home at night."

"Of course," Brandon agreed. "I'm grateful to be allowed to spend such long hours at the Clan Mother's house."

He could pretend to leave and sneak back in at night. The automatic security shutters would be a challenge, but perhaps one of Annani's Odus could be persuaded to help.

He'd find a way. He couldn't bear the thought of being away from Morelle for that long.

They made one more trip to collect the rest of the packages, and by the time they finished loading everything, the golf cart was packed.

"Enjoy your tour," Kian said. "I'll see you later at my mother's house."

45

MORELLE

Morelle finished the last spoonful of the sweet concoction Gertrude had said was fermented milk and fruit, savoring the unfamiliar taste. Everything on Earth was new and different, from the food to the clothing to the way people interacted, and so far, she liked it much better on Earth than on Anumati.

In fact, there was no comparison.

She felt liberated.

Then again, all she had seen so far was the inside of a clinic, and what she knew about the world outside these walls was what Brandon had told her.

She couldn't wait to see it.

She was scraping the bottom of the glass to get the last of the fruit and fermented milk when a knock sounded at the door.

"Who is it?"

"Brandon." He opened the door just a crack. "May I come in?"

"Yes. Of course." She pushed the rolling table away and straightened the blanket around her.

"Good morning, Princess." He walked in, arms laden with bags and packages and a big smile lighting up his face.

When he approached her bed, he leaned down as if to kiss her cheek but hesitated, hovering close but not touching his lips to her face.

Morelle held perfectly still, not wanting to discourage him. She did not know Earth customs, but Annani had kissed her cheek, so maybe it was a common way of greeting.

She wouldn't mind Brandon kissing her cheek or even her lips.

Oh, who was she trying to deceive? She wanted him to kiss her right on the lips and know what it felt like. She had never been kissed by a male like that before, and as her mother had said in her dream, it was long overdue.

When he pulled back without completing the gesture, disappointment fluttered in her chest. Was there something wrong with her? Or maybe Earth customs prohibited him from kissing someone who wasn't his relative?

At times, it seemed as if Brandon was trying to impress her or to make her like him, and she wondered if that was considered courtship.

According to the head priestess on Anumati, Kra-ell males competed for females by trying to impress them with their fighting talents through dueling. Other forms of showmanship were elaborate war dances and songs.

Brandon told stories, dedicated his time to her, and was now providing her with clothing. Was that constant attention and care his way of courting her?

The thought sent a warm flutter through her stomach.

But why would he want to court her? He knew nothing about her, and given how she looked, it couldn't be a physical attraction.

Perhaps he was doing all this on Annani's behalf?

The thought cooled her rising hopes.

"Good morning." She forced a smile. "What have you brought?"

"I come bearing gifts." He pulled a box from his pocket and opened it. Inside were two earpieces like the ones he wore. "These are for you, so you can understand what people who don't have a teardrop are saying."

When she reached for them, he shook his head. "Let me do this for you. They mold to the shape of your ear, so it's important to insert them properly the first time."

Morelle nodded. "What about when I want to speak to others? Does everyone have earpieces?"

"No." He looked down at his teardrop. "This should work in reverse as well. I will check with William, whose lab makes these things. If it does, I'll give you mine." He pulled one of the earpieces out of the box. "May I?"

"Yes, of course."

His fingers were very gentle as he inserted the device in her left ear, and as his hand brushed over her cheek, Morelle felt tingles on her skin.

"How does it feel?" he asked.

"It's comfortable, but I can't hear anything on that side."

"That's because I didn't activate it yet." He pressed on his teardrop and then tapped her earpiece. "Can you hear me now?"

She laughed. "I hear you talking in Kra-ell in this ear and your language in the other. It's so strange."

He lifted the other earpiece, and when she turned her head to allow him easier access, he put it in her ear, waited a moment, and then tapped it as he had done with the first one.

"How is it now?"

"Perfect. I hear Kra-ell in both ears." She touched the devices gently. "Do I ever take them off?"

"They need recharging every other day or so, but they don't need long. You can charge them while you are in the shower, and by the time you are done, they will be ready."

She looked confused. "How do they charge?"

"Simply put them back in the box, and then put the box on a charging circle." He pointed to one on the bedside table. "You can also carry the box in your purse or pocket and only put them in when you need to talk to someone who doesn't speak Kra-ell and doesn't have a teardrop device."

Morelle looked down at the gown that Gertrude had provided. "I don't have a purse or a pocket."

"Yes, you do." He took a step back and pointed at the bags and boxes he'd carried into the room. "I got you nice things to wear. I'll leave them beside the bed and ask Gertrude to help you get dressed, and some of them have pockets. The purse, though, is still in the cart. I just brought a small sampling for you to choose what to wear today."

When she just gaped at him, not sure what she was supposed to say, he chuckled. "It's a beautiful day outside, and I can't wait to take you out of here so you can enjoy it."

The prospect of going outside without veils or suffocating robes sent a thrill of excitement through her. She couldn't wait either.

"Thank you so much for the clothes and for everything you are doing for me. I don't know how I will ever be able to repay you."

Brandon reached for her hand, bringing it to his lips for one of those gentle kisses that made her heart skip. "Being with you is my reward. I don't need any repayment other than that."

"Why? You don't know me. What if I am a terrible person?"

His brow furrowed. "You are not terrible. Why would you say that? Is it because of all the stupid people on your planet calling you and your brother abominations?"

Morelle hadn't even thought of that. She was doing her best not to think about that vile world. "I didn't say that I was terrible. I said that I might be, and you would not know."

"I have good instincts, Morelle, and no warning bells went off when you were still asleep or when you woke up. I enjoy being with you."

"Why?"

He chuckled. "Get dressed, and I will tell you during our tour of the village. Deal?"

Morelle narrowed her eyes at him. "You don't know why. For some reason, you are drawn to me, and you don't know what that reason is, so you are going to use the time I need to get dressed to think it through."

"You are wise, Princess Morelle." His eyes danced with amusement, but he didn't deny it. "I will leave you to get dressed before we get into further discussion and prolong our departure even further." He strode to the door with fluid grace, closing it softly behind him.

She sighed. He was such a confusing male. But hadn't the head priestess said that males were impossible to understand?

Morelle had thought that the female was being bitter and spiteful, and she had been—the priestess had not liked anyone—but perhaps her words were true.

Moments later, Gertrude walked in. "Brandon told me that he got you some clothes." She glanced at the packages with curiosity. "Let's see what we've got here."

Morelle watched as the medic pulled the first item out of one of the bags and held it up for her to see.

"This is a very nice dress, but it looks too fancy for everyday wear." Gertrude draped it on the bed over Morelle's legs. "Now, let's see what's in here." She pulled out two items from another bag: a pair of soft gray pants that looked comfortable and a white blouse from a fabric similar to the pants but a little more delicate.

"I like these," Morelle said.

"Yeah, I like them too." Gertrude held up the two garments. "It's a little much for a ride through the village, but if you like it, go for it." She draped them over the bed and then leaned down to open the two boxes that Brandon had left on the floor, producing a pair of gray shoes that matched the pants. "Those will do just fine. They're flat and will look great with the slacks." She put them next to the bed. "Where do you want to get dressed, here or the bathroom?"

"The bathroom." There was a mirror in there, and Morelle wanted to see what she looked like in these new garments.

To her surprise everything fit perfectly, as if crafted specifically for her body. The pants were so wide that they looked like a long skirt, and the blouse's fabric felt wonderfully cool against her skin.

"You look stunning." Gertrude helped her to stand upright in front of the mirror. "What do you think?"

Morelle didn't know what to say. She had never worn anything like it nor had she ever even seen anyone wearing such things. The white blouse had short sleeves and a tie in the front that was part of it. Gertrude fussed with it a little until she was satisfied with how it looked, and then she tucked the blouse inside the wide waistband of the pants.

"Your waist is so tiny," Gertrude said. "It must be your Kra-ell half."

"Is it considered unattractive?" Morelle asked.

"No, it's perfect. The pureblooded Kra-ell are too thin, but you just look like a runway model."

Morelle frowned. "I must have misunderstood. Why would a model run away?"

Gertrude laughed. "Forget I said that. Are you okay with walking out of the room with my help, or do you want me to get you the wheelchair?"

The medic had shown her the chair with wheels she could use for mobility if her legs grew tired.

"I would rather walk."

"As you wish." The medic wrapped her arm around Morelle's middle. "Lean on me, Morelle."

46

BRANDON

When Morelle emerged from her room, a grin spread over Brandon's face. Even leaning heavily on Gertrude, she looked like a new female in the outfit his shopper had chosen. She looked elegant, refined, and, most importantly, like someone who belonged in this era.

"You look beautiful." He moved forward, offering his arm to take over from the nurse. "Thank you, Gertrude. I've got Morelle from here."

The nurse smiled knowingly. "Enjoy your tour of the village."

He had not yet told Morelle that she wouldn't be returning to the clinic, and Gertrude didn't know either. He should tell them both so they could say their goodbyes. But first, Ell-rom needed to see his sister transformed into a modern woman.

"Do you want to say hello to your brother before we go?" he asked.

She looked down at herself and then lifted her head and smiled. "I've seen Ell-rom this morning, but I should tell him that I'm going out and will be gone for a little while. I don't want him to worry about me."

Better to be honest now. "You're not coming back here. After the tour, I'll take you to Annani's house. Naturally, we will come here often for your rehabilitation and to see Ell-rom if Jasmine remains here for a while longer."

Her eyes widened. "I haven't seen my brother's mate yet. I should do so before I leave."

Morelle was already leaning on him heavily, and he wanted to get her to the golf cart as soon as possible so she could sit down, but he wasn't going to deny her wishes. If need be, he would carry her or ask Gertrude to get the wheelchair.

"Of course." He tightened his hold on her waist, supporting her as they waited.

"Congratulations," the nurse said from behind them. "It'll be good for you to move out of here."

Morelle turned to look at Gertrude over her shoulder. "Thank you for taking care of me. I would also like to thank the other medics. Bridget and Julian."

Brandon had noticed that Morelle called every medical practitioner a medic without differentiating between doctors and nurses. He wondered whether the Kra-ell had only one class of such providers or whether it was a translation problem.

"You're most welcome," Gertrude said. "And don't worry about the docs. You'll have plenty of opportunities to see them in person when you come for checkups and rehabilitation."

"I'm not sure Morelle needs it."

At the rate she was progressing, she would be jogging through the village in no time.

"We shall see." Gertrude smiled at Morelle. "The village is a small place, and you are bound to bump into everyone sooner or later." She walked to Jasmine's room and knocked. "Ell-rom, Morelle wants you to come out for a moment."

When Ell-rom emerged and saw his sister, there was wonderment in his eyes, and he pressed a hand to his chest. "You look like a completely different person. You have no idea how it makes me feel to see you like this. I don't remember much from before, but sometimes I have dreams, and I see you in long robes and veils. They were like a prison. Here, you are finally free."

Morelle nodded. "I feel free. Can I come in and see your mate?"

Ell-rom's smile grew broader. "I would love for you to see my Jasmine."

As Brandon helped Morelle into the room, Gertrude called from behind them. "I'll load the rest of Morelle's things into the golf cart while you're in there."

The room was quiet except for the beep of monitors and Jasmine's steady breathing.

Brandon watched as Morelle studied her brother's mate intently. "She's as beautiful as a goddess," she whispered. "No wonder you fell in love with her the moment you saw her."

Ell-rom sat on the edge of the bed and took Jasmine's hand. "It's more than her beauty. She has the kindest heart, and she sees the good in everyone." He looked up at his sister. "She sat with you too, you know. Talked to you, sang to you."

Morelle nodded. "I wish I remembered that, but I only heard Brandon for some reason. Perhaps I wasn't ready before."

When she wobbled on her feet, Brandon led her to the chair and helped her sit down.

"Thank you." She let out a breath. "I'm still so annoy-ingly weak."

Ell-rom chuckled. "You are doing so much better than I did when I first woke up that I feel embarrassed."

"Bridget said that you were still emaciated when you woke up. You didn't have the muscles to carry your weight."

"True," he conceded. "I owe everything to Jasmine, the doctors, and Gertrude." He waved at the nurse, who had returned and stood in the doorway. "Perhaps this is what I should do with my future. Become a doctor."

Something passed through Morelle's eyes that Brandon couldn't quite decipher.

Worry mixed with annoyance?

"You need to start with learning English first," Gertrude said. "Baby steps, Ell-rom. You can't run before you walk."

He laughed, which seemed to lift Morelle's spirits. "Yeah, you are right. I've been neglecting my studies." He turned to Brandon. "You should get Morelle a laptop with the program William's team designed for Kra-ell speakers for self-taught English. It's incredible."

Brandon hadn't known such a program existed, but he was certainly getting it for Morelle. "I will." He looked at his princess. "Are you ready to go?"

"Yes." She let him pull her up and then wrap his arm around her waist to support her.

"I can carry you to the cart."

She hesitated, and for a moment, he thought she would agree, but then she shook her head. "Is it right outside?"

"It is."

"Then I can make it." She turned to her brother. "I'm moving in with you and Annani today."

"I know. Annani told me."

Morelle frowned. "Was she here?"

He chuckled. "No. She texted me." He lifted his phone. "Brandon needs to explain how this thing works and get you one."

"I will do that as well." Brandon led Morelle out of Jasmine's room, and Gertrude opened the front door of the clinic for them.

Brandon didn't know what he'd expected Morelle would do once she saw the sky and the lush greenery of the village, but it hadn't been this silent wonder.

It tugged at his heart.

She was like a caged bird seeing the outdoors for the first time.

47

MORELLE

Morelle lifted her gaze to the sky, which was an incredible shade of light blue and was dotted with fluffy white clouds that drifted lazily overhead. It was like a dreamscape, or how the Fields of the Brave were described in hymns.

On Anumati, the thick atmosphere and their giant red sun had tinted everything in shades of red and amber, and the strong winds had battered at her robes and everything else, dictating that just the sturdiest survived, whether it was grass, trees, animals, or people.

Here, the sun was small and golden, and it warmed her face with gentle rays so unlike the humid heat she remembered.

Instead, a soft breeze played across her skin, carrying scents she couldn't identify but that made her want to breathe them in deeply. The air itself felt different, fresher somehow.

Brandon's arm around her waist was steady and strong, his touch both grounding and thrilling. No one had ever held her like this, with such care.

"Earth's sky is beautiful," she whispered. "No wonder my mother wanted the Kra-ell to settle here. This is like the Fields of the Brave but without having to die first to get here."

Brandon's arm tightened around her. "Many of the Kra-ell perished. Only a few pods survived, and the others are missing, with their occupants presumed dead. I'm so grateful that you are alive and that we found you and Ell-rom in time."

She felt him shift, adjusting his hold to better support her as she swayed with the breeze. The motion brought her closer to his chest, and she registered the subtle differences in his scent—something clean and masculine that made her want to lean in closer.

"I hope more will be found." She leaned her head on his shoulder. "It's so quiet here. On Anumati, it's rare for the winds to subside long enough for such calm."

"Is it always stormy there?" Brandon asked.

Morelle nodded. "The head priestess used to say that harsh conditions create tough people, and she was right. The gods solved the problem of heat and humidity by living underground, but the Kra-ell were made from hardier stuff and chose to live topside."

"That they are," Brandon admitted. "They are stronger, faster, and don't need much to survive. Very self-sufficient in the right environment, which this is not. There aren't beasts to hunt in the village, and they have to make do with domesticated animals and synthetic blood."

"They will adapt." She made a step forward. "The Kra-ell pride themselves on their ability to survive where others could not. But this place is more than habit-able. Even the gravity feels lighter." She straightened slightly, testing her balance. "Or maybe that's just because I'm not carrying so much fabric on me."

Brandon's arm tightened fractionally around her waist as she moved, ready to catch her if she stum-bled. "Take it slow," he said. "We can discuss all the differences between Earth and Anumati while sitting down."

Morelle turned her face to the sun again, marveling at how it could be so bright yet so kind. Everything about this world seemed designed for life to flourish rather than merely survive. No wonder the people here looked happier than those back home.

When he steered her toward a boxy-looking vehicle, Morelle was first struck by the large number of pack-ages loaded onto the rear seat. "What are all these?"

"They are all for you. You need a proper wardrobe." Brandon put both hands on her waist and lifted her onto the front seat. "You now have everything a beautiful princess needs, from casual wear to formal attire and everything in between."

"Thank you," she said when he got in the vehicle beside her. "That's very generous of you, and I don't know how to repay you." When he opened his mouth to protest, she put a finger on his lips. "Don't say that being with me is all you expect in return. I'll find a way to repay you. It might not be anytime soon, but I never forget a debt, whether it is a debt of gratitude or a debt of revenge."

He seemed taken aback by her words. "Who do you want to avenge?"

"My mother. She was murdered, and it is my duty as her daughter to find those responsible and kill them."

Brandon frowned. "How do you know she was murdered?"

"She told me. She came to me in my dreams and told me that I needed to wake up. She also told me to listen, and when I did, I heard you talking to me."

The truth was that her mother hadn't said anything about a murder, but that was the only way her life could have been cut short.

Brandon shivered even though it was a warm day and rubbed his arms. "That's profound. Do you often get dreams like that?"

Morelle shrugged. "Not at all, but then you have to

consider that I slept a dreamless sleep for seven thousand Earth years."

"And you still believe that it was your mother speaking to you?"

She nodded. "I'm positive."

"Did she tell you that she was murdered?"

"No, but she said that she crossed beyond the veil before her time. That can only mean that she did not die from natural causes."

He tilted his head. "Even if you are right, and she was assassinated, the killers are long gone by now."

"If they were Kra-ell, but I don't think they were. I think it was my grandfather's assassins."

Brandon nodded. "He would be my prime suspect as well, but since there is no way for you to get back to Anumati, there is no way for you to avenge your mother either."

That was another surprise. "The gods no longer send transports to collect the gold mined on Earth?"

"There is no contact with the planet of the gods. The Eternal King ordered Earth erased from the galactic maps." Brandon did something, and the vehicle started moving slowly. "Let's leave talk of Anumati for a later time. I promised you a tour, right?"

"Yes." She settled into her seat.

Morelle had so many questions about what Brandon had just said, but he seemed upset by her need for revenge, or maybe he just didn't want to spoil the mood by talking about dark topics.

"Over there is the playground, and as you can see, most of the children and mothers are Kra-ell. Immortals have a much lower fertility rate, and we don't have many children who can enjoy the playground. We hope for more, though."

The children looked happy, and then one uttered a joyful shriek that had her jump in her seat. Morelle had never heard a sound like that. She'd never even seen children at play before.

In the temple, even the youngest acolytes maintained strict decorum.

"That's the café." Brandon pointed. "You can get superb coffee, a sandwich, or a pastry and enjoy them on one of these outdoor tables or take them to go if you are in a rush."

People sat at tables in the open air, sipping beverages and chatting. They smiled and waved as the cart passed them so slowly that Morelle got to smile back and even tried to memorize some faces. A group of Kra-ell walked past, but they were not fully Kra-ell. They looked part human. Two of them stopped by one of the tables and started chatting with the immortals sitting there.

"They are on their way to training," Brandon said. "Many of the young Kra-ell want to join our Guardian force, and we welcome them with open arms. They are good fighters."

She turned to look at the group of five young males while Brandon navigated the cart into one of the paths forking from the one they were on. "They look half human."

"That's because they are. The Kra-ell also realized that their numbers were not sufficient to maintain a genetically viable society, but their experiment was less successful than ours."

She turned to him. "What do you mean?"

"When the gods took human partners, the children born of such unions were immortal. But when those immortals took human partners, their children were born human. Later, they discovered a way to activate the dormant genes of the children born to immortal mothers but not to immortal fathers. Our clan continued to grow through our females. Only their children can be turned immortal. The Kra-ell experienced a similar phenomenon, but the children born to their female hybrids can only be activated by immortal males, and the other problem is that only their hybrid males choose human partners. Their hybrid females almost never partner with humans."

"Why not?"

He shrugged. "Too weak, I guess. One hybrid Kra-ell female fought off three well-trained immortals, and they barely managed to subdue her."

Morelle tensed. "Why did they want to subdue her?"

"It's a long story, but it has a happy ending. Aliya joined our clan and mated another hybrid Kra-ell. She works at the café."

"You still didn't explain why she was fighting them. I don't want to hear only the nice stories. I want a balanced view of this world."

When Brandon didn't answer right away, she feared she had offended him by speaking too forcefully. He had been so good to her, and he deserved only kind words and the warmest of tones from her, but that wasn't who she was.

She had gotten in trouble with the head priestess so many times over her attitude.

"You are not the queen," the head priestess had told her. "And you will never be queen, so learn some humility, or I will beat that haughty attitude out of you."

She had never dared to actually make good on that threat, but she had found other ways to punish Morelle, like separating her from Ell-rom and locking her in a dark, windowless room.

Finally, Brandon nodded. "I'll tell you everything you

want to know except for the things the Clan Mother wants to tell you herself."

Morelle couldn't read in Brandon's tone whether he was upset or not.

"Thank you, and I'm sorry. I didn't mean to sound demanding. I shouldn't demand anything and only accept what is given to me freely. I'm not being a gracious guest. Can you forgive me?"

He reached for her hand, threading his fingers through hers. "You are not a shrinking violet to be coddled, not even on your second day of waking up from a coma. I should have realized that."

She was confused. "What does a shrinking flower have to do with me?"

Brandon chuckled. "It's a human expression that describes a shy and timid person."

"I'm neither."

Well, that was true for some things and not for others. She was shy about reminding him that he wanted her to kiss him and asking him whether he still wanted that.

48

BRANDON

B randon watched Morelle with a mix of admiration and amusement. Her feminine beauty was misleading, and so was her physical weakness. Behind the elegant and refined façade that he had helped to create with the clothing he'd gotten for her, there was a fierce Kra-ell princess who spoke of vengeance and killing her mother's murderer as if she were discussing the weather.

"I know that now, Princess. I will not make that mistake again. But I hate to disappoint you. The story of Aliya, the hybrid Kra-ell who beat up three strong immortal warriors, is not bloody or vicious. It's actually nice."

She tilted her head and looked at him from under lowered lashes. "You are not going to paint it in pretty colors for me, right?"

He lifted one hand off the steering wheel. "I promise

to tell you the truth, the whole truth, and nothing but the truth."

That seemed to satisfy her, and she leaned back in the cart's not-so-comfortable seat.

"First, though, let me show you something." He steered the cart toward the village's edge.

As they crested the gentle slope, the ocean came into view—a distant strip of blue meeting the horizon.

Morelle leaned forward. "It looks like the sky has fallen to earth."

"That's the Pacific Ocean." He parked the cart as close as he could to the bench that he intended them to sit on. "It stretches for thousands of miles and connects continents."

"It doesn't look that big, but that's because of Earth's curvature. We had seas on Anumati, but I never saw one. I never got to see even a lake."

He felt a twinge of sorrow for the secluded life she'd been forced to lead. "When you get stronger, I'll take you to see the ocean up close, and if you want, you can dip your toes in the water."

She recoiled. "Oh, no. Big bodies of water are dangerous."

He chuckled. "I've heard of the Kra-ell's aversion to deep water, which is somewhat justified. Their bodies are less buoyant. But you are built like a goddess, so you shouldn't fear the water."

She looked down at her body and then back at him. "I've seen goddesses on vids and in books, and now I have also seen Annani. I'm not nearly as beautiful as they are."

"Yes, you are." He took her hand and kissed the back of it. "Do you want to sit over there on that bench?"

"Yes." She started to turn.

"Stop right there and wait for me to get you. If you fall, it's back to the clinic. I'm sure you don't want that."

"No." She stopped with her feet dangling over the side of the cart. "I don't want to go back to that room."

He was learning how to speak to his fiercely independent and strong-willed princess. If he wanted her to do as he asked, he had to give her a good reason to do so.

Morelle was not a follower. She was a leader.

Still, he couldn't help himself, and instead of offering a hand to help her down, he put his hands on her tiny waist, lifted her out of the seat, and transferred her to the bench.

She gave him a baleful look but quickly followed it with a smile. "If you keep doing that, I will have to ask Gertrude to bring that leg exercising machine to Annani's home. Otherwise, I will not get stronger."

He sat beside her on the bench and took her hand. "That might be a good idea regardless of anything else. How are you feeling? Are you tired?"

"I've been sitting in that cart and talking. Those are not tiring activities."

He laughed. "You'd be surprised, but some people find talking exhausting. Not me, thank the merciful Fates, but for some, it's a problem."

She smiled. "I called you my storyteller when I didn't know your name."

His heart swelled. "You can call me anything you want as long as you add 'my' in front of it. I like the sound of it."

She blushed, which was completely unexpected. The fierce Morelle shouldn't feel embarrassed by some innocent flirting.

"Did I go too far?" he asked.

She looked around the small lookout point. "I don't know. Is this place considered far away for the village people?"

He stifled a laugh. "Never mind. Forget I said that. You wanted to hear Aliya's story, right?"

"Yes, please."

He turned to face her. "When we found her, she was living alone in a cave system in China, a different country that's very far from where we are. Her human mother took her to live with her people, and when the mother died, Aliya was left to fend for herself. If she'd continued looking human, she might have been okay, but after puberty, her features became more and more Kra-ell and her physical strength scared the people she lived with. She ran away and survived on her own, hiding from humans and other Kra-ell who she feared might come after her." When Morelle opened her mouth, he lifted his hand to stop her, knowing that she wanted to ask who the Kra-ell were that Aliya had feared, but if he branched into that story, they would never make it to Annani's, who was no doubt waiting for them to arrive.

"That's another story. Let's stay on this one, okay?"

Reluctantly, Morelle nodded. "A group of immortals from our community were touring the area when one of them had a vision of a child lost in those caves, so naturally they went to investigate. Turned out that the vision was from the past and that the child had grown up into the woman who'd turned the caves into a fortress, complete with traps that might have resulted in a catastrophe. Especially since one of these immortals was Alena, Annani's daughter, and another one, the seer who had the vision, was pregnant. "

That got Morelle's attention. "Did they evade the traps?"

"Not all of them, but most. At some point, they got trapped and couldn't get out, but then they spotted Aliya across an underground lake, and three of them swam after her, realizing that she could lead them to another exit."

"The three she fought off?"

"Yes. They chased her across the lake and some secret passages and barely caught up to her when she got topside. She fought like a tigress, inflicting injuries on all three males, and since they didn't want to hurt her, they were at a disadvantage. Finally, one of them bashed her with a rock."

Morelle winced. "Ouch."

"Yeah. Ouch is right. Anyway, the funny part is that one of them was a compeller, but in the heat of the battle, he forgot that he could force her to stop fighting by commanding it. He used that skill later to get her to help them free the others who were trapped and couldn't swim across the freezing water of the lake, especially the pregnant female. They also explained who they were and that they weren't there to harm her. After spending some time with them, she chose to come live in the village, met Vrog, another hybrid Kra-ell, and they lived happily ever after."

Morelle frowned. "Why are you talking about them in past tense? Did they die?"

"Fates forbid. Many fictional stories end with that line, so people started saying it when telling a real story with a happy ending."

"That's nice." She glanced at the ocean. "Kra-ell stories don't have happy endings. The best ending is for the heroes to sacrifice their lives in a brutal battle and end up in the Fields of the Brave."

"Yes, I've heard that. Your Mother of All Life is not a kind deity. She is vicious and bloodthirsty."

"I'm not a believer," Morelle said. "If I invoke the Mother, it is due to imitation and habit, not out of reverence. But life does not have many happy endings, if any. It is better to die in battle than from old age."

"I disagree, but then immortals don't age, and neither will you since you are half goddess."

"True." She let out a breath. "Do you know any stories with bad endings?"

"Regrettably, I know too many of them," he admitted. "But we should head to Annani's." He rose to his feet and offered Morelle a hand up.

She took it and let him pull her up. "Are the bad stories about the clan?"

"The clan has always been a force for good, and I'm not just saying that out of loyalty or bias. Some truths are universal." He helped her climb into the cart with just a little help. "But we have enemies, powerful ones, bent on eradicating Annani and her people over an ancient feud and twisted ideology." He started the cart and backed out of the lookout point and back onto the main path. "We have been forced to defend ourselves against them many times, and sometimes we had to go with preemptive strikes, but most of the time, we prefer to hide from them." He smiled at her. "If they can't find us, they can't kill us."

"Why don't you just fight to win and be done with them?"

"Several reasons, the main one being that they have superior numbers." He navigated around a curve in the path. "The other consideration is that the Clan Mother, your sister, has a soft heart, and she doesn't want to annihilate all those immortals. There aren't many of us on Earth."

Morelle looked like she didn't accept that argument, and Brandon had a feeling that she would discuss it with Annani later. His princess was not softhearted, and she wasn't merciful, and for some reason, it made him want her even more.

"What are they called?" Morelle's voice held that sharp edge again, which proved to him that he'd been right about her. "Your enemies. What are they called?"

"The Brotherhood of the Devout Order of Mortdh, or the Doomers for short. And before you ask, that's also one of the stories your sister will want to tell you herself."

MORELLE

T he cart slowed as they approached a bridge spanning a small ravine. The houses on the other side looked bigger than the ones they had passed so far and farther apart.

"We're crossing into the newest section of the village," Brandon explained as they started across. "This is where Annani and her children live, along with the council members and many of the Guardian force."

Morelle tried to follow as he detailed the village's expansion—something about phases and different groups settling in different areas. There was mention of someone named Kalugal wanting his own section, but she found her attention divided between his words and the overwhelming sensory experience around her.

A bird called from somewhere nearby, its song unlike anything she'd heard before. Even the air here carried different scents than the dense vegetation of her home planet, which always smelled a little of rot because of the humidity. It was much drier here and more comfortable.

Her mind kept drifting back to Brandon's story about Aliya. He had a gift for storytelling, making even the shortened version come alive in Morelle's imagination. She could picture Annani's daughter, he hadn't told her which one, touring with a group of immortals or maybe leading them in some remote area on Earth, and then someone having a prophetic vision about a girl. Poor Aliya, living alone in those caves, terrified when the warriors chased her...

Morelle wanted to ask about the seer, and whether it was common for immortals to have visions, but before she could voice the question, the cart came to a stop in front of a house with wide windows and a large porch. It wasn't much different in size or style from the other houses lining the pathways, but it was easily recognizable because each house had a few features that were different from the others. This one had straight white railing posts, while the one next to it had an iron railing with a scrolling design.

The front door opened and two squat males, who couldn't possibly be immortals given their weathered features, hurried out to meet them. They looked almost identical and were dressed similarly.

Were they human?

Did Annani employ human servants?

Despite looking elderly, they moved with an oddly fluid grace that set her instincts on edge, and when they bowed in perfect synchronization, she felt a chill run down her spine.

These were not humans.

"Welcome, Mistress Morelle, Master Brandon," one of them said. "We came to collect the packages."

"Thank you," Brandon replied as he exited the cart.

He came around to help her down and offered her his hand, but she was still observing the two strange males.

Something about them bothered her. Their scent was wrong. Not quite living, but not dead either. She wrinkled her nose, trying to place the strange chemical undertone. "Who are these people?"

Brandon's arm slipped around her waist, supporting her as they walked. "Have you heard about the Odus?"

A shiver ran through her body as she remembered what she had learned about the creatures. "I have, but I've never seen one. They were destroyed on Anumati, and no more were made. Is that what those two are?"

"Yes, and they serve the Clan Mother. You have nothing to fear from them. They were vilified on Anumati through no fault of their own. The gods reprogrammed their servants to become killing machines and fight the Kra-ell, and then they blamed the Odus for the bloodshed. It's like blaming the weapon for killing and not the person pulling the trigger."

"We were told that they malfunctioned."

"It was a lie." Brandon helped her climb the stairs to the porch, patiently waiting as she lifted one leg and then the other. "The Eternal King, your grandfather, realized that the Odus could be mobilized against him once everyone knew it could be done. That was why he ordered them to be destroyed, along with the blueprints for how to make them. Naturally, he put a benevolent spin on the move, making himself look like the victim and the savior."

After she had made it over the three steps, Morelle had to stop and catch her breath. "It is embarrassing how difficult it was for me to climb these. I should be able to leap over them."

"You will before you know it."

She looked over her shoulder at the Odus, who were done unloading the cart and were waiting for her and Brandon to clear the steps before following them with all the packages.

They seemed so accommodating, so harmless, and yet she couldn't shake the feeling that they were dangerous.

But Brandon was right.

They were just a device, a tool, possibly a weapon, and how they were used was up to their owner. She had to trust that Annani would only use them for good.

"How did they get to Earth? I thought they were all destroyed."

Brandon's arm tightened around her waist. "Someone must have sent them to Earth to save them. Perhaps the god who created them wanted his creations to survive. These two and five others were found wandering the desert, their memories of their past wiped away. One of the gods found them, and they were given as a gift to Annani."

"Excuse us," one of the Odus said as he and his twin passed them by, each carrying a mountain of packages.

They disappeared into the house, and a moment later, one of them returned. "Please, come in. The Clan Mother is awaiting you in the living room." He bowed and retreated inside.

"They are very efficient," Morelle whispered.

Brandon chuckled. "They're also excellent cooks, keep the house spotless, and never sleep. Your sister is very fond of them, and she treats them as if they are sentient, which we all believe they are becoming."

The hint was obvious. She needed to treat the Odus as if they were people because that was what her sister expected.

As they entered the reception room, Annani rose to her feet, looking resplendent in a green gown, her flowing red hair looking like a live flame in the light streaming through the large window.

"Welcome home, sister of mine," Annani said and opened her arms to Morelle.

KIAN

K ian was halfway to the door when his phone buzzed. Seeing Onegus's name flash across the screen, he paused, pulled out a chair next to the conference table, and sat down.

His mother hadn't specified a precise time for lunch since she didn't know when Morelle and Brandon would be done with their tour, so he could spare a few minutes to talk with the chief.

"Hello, Onegus," he answered.

"We may have stumbled onto something bigger than we anticipated," the chief said. "I put Roni on tracking potential targets, and what he found was shocking, to be honest."

"That bad?"

"There are entire networks, Kian. Services that broker children to perverts, all operating out in the open on the internet with apps that don't even try very hard to hide what they are used for. Roni has barely scratched the surface, and he's already uncovered an avalanche of leads."

Kian's free hand clenched into a fist. "If we want to run sting operations to address the infestation, we might need Turner's help. What are we looking at in terms of organization?"

"I'm still trying to organize my thoughts, Kian. To start with, it will need to be a completely separate department that will require someone to head it. We'll need specialized teams that are smaller than what we are using to bust the trafficker cells. This isn't just about the end users anymore. There's a whole layer of middlemen, the brokers who connect buyers with suppliers."

Kian groaned. "How come we didn't know about this?"

"We knew. We just didn't realize how big it was. We've started seeing really young kids only lately in our rescue missions, so we assumed that it was a fringe thing. But it's not. I think there are other traffickers who specialize in kids."

Bile rose in Kian's throat.

The level of depravity humans were capable of was really staggering.

"Roni also stumbled upon articles and stories about those pimps of kids collecting blackmail material on their clients. Politicians, actors, wealthy businessmen, you get the picture. Does that sound familiar?"

The question was rhetorical. They both knew exactly what this resembled.

"Doomers." Kian spat the word like a curse. "This fits their MO perfectly. They've graduated from drugs and prostitution to dealing in children. Demon spawn. They truly have no regard for human life, not even the most innocent."

"If the Doomers are involved, we'll need to structure our approach accordingly. Dealing with them is not like dealing with humans."

Kian ran a hand through his hair. "Guardian safety has to be our primary concern. We have to assume Doomer involvement in every operation."

"Agreed. It's going to strain our resources."

"We'll need to shift more of the Kra-ell trainees into the regular missions to free up Guardians. How is their progress going?" He rose to his feet and started pacing.

"They're incredibly strong fighters," Onegus said. "And they learn fast, but we are having disciplinary problems."

Kian frowned. "That's unexpected. After having lived under Igor's boot for so long, I would have thought they'd be more compliant. Discipline was enforced mercilessly at his compound."

"Igor ruled through compulsion and fear while we operate on loyalty, respect, and proper training. It's a completely different paradigm, and they're struggling to adapt."

The distinction was important. Fear might produce immediate results, but it created unstable foundations. The Guardians' strength came from their unity, their shared values, and trust in the chain of command.

"Don't forget that they have been training for weeks, not decades," Onegus continued. "I didn't really expect them to be combat-ready any time soon and have only used them in backup positions so far. But if we want to shift our operations in a new direction while continuing what we've been doing until now, we have no choice. Not unless you want to hire human mercenaries for the pedophile stings."

That was an option, but then Kian would need to rely on Turner, and the guy was too busy with his own operations to take on an entire new division.

"We can't work with humans. They are fine for the occasional job but not on a regular basis."

"So that leaves the Kra-ell, males and females," Onegus said. "The females are even more ferocious than the males, especially the purebloods."

"I will need to speak with Jade." Kian thought of Drova and whether it was a good idea to get her involved. She was still young, but she was capable, a good fighter, a powerful compeller, and she was chafing from having nothing to do.

She could be an asset if her abilities were properly harnessed. She could render even Doomers helpless.

The more Kian thought about it, the more he liked the idea, and he had a feeling that the girl would like it, too. She wasn't a bad kid. She just needed direction.

"We can't rush this," Onegus said. "Better to have fewer reliable teams than risk operations going sideways because of undisciplined elements."

Perhaps he shouldn't tell Onegus his idea about Drova.

Talk about undisciplined elements.

Kian checked his watch, grimacing at the time. "Start putting together profiles of potential team leaders for the specialized units. We need our most experienced people on this—Guardians who've faced Doomers before."

Onegus groaned. "First, I need to create the organizational chart in my head. Roni is also still digging, but he says the network is extensive. This could be bigger than anything we've tackled before."

"Do you have anyone in mind who can head the new division?"

"My first thought was Arwel, but I can't do that to the

guy. It would break him. We need someone more emotionally resilient."

"Turner would have been great if we could persuade him to close his private operations. He doesn't get emotional, and he can deal with shit that would devastate anyone else."

"Good luck with that," Onegus said. "You've dangled better positions in front of him, and he didn't bite. We need someone else."

"Make a list of potential candidates, and we will go over them together."

"Will do, boss." Onegus ended the call.

Kian's earlier good mood had thoroughly evaporated.

If the Doomers had indeed moved into trafficking children, it represented a new level of depravity even for them. But it made tactical sense. What better way to control powerful people than to have evidence of their worst crimes?

Spending a night with a prostitute was no longer a big deal, and holding evidence of that over someone's head was not enough leverage. Sex with minors, especially really young ones, though, was enough to ruin someone's life.

That was powerful leverage.

ANNANI

"T hank you for welcoming me into your home," Morelle said as she walked into Annani's arms, bending down to kiss her cheek.

She was nearly as tall as Amanda and was even skinnier, which Annani resolved to remedy.

She took a step back to give her sister another once-over. "You look wonderful."

Annani was delighted to see Morelle looking so well so soon. Her sister was still recuperating, though. There were dark circles under her eyes, and she was still much too thin, but there was vitality in her gaze, and the outfit Brandon's shopper had chosen for her was absolutely perfect. It was elegant and comfortable, suitable for all-day wear, and it fit nearly any occasion.

"I knew I was right to let Brandon handle your wardrobe." She took Morelle's hand and led her to the couch. "Since I absolutely detest pants, I would have chosen dresses, but this suits you perfectly." She turned to Brandon. "Thank you for doing this for Morelle. Naturally, I will cover the expenses you incurred."

Brandon, who was about to sit down on one of the armchairs, froze midway, looking like she had slapped him, and Annani immediately regretted making the offer.

"It was my pleasure to provide for Morelle, Clan Mother. Please don't deprive me of it." He lowered himself into the armchair.

Annani was a little saddened that Morelle would not be a candidate for her companion. It seemed that the Fates had already paired her with Brandon. On the other hand, she was happy for her sister. Finding her fated mate was much more important than keeping Annani company.

"Lunch is ready." Annani patted Morelle's hand. "But we are waiting for Kian and Ell-rom to arrive. In the meantime, we can have tea." She lifted her hand, signaling for Ogidu.

"Right away, Clan Mother." He bowed and rushed into the kitchen.

"I didn't know that Kian and Ell-rom were coming,"

Morelle said. "Ell-rom didn't mention it when we spoke at the clinic."

"That is because it was decided after you left with Brandon." She smiled. "I wanted to invite the entire family, but Kian wisely pointed out that Syssi and Amanda are at the university today and that we shouldn't overwhelm you with too many relatives at once."

Morelle returned a sheepish smile. "It has been a very full day, but after seven thousand years of slumber, I feel like I have to keep moving and experiencing to compensate for lost time."

"Oh dear." Annani patted Morelle's hand again. "You are immortal. You do not need to rush to do anything."

"I know." Morelle sighed. "And I'm far from being at my best, but I have this feeling inside that is propelling me to keep going." She touched a hand to her belly.

"You are hungry," Annani said as Ogidu returned with the tea service.

Morelle nodded. "Yes, I am hungry for experiences."

Annani chuckled. "You are also hungry for food. Your body is still rebuilding itself after the long stasis, and you need more than just tea." She turned to her Odu. "Ogidu, please bring out some appetizers."

"Of course, Clan Mother." He finished pouring the tea and then retreated to the kitchen.

"Thank you." Morelle pressed her hand to her belly again. "I didn't realize that I was hungry."

"I should have thought of that," Brandon said. "I'm not a very good caregiver."

Morelle cast him a reproachful look. "I'm not a child, Brandon."

"Oh, I know that you are not a child and thank the Fates for that."

Morelle looked confused while Annani laughed. "Oh, Morelle. There is so much you are about to learn about the way we use language here and all the cultural references that are lost on you. What Brandon meant was that he sees you as a desirable female. He is glad that you are old enough for him to pursue. It was a compliment."

"A strange one, that's for sure." Morelle frowned at Brandon. "Do I look so young that it might be confusing?" She lifted her hand to her head and touched the fuzzy growth. "It's because of this. I look different with hair."

"It was just a bad joke," Brandon said. "Forget that I said it."

Thankfully, Ogidu returned with plates of small sandwiches, fruit, and cheese, and Morelle got distracted by the food.

Annani cast Brandon a knowing look, and in response he lifted his hands in defeat.

Falling in love was difficult, and even an experienced male like Brandon was faltering. It was much easier to feign confidence when the stakes were not as high as impressing the one person that he hoped to spend eternity with.

Did Morelle feel the same toward him, though?

It was hard to tell. Her sister was a mix of contradicting traits, and Annani was eager to get to know her.

Was she also harboring a deadly talent like her twin brother's?

Once Morelle had filled her belly with a few of the small canapés, she wiped her lips with a napkin and put it down. "My stomach seems to be able to process only tiny quantities of food at a time, and Bridget told me to listen to my body and not to try to push it."

"That is natural, my dear. Your stomach has not been active for a very long time. You need to be patient."

"I'm not a patient person by nature, but I will try." Morelle drummed her fingers on her knee, looking anything but patient. "While we wait for Ell-rom and Kian, perhaps you could tell me about our father? I realize that it might not be a comfortable subject for you, but it might be better to get this story out of the way."

"It happened a very long time ago." Annani sighed. "The pain has dulled, though when you lose a loved one, it never truly goes away." She had wanted to wait, to let Morelle grow stronger before burdening her with this knowledge, but she could see the determination in her sister's eyes. Morelle would not rest until she knew everything.

"Perhaps my reluctance to tell you the story has to do with my part in the gods' demise and the guilt I feel to this day."

Morelle was taken aback. "What happened?"

"I did not want to mate the god my father chose for me, and I fell in love with another. My Khiann, my one and only, my fated mate."

ELL-ROM

E ll-rom stood at another unfamiliar intersection, frustration mounting as he realized he'd gotten turned around again. The paths in this section of the village all looked the same to him, lined with identical manicured shrubs and the occasional bench.

His mind had been so preoccupied with worry for Jasmine and excitement about Morelle that he'd barely paid attention to where he was going, and his sense of direction wasn't great.

What had happened to the Guardians who were supposed to be watching him? Had Kian dismissed them? Or were they hiding in the perfectly trimmed bushes, amusing themselves by watching him wander in circles?

The sound of gravel crunching under wheels made him step aside to let a golf cart pass, but instead of continuing on, it slowed to a stop beside him.

"Get in," Kian said from the driver's seat. "I was late too, so I grabbed the cart."

Relief flooded through Ell-rom as he climbed in beside his nephew. The relationship still felt strange. He was an uncle to someone who had much more life experience than him and led a community with natural authority. "No bodyguards?"

"Don't need them in the village." Kian guided the cart around a curve.

"What about the Guardians who are supposed to watch over me?"

"There's only one now, and he's trailing you." Kian looked into the shrubs as if he could see a Guardian galloping through them to keep up with the cart.

Ell-rom scanned their surroundings as well, seeing nothing but pristine landscaping and empty paths. "I can't see him. And if he's around, couldn't he have told me I was walking in the wrong direction?"

"He's probably taking a shortcut to my mother's house. He knows that we are heading there. And as for not pointing you in the right direction, he was told to keep his distance. I want to see if anyone tries anything when they think you're on your own. If nothing suspicious happens by the end of the week, I'm going to remove the last Guardian assigned to you. We need them for other things."

"What about my sister? Is anyone watching over her?"

"Same protocol as you, and it will also remain in effect only until the end of this week."

Something dark lurked behind Kian's polite expression, a tension that suggested problems Ell-rom wasn't privy to. He decided not to press. Kian would share what he deemed necessary, and since Ell-rom was not one of his advisors, if he had any, he wouldn't tell him anything even if he asked.

Besides, Ell-rom had enough worries of his own without taking on whatever was troubling Kian.

"How is Jasmine doing?" Kian asked.

"According to Bridget, she's doing well." Ell-rom shifted in the seat. "She's grown a full inch so far, and I know she's not going to be happy about it."

"Why not?" Kian frowned. "She's tall, but not even as tall as Amanda. Another inch isn't going to make much of a difference."

"I know," Ell-rom sighed. "And I don't mind if she grows even five inches taller. I'm just worried that she won't like it."

A knowing smile crossed Kian's face. "Here is what you should do. The moment she wakes up, tell her how beautiful she is and keep saying it until she has no choice but to believe you. She won't even notice the additional inches."

The simple advice struck Ell-rom as profound. Jasmine was always beautiful to him, whether she was dressed up for a formal occasion or just waking up in the morning. He needed to remember to tell her that as often as he could.

"I miss her voice," he admitted. "Her laugh. The way her eyes light up when she's excited about something." He looked up at the sun through the canopy of trees. "She is my sunshine."

"She'll wake up soon," Kian assured him. "The fact that she is growing is an excellent sign and probably the reason she hasn't woken up yet. Can you imagine how hard her body is working to make her grow an inch in just a few days? Not only that but if she had been awake, she would have been very uncomfortable. It hurts to grow so rapidly."

Ell-rom nodded. "Bridget said the same thing."

As Kian stopped the cart in front of Annani's house, Ell-rom spotted Morelle through the large living room window. She was sitting on the couch beside Annani, looking animated as she told Annani something. She waved her hands to accompany her story.

"Morelle retained her memories. I yearn for time to sit with her and talk about our life on Anumati, but I can't leave Jasmine's side, and Brandon is monopolizing Morelle's time. Not that I begrudge him it. She is awake, thanks to him. I just want the opportunity to get to know my twin sister."

ROB

Rob balanced two coffee cups and a paper bag of sandwiches as he left the café, planning to surprise Gertrude with lunch. Hopefully, she hadn't eaten yet and would be glad to see him. His game was rusty, and he had never flirted with an immortal before, but she seemed to like him.

He'd barely taken two steps when a familiar voice called out.

"Hey, stranger!"

Lusha sat at one of the outdoor tables, her dark hair gleaming in the sunlight. She'd been friendly since his arrival in the village, maybe a little too friendly considering that she was dating a Guardian, but maybe that was just her style, and she didn't mean anything by it. She was smart, and she knew a lot about the village, given that she hadn't been a resident long either. He liked talking to her, and he hoped she wouldn't be too put off by him pursuing Gertrude.

"Hi, Lusha." Rob stopped beside her table. "How are you?"

She gestured at the drinks in his hands. "Are you meeting Margo?"

Was he so pathetic that the only person Lusha could imagine him meeting was his sister?

"No, actually, I'm bringing lunch to Gertrude at the clinic."

"Oh." Lusha's eyebrows rose. "Is something going on between you two?"

"Not yet," Rob admitted. "But I'm hoping there might be. She's..." He searched for words that wouldn't sound too eager. "She's fun." *And beautiful, and warm, and assertive without being overbearing.*

He really liked Gertrude.

Something flickered across Lusha's face—disappointment? Annoyance? "Well, good luck." She waved a hand. "Just don't get too attached." She looked around and then leaned toward him and whispered, "These immortals are so promiscuous. They love having a variety of lovers."

He'd heard the same from Mia, but Gertrude didn't fit the profile.

"Thanks for the advice. I'll keep it in mind." He shifted the drinks. "Say hi to Alfie for me."

"I will." She gave him a saccharine smile.

What was her deal?

He'd deliberately kept things purely in the friend zone with Lusha despite her occasional flirting, respecting her relationship with Alfie. Perhaps she liked to keep her options open and collect male attention, like insurance policies, just in case her current relationship didn't work out.

Rob had known plenty of women like that, including his former fiancée.

No, that wasn't right. Lusha wasn't like that. Perhaps she just didn't like Gertrude for some reason, though he couldn't imagine why. Gertrude was awesome, and unlike some of the immortals who seemed to float above it all, she felt really approachable.

Maybe it was time to stop overthinking everything and just ask her out on a proper date.

As he entered the clinic, he found Gertrude sitting in Bridget's office, and when he walked in and put the coffee and sandwiches on the desk, she laughed.

"Are you trying to win my heart through my stomach?"

"Is it working?"

"Definitely. I'm starving, and the café makes the best turkey club in existence."

He frowned. "How did you know that was what I got?"

She tapped her nose. "Immortal sense of smell." She rose to her feet. "But we shouldn't eat here. Let's move the party to the waiting room."

"Of course." He handed her a cup and lifted the other one and the bag. "Will Bridget get mad if we eat in here?"

"She will give me the look, and I'd rather avoid it." Gertrude sat on one of the chairs. "But seriously, it would just be disrespectful."

"True." Rob suddenly noticed how quiet the clinic seemed. "Where is everyone?" The doors to both patient rooms were open, but the princess wasn't in hers, and Ell-rom wasn't sitting by Jasmine's side.

"Big changes today," Gertrude said, unwrapping her sandwich. "Morelle was released this morning, and she is moving to the Clan Mother's house."

Rob blinked in surprise. "That was fast. She just opened her eyes yesterday after thousands of years in stasis."

He was still trying to wrap his head around those numbers. The princess was nearly as old as human civilization, but since she'd spent most of that time unconscious, did it even count?

"Morelle is doing remarkably well. She's half goddess, after all, so that's not surprising. She just needed a jumpstart to take off like a race car."

Rob laughed. "I like the analogy. Are you a racing fan?"

"Not really." She took a sip of her coffee and sighed. "I needed this. Anyway, Brandon took her on a tour of the village first, and then they are heading to the Clan Mother's, or maybe they are already there because Ell-rom left a while ago to join them for lunch." She took another sip. "So, now it's just me watching over Jasmine. Bridget took advantage of the quiet to handle some paperwork in her other office." She took a big bite of her sandwich and moaned in pleasure.

The sound did all kinds of things to him that were too embarrassing to admit.

"Sounds like an opportunity for mischief," he said teasingly, but his pulse quickened at the thought.

Gertrude's eyes met his, and the way she slowly licked a crumb from her bottom lip sent more heat rushing through his body. "What kind of mischief did you have in mind?"

The invitation in her voice was unmistakable. Before he could overthink it, he leaned in and pressed a quick, soft kiss to her lips.

When he pulled back, Gertrude studied him with an unreadable expression, and he prepared to apologize for misreading the situation. But then she carefully placed both their cups in the tray on the side table next to their sandwiches, and the next thing he knew, her lips were on his again.

It was no gentle peck, though. This kiss was fire and sweetness and need all rolled into one. Her hands came up to frame his face as she deepened the kiss, and Rob saw stars behind his closed eyelids.

When they finally broke apart, they were both breathing heavily, and Gertrude's eyes were darker than usual, her lips slightly swollen. She looked even more beautiful than before, if that was possible.

"I've wanted to do that since I saw you training in the gym," she admitted.

That was a big surprise.

"Really? Even when I was pretending to know how to box?"

She laughed, the sound rich and warm. "Especially then. You were so earnest about it, even though we both knew I was holding back."

"I knew it!" He grinned. "I kept wondering how an immortal could punch so weakly."

"I didn't want to bruise your ego." She traced a finger along his jaw. "Or the punching bag, although the thing is probably specially designed for immortals, so I shouldn't have worried about it."

The casual reminder of her strength sent a shiver through him that had nothing to do with fear. "I appreciate your valiant effort to save my ego, but I assure you I have no problem with a female kicking my butt, as long as it's by besting me in something and not by cheating on me with her ex."

He didn't know why he had blurted it out, but now it was too late to take it back.

"I would never do that to you." She cupped his cheek. "I mean about the cheating. I abhor dishonesty in all forms, and that's what cheating is."

Rob swallowed hard. "Would you like to have dinner with me sometime?"

She smiled. "Are you asking me out on a date?"

"Yes, I am."

"I'd like that." She leaned in again, her breath ghosting across his lips. "But right now, I need more of this."

The second kiss was even better than the first, and Rob lost himself in it. The softness of her lips, the strength of her hands, and the perfect rightness of holding her.

He'd kissed plenty of women before, but none of them had made him feel like this—like he was falling and flying at the same time.

A door opened somewhere in the clinic, and they jumped apart. They were both trying to look innocent as footsteps approached. But it was just one of the Odus going about his cleaning routine.

"Good afternoon, Mistress Gertrude, Master Rob. May I clean the doctor's office?"

"Yes, please," Gertrude said.

He bowed, collected his cleaning tools, and walked into the office.

"I forgot about Onidu," Gertrude whispered. "He always comes to clean the clinic on Wednesdays, which was probably why Bridget left to work in the office building." She lifted her sandwich and coffee cup. "We should finish our lunch."

"Probably wise," Rob agreed, though his appetite had shifted to something food couldn't satisfy. "I hope we can continue our discussion later."

Her smile was humorous and playful wickedness mashed into one sexy-as-hell look. "I'm counting on it."

GERTRUDE

Damn. What had she been thinking, letting herself get carried away like that?

Getting involved with someone who lived in the village was a recipe for disaster. Gertrude should have learned that lesson with Negal, and he and Margo weren't even living in the village yet. Just seeing them in the keep while taking care of the twins had been an ordeal.

If Hildegard hadn't been taking that continuing education course, Gertrude would have asked to trade places with her, but it would have been a silly move just to avoid some awkwardness.

It wasn't as if she was in love with Negal or anything like that, but she had been infatuated with him for a little while until Margo arrived on the scene. She should put that entire awkward episode behind her and move on.

363

Rob was a catch. He was a Dormant, and Fates knew those didn't come around every day, and he was also sweet, handsome, and fun to be with.

The guy needed some tender loving after what had been done to him, and the combination was irresistible to her. She just wanted to wrap him up in her love and attention and shield him from his mean former fiancée.

It wasn't like she was in love with him or thought that he was her fated mate or that he could be the father of the child she so desperately wanted or anything like that.

He could be, though, whispered a small voice in the back of her head.

Don't get your hopes up, Trudy. It was just an attraction, and two lonely people finding comfort in each other.

Perhaps she should have treated this as something much more casual instead of calling it a date.

Besides, she had responsibilities. The gods were already interviewing the candidates Turner was sending their way for their tracker implants, and if the commander didn't react by week's end, they would go ahead with the procedures. She'd be spending the weekend at the keep, helping with the extractions and implantations and monitoring the humans who didn't heal as fast as her other patients.

Rob crumpled the wrapping of his sandwich and tossed it into the trash bin. "So, what are our options for fine dining? We could go into the city or maybe Callie's if you don't want to leave the village?"

Gertrude folded the wrap over the remaining half of her sandwich. "I'll probably be tied up at the keep this weekend with the tracker procedures. Tomorrow and Friday, I need to be here until six, so the city's not an option." She gave him an apologetic smile. "And Callie's is booked solid for weeks in advance."

"Oh." His face fell, and something in her chest tightened.

"You could come to my place tomorrow evening," she found herself saying. "I'll cook."

What had possessed her to suggest that?

"That's not really a date if you have to do all the work."

"I love cooking." The words came faster now. "Hildegard, my roommate, is handling the night shift in the clinic, so we'll have the place to ourselves." The moment the words left her lips, she realized how blatant her invitation had sounded.

Rob actually blushed, the pink spreading across his cheeks, making him look adorably young. Gertrude closed her eyes, forcing her hands to remain by her sides and not reach for his face.

"I would love that," he said. "Thank you for going to all this trouble."

"I should be honest." She let out a breath. "I've been fighting this attraction because I don't want a repeat of what happened with Negal. Dating someone who lives in the village is not a good idea."

He nodded. "I get it. Margo told me that you had a thing with him."

Gertrude waved a dismissive hand. "It was a cruise fling, and nothing happened. It just became awkward later because he dumped me for your sister like I was yesterday's news."

"It was fated," Rob said quietly. "Neither of them had a choice."

"I know, but that made me feel even worse. Getting a fated mate is like winning the lottery of life. I was so damn jealous." She cast him a sidelong glance. "But don't tell Margo. It will only make her feel bad."

"I won't." He raked his fingers through his hair. "But if you don't want to date anyone who lives in the village, who do you usually date?"

Gertrude chuckled. "I don't date. I occasionally hook up with humans in the city when I need to blow off steam." She met his eyes. "That's how most immortals handle it. Getting attached to a human isn't smart."

"I'm human."

"That's temporary." She put her wrapped half-sand-wich on the side table. "As Margo's brother, there is no doubt that you will transition. Look at Marina and Peter as an example. Do you know who I'm talking about?"

"Yes. I've met Marina, but not Peter."

"He's a Guardian, and she's a human who is not a Dormant. They met during the cruise and fell in love. I feel terrible for them. Bridget thinks that getting regular doses of venom might extend Marina's life, but by how much? Even if it doubles her lifespan, it's still just a blink of an eye to Peter."

"Nobody knows what the future holds," Rob said. "Love is precious, and we shouldn't dismiss it just because we're afraid of what might be." He chuckled. "Look who's talking. I'm terrified of falling for someone like Lynda again."

"I'm not Lynda," Gertrude said, the words once again tumbling out of her mouth as if she had no control over them.

She wasn't like Rob's ex. She would never manipulate someone's feelings or use them for personal gain. But Rob hadn't said anything about falling for her, and one little kiss didn't mean that he would.

Was she so desperate for a connection that she was clutching at straws?

"No." He reached for her hand. "You're nothing like her. You're real. What you see is what you get, and I love that about you."

He really shouldn't throw the word love around like it meant nothing.

"Tomorrow night, then?" she asked. "I make a mean coq au vin."

His eyebrows rose. "Impressive. I don't even know what that is, but should I bring wine?"

She smiled. "Do you have a vehicle to drive to the city? Because there is nowhere in the village to buy wine."

He winced. "I don't, but I could ask Mia to give me a lift."

"Don't worry about it. You don't have to bring anything." She took his hand. "Just bring yourself and a healthy appetite." She gave him a mock stern look. "When I cook, I expect my guest to eat."

"Oh, don't worry about that. I can definitely eat. Whatever that dish you mentioned is."

Gertrude studied their joined hands. "It's a French dish of chicken and mushrooms braised in wine. It sounds much fancier than it is." She looked up at his hopeful eyes. "It's just dinner, Rob. No expectations and no promises. Just two people sharing a meal and some nice conversation and seeing where it leads them."

His answering smile was like sunshine breaking through clouds. "I can work with that."

55

BRANDON

After Ell-rom and Kian had finally arrived and lunch was served in the dining room, Brandon couldn't focus on the delicious mushroom gnocchi on his plate, let alone on what was being said around him. Every small movement Morelle made sent electricity crackling through his awareness—the hesitant way she handled her silverware, watching Annani and imitating her sister, the way her throat moved when she swallowed, the occasional brush of her arm against his when she reached for something.

The connection between them sizzled like a living current.

He wondered if she felt it, too, or if these sensations were completely foreign to her. She wasn't emitting any scents of arousal, but then she didn't emit any emotional scents, probably because of her Kra-ell genes, so he was left guessing, and it was a humbling experience even though he wasn't completely clueless.

Thankfully, after many decades in the entertainment industry, he had learned what to look for. On movie sets, actresses had to fake feelings of attraction toward their male costars even when they detested them, which happened more often than people realized.

Big egos clashing and all that.

So, he knew what to look for and wasn't fooled even when he couldn't rely on his sense of smell.

Still, Brandon could empathize with human males who couldn't rely on scent to tell them whether a woman was attracted to them and had to figure it out from what she was saying, how she was saying it, and her body language.

Morelle, on the other hand, was a complete novice who hadn't even seen others engage in flirting. She had grown up in a temple surrounded by celibate priestesses, and her only companion had been her twin brother.

She needed to learn everything from scratch, and the thought of being her teacher in the carnal arts thrilled Brandon, sending heat coursing through his veins. He wanted to introduce her to every possible pleasure and watch her discover not just the world around her but her own desires as well.

"How is Jasmine doing?" Annani's question pulled him from his increasingly dangerous thoughts.

"She's grown a whole inch," Ell-rom reported, worry creasing his brow. "Bridget says that it's an excellent sign that she is doing well, but Jasmine might not like that when she wakes up."

Annani's musical laugh filled the dining room. "I'll gladly take that inch if she doesn't want it."

"You're perfect exactly as you are, Clan Mother," Brandon said, meaning it. Annani's petite stature did not diminish her presence. "Your greatness comes from the brightness of your soul."

"And your beauty," Ell-rom added.

Kian just nodded while refilling his plate with more of the delicious mushroom gnocchi.

"Such charming males you two are." Annani's eyes twinkled as she accepted the compliments.

Kian lifted his wine glass and took a long sip. "Despite my loving wife's efforts to convince me that I am charming, I know that I'm not, but I agree with those two."

Annani smiled. "You are charming in your own way, my son. Speaking of your lovely wife, though. Has Kalugal's inquiry about the ruins in Syssi's vision uncovered anything?"

"What ruins?" Brandon asked. And what vision, but

he didn't add that. If Kian wanted to tell him, he would.

Kian set down his wine glass. "Syssi summoned a vision asking for clues as to Khiann's fate." He turned to his mother. "Can I share more?"

"Of course." She waved a hand. "Ell-rom already knows about it, and while we were waiting for you, I told Morelle about the sad history of our people and what happened to my Khiann. Brandon is a trusted council member, and I can share my latest hopes with him, even if they are based on a very shaky foundation." She sighed. "I realized that my father, who was a powerful compeller, could have compelled those two witnesses who testified that Mortdh murdered Khiann. He needed to get rid of Mortdh, who was threatening his position, and convicting him of murder was an excellent way to do that without appearing as the aggressor. I suspect that Khiann and his entire caravan fell victim to the massive earthquake that shook the Arabian Desert, and if so, he might be buried under the sand in stasis the same way Wonder was. The biggest hole in my theory is how my father knew about that. No one survived other than those two witnesses."

"Maybe those witnesses told him," Morelle said. "And after they did, he compelled them to tell a different story."

Kian chuckled. "Amazing. It's such a simple explanation that I don't know how none of us thought of it."

Morelle straightened in her chair, looking smug. "Sometimes it takes someone on the outside who isn't familiar with the story to think of the obvious."

Annani beamed at her sister. "Bravo, Morelle. You have given me renewed hope."

"I'm glad." Morelle reached for Annani's hand. "You deserve happiness."

Brandon had a feeling that the Clan Mother was fighting tears, and decided to help her save face. "That's a fascinating new theory, but I'm eager to hear about Syssi's vision."

"I can take it from here," Kian said. "Syssi saw a woman standing on a dune, with mountain peaks in the distance behind her and some ruins ahead of her. She wore traditional male desert clothing, with a scarf wrapped around her head and another one covering her lower face, but her curvy shape betrayed her as a woman, and she also had very distinctive eyes—brown with gold flakes swirling around the irises." He paused. "Syssi figured that the vision was trying to tell her that Jasmine was instrumental to finding Khiann and that he was buried somewhere in the area of those ruins. She sketched what she saw, and I gave it to Kalugal, who reached out to his archaeological contacts. So far, no one has seen anything matching the description. So, we are back to square one. Even with Jasmine's scrying talent, we can't start looking for Khiann without a

373

clue to point us in the right direction and where to start."

Something tickled at Brandon's memory. "That reminds me of a movie, but I can't quite place which one."

"*Stargate?*" Kian suggested.

"No, but similar vibe." Brandon rubbed his chin thoughtfully. "Desert, ruins, mysterious figures..."

He caught identical looks of confusion on Ell-rom and Morelle's faces and couldn't help but smile.

The twins might look different in many ways, but that particular expression of puzzlement was mirror perfect. "Your cultural education needs to include some iconic films."

"Is *Stargate* really iconic?" Kian asked skeptically.

"Absolutely." It was one of Brandon's favorites, and talking about it was a perfect distraction from his hyper-awareness of Morelle's presence beside him. "It perfectly captured that moment in sci-fi when we were transitioning from pure space opera to more grounded, military-focused science fiction. Plus, it spawned multiple successful TV series and influenced countless other works."

Morelle still looked just as confused as she was before, and he realized that he had used industry jargon that Annani and Kian would have no trouble understanding but was probably meaningless to the twins. "The movie is about ancient aliens visiting Earth sometime in a distant past and leaving behind technology that looked like magic to the primitive humans."

Morelle nodded. "That sounds like an interesting story."

Brandon chuckled. "I suppose that, in your case, that's less fiction and more of a historical documentary."

She tilted her head. "The gods presented themselves as deities to the people they created, but they didn't leave technology behind for the primitives to use or figure out that their gods were just people who came from somewhere else in the universe." She looked at Ell-rom. "Or at least that was what the head priestess told us."

Ell-rom smiled apologetically. "I don't remember much from my old life, so I can't help you there."

For some reason, his statement seemed to please Morelle when it should have upset her, and Brandon wondered what the reason for that was. Did Ell-rom know things about her that she preferred he didn't remember?

What if she was hiding some terrible talent?

"Actually," Kian said, "things were a little different on Earth because the gods brought with them advanced tech for their own use, and we have one such relic in the clan's possession." He looked at Annani. "A tablet that my mother pilfered from her uncle and that helped us propel the development of human technology faster than it would have otherwise happened."

"I did not pilfer," Annani voiced her indignation. "I borrowed, and Ekin was perfectly fine with me doing so. He let me use his tablet whenever I wanted."

Kian cast her a fond smile. "Borrowing without intending to return an item is called stealing. I used the word pilfer to make it sound less egregious."

Annani waved a dismissive hand. "It was for a good cause. I knew that I was going to start a new civilization, and I could not do that without the necessary blueprints. Ekin's tablet had everything I needed and more."

MORELLE

Morelle gratefully latched on to the conversation about visions and mysteries, hoping it would distract her from thinking about kissing Brandon.

She had no frame of reference for how to approach it and how it was done, which turned the urge into an obsession. The head priestess had only talked about the struggle for dominance that Kra-ell sex was all about, and kissing had not even been mentioned.

Biting was the norm, not kissing.

The gods had a softer approach to intimacy, but she hadn't been allowed to watch their vids except for those approved by the head priestess, and there had been no kissing in those. The same was true for literature.

All she had was pure instinct, and that instinct was

whispering all kinds of crazy things that she was sure would send Brandon running away.

"You did the right thing, Mother," Kian said. "And by taking Ekin's tablet, you ensured that your father's work and Ekin's would continue, but you can't deny that you stole it."

"Fine." Annani hmphed. "I admit it. I stole the tablet and saved the world."

The revelation cast Annani in a fascinating new light. She wasn't purely good, as she had tried to portray herself in their previous conversations. There was a hint of darkness in her that made her a more effective leader, and Morelle liked her all the more for it.

It aligned perfectly with one of the central tenets of Kra-ell philosophy: good could not exist without evil, and evil could not exist without good. The Mother of All Life was both creator and destroyer, but the key was finding the proper balance.

The priestess had taught her and Ell-rom that good required just a touch of darkness to be truly effective, while evil needed a substantial amount of good to survive, or it would destroy itself. This was why good formed the majority and evil the minority. It was a natural law, one the priestesses were tasked with maintaining.

Disturbingly, though, what Annani had shared before about humans abducting young girls and women and selling them to be exploited in all kinds of unconscionable ways painted a picture far darker than anything Morelle had witnessed among the Kra-ell.

The Kra-ell were savage, and if left free to do as they pleased, they would kill each other off in endless duels and tribal battles, but they obeyed a strict code of honor and were not as depraved.

Humans might be physically weaker, but they lacked honor and were capable of greater cruelty. After what Morelle had heard, she resolved to be very cautious once she ventured among the humans. Brandon had promised to take her to the big city and to see the beach, but now she wasn't sure she wanted to be among people who could stoop so low.

"I was thinking…" Ell-rom's voice pulled her from her dark musings. "What if the woman Syssi saw in her vision wasn't Jasmine but her mother?"

Kian turned to him sharply. "Why would a vision about Khiann show Jasmine's mother?"

"Isn't she supposed to be dead?" Brandon added.

"That's why I think it might be her." Ell-rom shifted in his chair so he could address everyone. "Syssi asked whether Khiann was dead or in stasis. Instead of showing her that truth, maybe the vision revealed something about Jasmine's mother, who might not be dead and could somehow be instrumental in finding Khiann. I know that I'm reaching, but I've had a lot of time to think about it as I sat by Jasmine's bedside." He paused. "Her father never talked about her mother. Jasmine doesn't even know where she's buried or how she died, and it all feels suspicious. She wants to visit her father once she can thrall, and peek into his memories."

Morelle could respect that. It was personal, and Jasmine didn't want anyone looking into her father's head on her behalf.

Annani regarded her from the head of the table. "You seem to agree, Morelle. Should we follow Ell-rom's hunch that the woman in Syssi's vision was Jasmine's mother and not Jasmine herself?"

She set down her glass. "In my opinion, it's worth investigating. You have no other viable leads at the moment, so pursuing this will not delay other avenues of investigation, and if nothing else, it would provide Jasmine with closure. If she discovers that her mother was murdered, she will probably want to avenge her, as is her right."

Ell-rom cleared his throat. "This is not how things are done on Earth. Jasmine would not go after her mother's murderer in order to kill him."

Morelle regarded her brother with a raised brow, but she didn't say what was on her mind because she didn't know whether Ell-rom had told anyone about his ability. As Jasmine's mate, he could avenge her mother. It would be within his rights, and given what he could do, it would be as simple as wishing the death of the killer. But Ell-rom was soft, and his

380

ability had terrified him since the first he learned of it.

"Yes, well." Annani turned to her son. "I assume Roni did a background check on Jasmine and found out who her mother was and what happened to her?"

Kian's expression tightened. "He found her name. Kyra Fazel. She came from Iran on a student visa in 1988 and a year later married Jasmine's father, Boris Orlov, dropped out of the university and changed her name to Kira Orlova. Roni tried tracing her family in Iran, but there isn't much to hack into there, so we don't know her history. There's no death record, so if she died, it wasn't in a hospital and wasn't reported. She also wasn't buried by any traditional means. She simply vanished from all records around the time of her supposed death." He refilled his wine. "We kept it quiet to avoid upsetting Jasmine. I planned to wait for her to go through her transition and get settled here before sharing this information with her."

"I appreciate that," Ell-rom said. "Jasmine has been under a lot of stress lately."

"What about her stepmother and stepbrothers?" Annani asked. "Did Boris divorce Kira in her absence?"

"Roni didn't check that." Kian drummed his fingers on the table. "Maybe I'll ask him to do it when he is done with his current project."

Morelle thought of the possibilities. "The mother might be alive. Perhaps she had a good reason to leave. Maybe there was a family emergency back home, and she couldn't return for some reason. Or she could have been murdered, and her body was hidden. Or she could have been taken. If she was as beautiful as Jasmine, she could have been targeted by those terrible humans who steal women and girls and sell them."

Kian's eyes narrowed at her, and then he turned to his mother. "What exactly have you been telling Morelle?"

Annani shrugged. "My sister wanted to know what we are about and what we do. Our important charity project has become a big part of our identity as a clan, so I started with that."

"It was very disturbing to hear," Morelle confirmed. "The Kra-ell society has many problems, but it is not depraved. Females are cherished and valued, and males die to protect them. The disregard for women's dignity and well-being on Earth is abhorrent."

Kian nodded his head. "It certainly is, but I don't want you to think that all humans are like that." He sighed. "We've worked very hard to change that, and we have succeeded in many places, but our enemies' influence over large portions of Earth is palpable, and things seem to have gotten worse lately." He looked at his mother. "But Annani, and by extension the clan, will never stop fighting for women."

Annani nodded. "Women. Life. Freedom."

Kian tilted his head. "I've heard that somewhere before."

"Of course, you have." Annani smiled. "It is the Kurdish Women's Freedom Movement's official motto, which was later adopted by Kurdish fighters. In their language, it rhymes: Jin, Jiyan, Azadî."

Kian turned to Brandon. "Is this our doing?"

Brandon shook his head. "It's a grassroots movement, but since it was influenced by the freedoms women enjoy in the West, then it is our doing in a round-about way."

Morelle was really starting to dislike humans. "Why do human women need to fight for life and freedom? Isn't it their goddess-given right?"

"It is." Annani smiled sadly. "When the gods created humans, they made them easy to influence, so they could control them with very little effort. That weakness, or perhaps backdoor into their psyche, is exploited by bad players who manipulate them to their advantage."

Morelle felt her blood electrify, and not in a pleasant way. "How do we get to those bad players and eliminate them?"

Kian chuckled. "Welcome to my world, Morelle. Regrettably, there are too many of them and too few of us, and right now, it seems like the bad players have the upper hand, but not for long. In the end, good always triumphs over evil."

BRANDON

randon liked Kian's optimism. A few days ago, he wouldn't have shared it, but now that Morelle was in his life, everything seemed a little brighter, and as her hand found his under the table and clasped it, he was surprised and delighted.

He turned to her and smiled, so mesmerized by her incredible blue eyes and the black lashes framing them that he found he had missed the first half of what the Clan Mother had just said.

"...Jasmine's father?" Annani asked. "He must know something."

"Please don't," Ell-rom interjected. "She is really adamant about doing it herself when she gains the ability to thrall. Edgar, the pilot she was briefly with, offered to question her father, but Jasmine prohibited him and me from doing that."

"It is not guaranteed that Jasmine will ever be able to thrall." Annani lifted her glass, and Ogidu rushed to fill it with more sparkling water. "Most transitioned Dormants cannot. It seems that it needs to be learned at a young age when the mind is still developing."

"I'm learning to thrall," Ell-rom said. "I'm even getting good at it."

"That's because you knew how to do it before you entered stasis and just forgot how." Kian glanced at Morelle. "Am I right?"

She nodded. "We both can thrall and shroud, and we are good. Otherwise, we couldn't have fooled all the gods in the spaceport into thinking that we looked like Kra-ell. Then again, it was possible that our mother was doing that. She walked with us most of the way." Morelle closed her eyes. "I wish I could have hugged her. I should have done that, even if it was risky. I didn't know that I would be traveling for seven thousand years, but I knew that I would never see her again. Well, not in the flesh anyway. She came to me in a dream."

"Oh, do tell." Annani leaned forward. "What did she say?"

Morelle squeezed Brandon's hand under the table. "She told me that I needed to wake up and that I needed to listen."

"Listen to what?" Ell-rom asked.

"The storyteller." She cast Brandon a smile. "She also said that life is worth living and that I should not keep wasting it in sleep or something to that effect. I don't remember her exact words."

Brandon had a feeling that she wasn't telling the whole truth, but it was her prerogative. She didn't need to disclose everything her mother had told her.

Kian glanced at his watch and then reached for his glass and refilled it with wine. "I'm glad that you chose to wake up and join us, Morelle. But speaking of abilities, do you have any talents other than thralling and shrouding?"

Morelle's fingers closed almost painfully around Brandon's, and Ell-rom seemed to turn a shade paler.

"I don't, or rather, I don't know if I have any other talents. The head priestess tried to find out by testing me in various ways, but I had nothing special. She was very disappointed with me."

The color seemed to return to Ell-rom's face, and Brandon wondered what that was all about.

"My sister Amanda is a researcher of special abilities." Kian took a sip of his wine. "Would you agree for her to test you?"

Again, Morelle's fingers tightened around Brandon's, and she and Ell-rom exchanged glances. "Perhaps when I feel stronger. Right now, I'm still too weak, and my mind feels a little fuzzy."

Morelle's mind seemed perfectly sharp to Brandon. He suspected that she was trying to avoid being tested.

What was she hiding?

"It can wait," Annani said. "Morelle is still in no state for even the gentlest of tests." She smiled at her sister. "Do not think that I cannot see the effort you are putting into just sitting up straight. You should be in bed."

Morelle shook her head stubbornly. "I've spent enough time in bed."

"You have a backbone." Annani smiled knowingly. "Our father would have been proud of you."

Morelle's shoulders squared, and she held herself straight once more as if her sister's words infused her with strength.

"I would have liked to know him," she said. "But perhaps I'll get to see glimpses of him in you."

"You certainly will, and one of those traits is impatience. I cannot wait for Jasmine to learn how to thrall to follow the lead to her mother and see whether she is somehow connected to finding my Khiann."

Ell-rom looked pained. "Please. Can we at least wait until Jasmine is awake and ask her consent?"

"Of course." Kian cast his mother a warning look. "We will never contravene her wishes. Besides, thinking that the woman in Syssi's vision was Jasmine's mother is pure speculation. I still think that it was Jasmine and that she is supposed to help us locate Khiann. We just need to find out the starting point of the search for her to use her scrying. The problem is that the Arabian Desert is huge, and there are many other deserts, any of which could have been the one in the scene Syssi saw. It could have happened anywhere in the world."

"There is only one solution then." Annani leaned back. "Syssi needs to summon another vision and get more clues."

Kian shook his head. "It doesn't work like that, Mother. She might ask and again get a vision that doesn't tell us anything or tells us something that is unrelated to Khiann. I don't want you to get your hopes up, thinking that it's as easy as calling a helpline."

Annani laughed. "It actually is, but the person answering the line is a trickster. The Fates sometimes have a strange sense of humor."

Brandon brushed his thumb over Morelle's palm. "Sometimes, the Fates are generous, though, and merciful, and they surprise us in the most unex-pected ways."

"I agree." Ell-rom nodded. "Who would have thought that at the end of a seven-thousand-year journey, my sister and I would find a family and a home on Earth."

8

MORELLE

After Ell-rom and Kian left, Annani led Morelle and Brandon to a room that was much larger than the one Morelle had occupied in the temple, with a massive bed that could have slept four acolytes comfortably.

A plush couch and an armchair created an intimate seating area, and floor-to-ceiling bookcases lined one wall, filled with volumes she couldn't read but wished she could.

Books were cherished on Anumati, or at least they had been when she was an acolyte, and religious texts were copied by hand. She and Ell-rom had been tasked with that project since they were old enough to produce the beautiful penmanship required, and it had been boring and arduous, and the subject matter wasn't any better. After a while, she'd stopped paying attention to the words she was copying, and it had become a routine chore.

390

"You need to sit down." Brandon guided her to the couch and lowered her to a sitting position as if he feared that her thigh muscles weren't strong enough to complete the movement without assistance.

The truth was that her legs still felt weak, even wobbly, and her arms weren't much better, but she was determined to build her strength back quickly.

One of the Odus, she couldn't tell them apart, entered the room behind them. "If Mistress will allow, I will unpack your belongings and arrange them in the closet."

Morelle tensed involuntarily. Despite what Brandon had told her, she still didn't feel comfortable around the Odus.

Brandon caught the hesitance in her expression. "Thank you, but I'll handle it." He smiled at the Odu. "I haven't even seen what's in these packages myself."

"Well, I will leave you to it." Annani excused herself. "If you need me, I will be in the living room."

"Thank you for hosting me," Morelle said.

Annani smiled. "It is my pleasure, sister of mine." She laughed. "I just love saying the words sister and brother." She flounced out the door, leaving them alone with the mountain of packages.

"You didn't buy all of this?" Morelle asked after the door closed behind Annani.

She had assumed that he bought the items himself, but she should have realized that he hadn't had time to do so unless commerce could be conducted during the night on Earth.

"I know a lady who specializes in putting together wardrobes for performers." Brandon crouched next to a pile of boxes but then looked up at her. "Do you have performers on Anumati?"

"The gods have professional performers who get paid for playing fictional characters, but the Kra-ell consider that frivolous. Performances are done only by warriors to enact stories of famous battles. They also dance and sing."

"Well, here on Earth, we have professional performers who get paid a lot of money for what they do because people are willing to pay to see the fictional stories they bring to life. Your brother's mate is a professional performer, so maybe you shouldn't sound so dismissive of her chosen profession when she wakes up. Also, up until recently, I was involved in producing those fictional stories, which was how I knew a professional wardrobe procurer."

That was what Morelle wanted to hear more about. She needed to know what the female meant to Brandon. "How did the lady who bought all these things know what will fit me?"

"I sent her your measurements and some general guidelines. Melinda has excellent taste, and she gets what I want."

The fondness and appreciation in his voice when he said the woman's name made something dark curl in Morelle's stomach. Was this Melinda a former paramour? Or perhaps a current one?

"This Melinda, how close is she to you?"

Brandon paused in his unpacking, turning to look at her with an expression of confusion that quickly shifted to understanding. "She's a professional who provides a service, nothing more. She's never been my lover if that's what you're asking."

"But there have been others." The words came out almost accusatory.

He left the box open on the floor and sat beside her on the couch, close enough that she could feel his warmth but not quite touching. "Yes, there have been others. I was not a celibate priest, and I am also not an inexperienced youth."

"How many?" The question burned in her throat.

"Quite a lot. They were all human, and none of them meant much to me. They couldn't have because there was no point in getting attached to someone who could not be mine forever. Besides, none of them kindled in me the kind of feelings that you do." His eyes held hers. "I've never experienced anything like this connection with anyone before."

"You don't even know me," Morelle protested, but her heart was racing at his words and his proximity.

"I think I do." Brandon pulled her into his arms. "May I kiss you, Princess Morelle?"

His lips were hovering so close to hers that all she needed to do to join them was move forward a fraction.

That was all the permission he needed, and as he took over the kiss, the avalanche of sensations and feelings Morelle felt was indescribable. This was fire and need and something that squeezed her heart and filled it at the same time, the intensity making her head spin.

She had no reference for this, no way to know how to respond, and no way to know what to do with her tongue and her hands. Acting on instinct, her hands found their way to his shoulders as she pressed herself closer to his chest, wanting more of this incredible sensation.

She felt as though she was simultaneously drowning and flying.

When they finally broke apart, she was breathing heavily, her whole body tingling with awareness. If one kiss could feel like this, she wanted hundreds more, thousands. She wanted to spend eternity learning every possible way to kiss Brandon.

"That's how well I know you," he said softly, his forehead resting against hers. "I don't need words or time to recognize what's between us. My whole existence, I've been waiting for you without even knowing it."

Morelle lifted a shaking hand to touch her lips, which still burned from his kiss. Everything she had thought she knew about what happened between a female and a male needed to be rewritten.

"Kiss me again!" she half pleaded, half demanded.

"Always."

COMING UP NEXT
The Children of the Gods Book 90
DARK PRINCESS
EMERGING

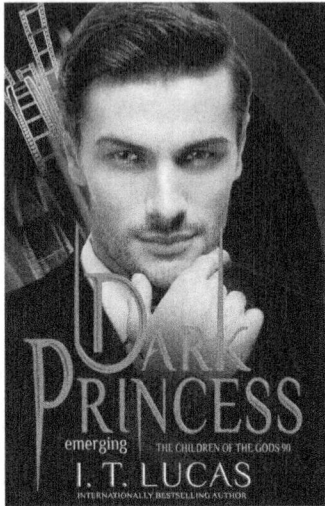

WHILE THE CLAN wages war against humanity's darkest elements, Morelle learns to navigate an unexpectedly complex Earth, explores unfamiliar feelings, and discovers powers that make her both invaluable and dangerous to her newfound family.

Don't forget to check out this fun, feel-good read

ADINA AND THE MAGIC LAMP

In this post-apocalyptic virtual reimagining of Aladdin, James, the enigmatic prince, and Adina, the fearless thief, navigate the treacherous streets of Londabad, a city that echoes London and Ahmedabad and fuses magic and technology. In the face of danger, the chemistry between them ignites, and the lines between prince and thief, royalty and commoner blur.

Join the VIP Club

To find out what's included in your free membership, flip to the last page.

NOTE

Dear reader,

I hope my stories have added a little joy to your day. If you have a moment to add some to mine, you can help spread the word about the Children Of The Gods series by telling your friends and penning a review. Your recommendations are the most powerful way to inspire new readers to explore the series.

Thank you,

Isabell

Also by I. T. Lucas

THE CHILDREN OF THE GODS ORIGINS
1: GODDESS'S CHOICE
2: GODDESS'S HOPE

THE CHILDREN OF THE GODS
DARK STRANGER
1: DARK STRANGER THE DREAM
2: DARK STRANGER REVEALED
3: DARK STRANGER IMMORTAL

DARK ENEMY
4: DARK ENEMY TAKEN
5: DARK ENEMY CAPTIVE
6: DARK ENEMY REDEEMED

KRI & MICHAEL'S STORY
6.5: MY DARK AMAZON

DARK WARRIOR
7: DARK WARRIOR MINE
8: DARK WARRIOR'S PROMISE
9: DARK WARRIOR'S DESTINY
10: DARK WARRIOR'S LEGACY

DARK GUARDIAN
11: DARK GUARDIAN FOUND
12: DARK GUARDIAN CRAVED
13: DARK GUARDIAN'S MATE

DARK PRINCESS

PERFECT MATCH

TRANSLATIONS

DIE ERBEN DER GÖTTER
DARK STRANGER

DARK ENEMY

The Children of the Gods Series Sets

Books 1-3: Dark Stranger trilogy—Includes a bonus short story: **The Fates Take a Vacation**

Books 4-6: Dark Enemy Trilogy —Includes a bonus short story—**The Fates' Post-Wedding Celebration**

Books 7-10: Dark Warrior Tetralogy
Books 11-13: Dark Guardian Trilogy
Books 14-16: Dark Angel Trilogy
Books 17-19: Dark Operative Trilogy
Books 20-22: Dark Survivor Trilogy
Books 23-25: Dark Widow Trilogy
Books 26-28: Dark Dream Trilogy
Books 29-31: Dark Prince Trilogy
Books 32-34: Dark Queen Trilogy
Books 35-37: Dark Spy Trilogy
Books 38-40: Dark Overlord Trilogy
Books 41-43: Dark Choices Trilogy
Books 44-46: Dark Secrets Trilogy
Books 47-49: Dark Haven Trilogy
Books 50-52: Dark Power Trilogy
Books 53-55: Dark Memories Trilogy
Books 56-58: Dark Hunter Trilogy
Books 59-61: Dark God Trilogy
Books 62-64: Dark Whispers Trilogy
Books 65-67: Dark Gambit Trilogy
Books 68-70: Dark Alliance Trilogy

Books 71-73: Dark Healing Trilogy
Books 74-76: Dark Encounters Trilogy
Books 77-79: Dark Voyage Trilogy
Books 80-81: Dark Horizon Trilogy

MEGA SETS
The Children of the Gods: Books 1-6
INCLUDES CHARACTER LISTS
The Children of the Gods: Books 6.5-10

Perfect Match Bundle 1

CHECK OUT THE SPECIALS ON
ITLUCAS.COM
(https://itlucas.com/specials)

FOR EXCLUSIVE PEEKS AT UPCOMING RELEASES &
A FREE I. T. LUCAS COMPANION BOOK

Join my *VIP Club* and gain access to the VIP portal at ITLUCAS.COM

To Join, go to:
http://eepurl.com/blMTpD

Find out more details about what's included with

your free membership on the book's last page.

**TRY THE CHILDREN OF THE GODS
SERIES ON
<u>AUDIBLE</u>**
2 FREE audiobooks with your new Audible
subscription!

FOR EXCLUSIVE PEEKS AT UPCOMING RELEASES & A FREE I. T. LUCAS COMPANION BOOK

Join my *VIP Club* and gain access to the VIP portal at ITLUCAS.COM
To Join, go to:
http://eepurl.com/blMTpD

INCLUDED IN YOUR FREE MEMBERSHIP:

YOUR VIP PORTAL

- Read preview chapters of upcoming releases.
- Listen to Goddess's Choice narration by Charles Lawrence
- Exclusive content offered only to my VIPs.

FREE I.T. LUCAS COMPANION INCLUDES:

- Goddess's Choice Part 1
- Perfect Match: Vampire's Consort (A standalone Novella)
- Interview Q & A
- Character Charts

If you're already a subscriber and you are not getting my emails, your provider is sending them

TO YOUR JUNK FOLDER, AND YOU ARE MISSING OUT ON IMPORTANT UPDATES. TO FIX THAT, ADD isabell@itlu cas.com TO YOUR EMAIL CONTACTS OR YOUR EMAIL VIP LIST.

Check out the specials at
https://www.itlucas.com/specials

Printed in Great Britain
by Amazon

57467623R00235